PRAISE FOR *Willful Machines*

★ "From a first-person perspective, Lee fumbles from self-deprecation to self-confidence. As varied as his opinions are of himself, so too is the landscape, mixing technology with gothic settings à la Poe and Stoker. Gothic, gadget-y, gay: a socially conscious sci-fi thriller to shelve between *The Terminator* and *Romeo and Juliet.*"

—*Kirkus Reviews*, starred review

"Smart, brave, and utterly original, *Willful Machines* asks questions that matter. Tim Floreen's unforgettable debut will stay with you long after you've finished reading."

—Amie Kaufman, *New York Times* bestselling author of *These Broken Stars* and *Illuminae*

"*Willful Machines* is as exciting as it is heartbreaking. A deft mixture of science fiction, gritty action, and sweet first love, Tim Floreen's debut is everything I want from a book."

—Shaun David Hutchinson, author of *The Five Stages of Andrew Brawley* and *We Are the Ants*

"*Willful Machines* is a thought-provoking thriller wrapped around a fascinating concept—skillfully mixed in with basic human dilemmas. Tim Floreen's tale convincingly depicts a world where machines can pass as human, but humans still struggle with age-old questions: 'How much control do I have over my own life? Who can I dare to trust? Who can I dare to love?'"

—Margaret Peterson Haddix, *New York Times* bestselling author

ALSO BY TIM FLOREEN

Willful Machines

TIM FLOREEN

New Y

SIMON PULSE
An imprint of Simon & Schuster Children's Publishing Division
1230 Avenue of the Americas, New York, New York 10020
First Simon Pulse hardcover edition October 2016

Jacket designed by Regina Flath
Interior designed by Mike Rosamilia
The text of this book was set in Minion Pro.
Manufactured in the United States of America
10 9 8 7 6 5 4 3 2 1
This book has been cataloged with the Library of Congress.
ISBN 978-1-4814-3280-1 (hc)
ISBN 978-1-4814-3282-5 (eBook)

for Duncan

1

Almost a year after Franklin Kettle shot my friend Pete Lund through the head, a squad of cops took Franklin to my mom's lab so she could put a hole in *his* head and slide a small electronic capsule inside.

The three police cruisers swerved to a stop in front of the sleek glass structure, their tires kicking up snow, their sirens for some reason blaring. The noise seemed to reach all the way around the lab and spread across the surface of the frozen lake beyond. Then there was a clattering of car doors opening and closing and booted feet stomping the slushy pavement. Gruff voices barked orders back and forth.

Franklin appeared to be enjoying all the fuss. When the cops helped him out of the middle cruiser's backseat, the chains on his wrists and ankles clinking, he had a tiny, secret smile on his face.

The police walked him past a sign that read MINNESOTA INSTITUTE OF NEUROLOGICAL RESEARCH and into the lab. An elevator sliced through the building without a sound as it carried them to the top floor. The door whispered open on a bright corridor, where a lab tech with a pierced nose, an asymmetrical wedge haircut, and a badge on her white coat that said GERTRUDE THOMAS waited. She blinked at the sight of the six huge cops packed into the elevator, but then she recovered herself and shifted her gaze to the skinny seventeen-year-old kid they were guarding.

"Hi, Franklin. I don't know if you remember me." She dipped her head a little but didn't manage to catch his eyes. "I'm Gertie. We met the first time you came here last year?"

Franklin responded with a slight tilt of his head that might've meant he remembered her and might've meant he didn't. His eyes never left the elevator floor.

"Why don't you follow me?" Gertie said. "I'll take you to Dr. Braithwaite."

She led them all down the corridor, only once throwing a flustered glance back at the mob of cops tromping after her. At the end of the corridor she grabbed the badge clipped to her lab coat and touched it to a card reader next to a door. The door clicked open. The group entered a big room with a floor-to-ceiling window spanning the rear wall. It looked out onto Lake Superior, which was solid and gray, like a continuation of the room's concrete floor. A table stood in front of the window.

My mom sat behind it.

A middle-aged man with a comb-over stepped forward and offered Franklin his hand. "Welcome, Mr. Kettle. I'm Dr. Hult, the head biomedical engineer. We're all thrilled to have you back. We can't wait to get started."

Franklin didn't look at him, either. Instead he let out a quiet snort, like he'd just told himself a private joke.

Dr. Hult glanced at his outstretched, unshaken hand and stuffed it into his lab coat pocket. He nodded at Mom. "I think you know Dr. Braithwaite."

"Hello, Franklin," Mom said. "Thanks, Gertie. You can go now."

Gertie cast one more uncertain look at Franklin before slipping out of the room.

Mom gestured toward a chair across the table from her. While one of the cops guided Franklin over and sat him down, Mom smoothed her straight hair—iron gray, like the concrete floor and the lake, shot through with a single thick streak of white near the front. She'd always refused to dye it. I'd told her once I thought the white streak made her look like a mad scientist, especially when she had her lab coat on, but she'd just replied, "Then it's a good thing I *am* one."

"It's been a while," she said to Franklin now. "How are you doing?"

He raised his hands—he had to raise both of them, because the chains bound his wrists close together—and pointed at the chair next to her. Something rested there, some kind of box, with a white cloth draped over it. The top of it was just visible above the table. A soft scratching sound came from within.

"What's that?"

"We'll get to that in a moment," she said. "I want to talk to you first. Do you understand why you're here?"

He slouched down low in his chair and stared at the box.

"Franklin? It's important that you answer the question."

"You want to open up my head."

"That's part of it, yes. Now, I know you must be nervous."

"I'm not nervous."

"I'm glad to hear that."

"Why do you think I'm nervous? Do I look like I'm nervous?"

"No."

He didn't look like he was anything. Franklin Kettle had a face empty of expression—except, sometimes, for that half smile of his—and a low, weirdly calm voice, like the computer from *2001: A Space Odyssey*. Kettlebot, kids had sometimes called him at school. His eyes, partly hidden behind spiky chunks of hair and glasses with bulky black frames, looked like dull gray stones.

"I've undergone thousands of hours of military training," he said. "I think I know how to keep my cool."

Mom pursed her lips. "You're talking about that video game you play. It isn't quite the same thing, is it?"

"It's not just a video game," he replied, still in that same calm tone. "Military training programs all over the world use Son of War to help prepare soldiers for combat. And I have one of the all-time high scores. You don't think that says something about me?"

"I'm sure it does."

"I do see your point, though, Madame Doctor. Can virtual combat make a person fearless for real? It's an interesting question. The kind of question you probably think about a lot, being a brain scientist and all." His smile had returned. "Sort of like: can sticking some gadget in the head of a cold-blooded killer make him not a killer anymore?"

Mom was unfazed. "Actually, that's what I want to talk to you about, Franklin: why you're here. Do you understand what we hope to accomplish when we—"

The chains clanked as he pointed again. His eyes hadn't budged from the box covered by the white cloth. "What is it? Why is it making that noise?"

She glanced at the thing on the chair next to her. "It's a gift. I was planning to give it to you a little later."

"Give it to me now. The noise is distracting me."

Mom hooked her hair behind her ear while she thought about it. "All right then."

She lifted the box onto the table and, drawing off the cloth, revealed a Plexiglas cage with half a dozen mice inside.

Franklin pulled himself out of his slouch so he could set his hands on the table, reaching them as far as his chains would allow. He tapped a fingernail on the white tabletop and watched the mice react.

"How come?" he said.

"I beg your pardon?"

"How come you're giving me these mice? What do you want me to do with them?"

He still didn't make eye contact with Mom. That was another thing about Franklin: he never looked anyone in the eyes. Not out of shyness. At least it didn't seem that way. He just appeared uninterested in connecting with other human beings.

"Whatever you like," Mom answered. "I thought you might enjoy them." To one of the police officers standing behind him, she said, "Would you take off his wrist restraints, please?"

The cop unchained his hands. Without hesitating or pausing to ask permission, Franklin opened the door to the cage and reached his hand inside. His fingers closed around a mouse with a coat of white and brown splotches. He brought it to his chest and stroked its head. The mouse's tiny pink paws scraped his fingers.

"I know what you want me to do with them," Franklin said. "You want me to hurt them."

Mom sat up a tiny bit straighter. "Why would I want you to do something like that?"

"So you can study my behavior. Gather data for your project. See for yourself what a psycho I am. You and whoever else is watching." He nodded at one of the cameras hanging from the ceiling. "You're all thrilled to have me back," he added, slitting his eyes at Dr. Hult, who was standing by the door. "You can't wait to get started." His chains rustled as he faced Mom again. "You're hoping I'll put on a show."

"What do you mean, 'put on a show'?"

He shrugged. "Maybe I'll smash this mouse on the table. Maybe I'll squeeze him until his eyes pop out. At least, that's what you're hoping, Madame Doctor."

Mom pressed the nail of her left index finger into the pad of her thumb. A couple years ago, while making dinner, she'd accidentally sliced off the tip of that thumb. A doctor had managed to sew it back on, but it had been numb ever since. Prodding the thumb had become a habit, something she always did when she got tense. Aside from that, though, she kept up an appearance of calm that matched Franklin's. "You don't really want to do that, do you?"

"No. I like this mouse."

The animal had started clawing at Franklin's hand more frantically, like it could understand the various fates he'd described for it. He brought it close to his cheek and shushed to calm it down.

Dr. Hult raised his eyebrows at Mom. She gave her head a small shake for him to stay put.

"I'm not stupid," Franklin said, the two stones behind his glasses fastened on the Plexiglas cage and the other mice inside it.

"I know that," Mom answered. "I know you're very intelligent."

"I'm onto your brain-doctor tricks."

"I'm not playing any tricks, Franklin."

He tipped his head forward, so his hair fell in front of his eyes in a curtain. "Stop watching me. I don't like it when people watch me."

"I'm not watching you. I'm looking at you. I'm having a conversation with you."

"No, you're not. You're studying me."

"That's not true. I want to talk to you about what's going to happen over the next few days. I want to make sure you understand—"

Franklin opened his mouth wide and stuffed the mouse in.

Mom's metal chair screeched across the concrete floor as she sprang to her feet. "What are you doing, Franklin?"

The cops took a few steps forward, but Mom put up a hand to stop them. Franklin's bulging cheek rippled as the mouse struggled inside.

"Take out the mouse," Mom said. "You just told me you didn't want to hurt him."

Franklin settled back into his slouch in the chair. He laced his fingers together on his lap. Even with the mouse struggling behind his cheek, you could still see the little smile on his lips.

"Listen to me, Franklin. Right now you have a choice. You can—"

His jaws closed with a sound like someone crunching into a mouthful of almonds. A trickle of blood snaked from his lips. He chewed a few times and spat the mouse onto the table. Tiny black beads of blood flecked the white surface and the Plexiglas cage and even Mom's lab coat. One of the mouse's hind legs continued to kick.

With sudden energy, Franklin sprang to his feet and banged his hands on the table. "Happy now? Happy?"

The police finally snapped into action. As they rushed to grab him, he kept repeating that word over and over, blood spraying from his mouth, his normally quiet, empty voice filling with rage, rising to a yell.

"Happy? Happy?! HAPPY?!"

2

Of course, I didn't actually see any of that firsthand. But a while ago I got a message on my phone with a link to a Dropbox folder containing a bunch of surveillance footage from the lab. I went through it a few days later, beginning with those first minutes after Franklin Kettle's arrival. It felt important that I watch all of it. I'd already decided I wanted to set down the whole story of the days before and after Mom performed her procedure on Franklin, start to finish. Lots of rumors had been flying around online, and I figured someone who'd been there, for most of it at least, should make a record of what had really happened. Or try.

Not that I knew whether I'd actually show what I wrote to another human being. If the truth got out, lots of people would get hurt, me included. Maybe I was really just doing it for myself. Maybe I was hoping it would give me a way to dump out all the unwelcome memories crawling around in my mind. Sort of like what I imagined happening when I drew in my Tattoo Atlas, even though I realized the brain didn't actually work like that. Probably the only way I'd ever get rid of my memories was if

Mom figured out how to open up *my* head and pull them out, one by one.

But I'm getting ahead of myself.

That Monday morning, at the same time Mom was attempting to talk to Franklin about the hole she wanted to drill in his skull, I was at home, out in the garage, warming up my car, a bright yellow 1972 Saab station wagon my older brother had bought and fixed up years ago. I wasn't exactly what you'd call a gearhead, but I did my best to take good care of it. My friends and I had a tradition of riding the seven blocks to school in the wagon every morning. I'd put up the garage door and sit there with the heater on full blast and wait for the others to slide into their usual seats one by one: Tor Agnarson in front next to me, Lydia Hicks and Callie Minwalla behind. Pete Lund, when he was still alive, had sat in the way back. For years we'd called ourselves the Boreal Five because we'd all grown up together on Boreal Street, but there were only four of us now.

The seating arrangement had undergone another change more recently, when Tor and Lydia had started dating. An unexpected development, and one that had caused some dissension in the Boreal Five's ranks.

Today as I sat in the driver's seat, the Saab's engine chugging and its heater roaring, Lydia showed up first, her freckly cheeks flushed from the cold, her auburn hair pulled into a neat ponytail under her knit cap, a stack of posters under her arm. She slid into the backseat.

"What have you got there?" I said.

"More publicity for the memorial." She turned the stack face-up on her lap. The poster showed Pete Lund's round face haloed by a haze of silver glitter. The words FOREVER IN OUR HEARTS appeared at the top. "Abigail dropped them off last night. She wants us to put them up before class this morning."

Abigail Lansing was the head organizer of the assembly that would mark the one-year anniversary of the shooting. On the basis of a single dance she'd gone to with Pete sophomore year, she'd seized the role of Pete's bereaved girlfriend and mourner-in-chief—even though she'd basically just hung out with him that one time, and even though she hadn't even seen him die. The girl was a colossal phony. But none of us in the Boreal Five—Pete's actual friends, in other words—had the heart to be our school's unofficial grief coordinator, so we pretty much left her to it.

When she'd asked us to help her organize the Big Bang memorial, though, grabbing our hands and whispering, "Pete would've wanted you to be part of it," we all agreed. She was right, not that she had any real idea what she was talking about.

Lydia jangled a couple rolls of tape she'd looped around her wrist. "You up for it?"

"Sure, but haven't we put up enough?"

"Apparently the other posters were just teasers. Now we're starting phase two of the marketing rollout. These have all the information about where and when the memorial's taking place printed at the bottom."

"But it's a mandatory school assembly. Doesn't that sort of make marketing beside the point?"

"Maybe." Her feathery eyebrows knitted and her eyes dropped to the posters. "I think Abigail just wants to make sure nobody ditches. She wants people to understand how important this is."

"She wants them to hear her make a speech and watch her cry. *That's* what she wants."

"She means well, Rem." Lydia touched her fingertips to Pete's cheek, her forehead still furrowed. We both went quiet as we stared at the image. For the past few weeks Pete's face on that sappy poster had been everywhere, all over the walls at school, but seeing it was still like a spike in the ribs every time.

Tor yanked open the Saab's other rear door and scooted in next to Lydia. Unlike us, he didn't have on a coat or a hat. Just a UMD sweatshirt—slightly too small, so as to better showcase his muscles—and, randomly, a pair of earmuffs. Like only his ears ever got cold. That was typical Tor, though. He was an underdresser: whatever the situation, he always had on at least two fewer layers than everyone else.

He slung a huge arm over Lydia's shoulders and gave her a kiss. "Morning, Strawberry."

Lydia turned red. She'd had a thing for Tor for years, everybody had always known it, but now that she had him, it was like she'd won the lottery and didn't have a clue what to do with the money. She took his public displays of affection with a mix of pleasure, mortification, and bafflement.

Tor leaned forward to ruffle my hair. "Morning, Nice Guy."

My name's Jeremy, Rem for short, but he liked to call me Nice Guy. Mr. Nice Guy if he was in a formal mood. Tor was into nicknames—he was the one who'd started calling us the Boreal Five—and he had one for each of us. In my case the nickname had caught on around school, too, and I suppose it fit well enough. Maybe I hadn't done anything as impressive and altruistic as my brother, who'd single-handedly started the crisis hotline at Duluth Central during his time as a student there, but I knew how to get along with people. I didn't gossip. I didn't pick fights. I didn't have enemies. None I knew of, at least.

Callie appeared next. She opened the back door and found Tor occupying what had been, up until a few weeks ago, her usual spot. "Oh. Right." Scowling, she slammed the door shut, flung open the front passenger door, and dumped herself into the seat.

"Think of it as a promotion," I said.

She cut a black look at me.

"I don't get what the problem is," Tor said. "It's a free country, isn't it? We're all friends, right? What's the big deal if Lydia and I want to get a little friendlier?"

Callie let out a noise halfway between a sigh and a groan as she pushed at the coiled mass of black hair piled on top of her head, a precarious hairdo that had given rise to Tor's name for her—Elvira. "It threatens the integrity of our group, Tor."

"'The integrity of our group'?" Tor repeated. "What are we, a team of Navy SEALs?"

"We didn't mean for it to happen, Callie," Lydia said. "It just sort of did. We were spending all that time together in the bio lab after school."

"Right," Callie muttered. "There's nothing like a little cat dissection to get two young lovers in the mood." She seized the rearview mirror and angled it so she could look Tor in the eyes. "We're graduating in June, Tor. We don't have much time left together. I don't want you ruining it."

"Why would—"

"Come on," she snapped. "You've never in your life dated anyone for more than a month. So what's going to happen one week from now when you kick Lydia to the fucking curb just like you do every other girl?"

"Who says he's going to kick me to the effing curb?" Lydia said, crossing her arms over her chest.

"Don't kid yourself, missy."

Lydia's freckle-strewn cheeks turned crimson again. "You know what really threatens the integrity of our group? The mean things you say."

Callie ignored her. "What do you want with Lydia anyway, Tor? She's a prude who can't even bring herself to say the word 'fuck.' Don't you prefer the slutty types?"

"That's enough, Callie," I said. "Give them a break. You can't control who you fall for."

"Thank you, Rem," Lydia said.

Callie turned to glare at me again, her mouth open as if she wanted to say something. But then she grabbed one of my hands from the steering wheel instead and lifted it up. "For God's sake, Rem, don't you ever wash?"

I'd been painting that morning, lost track of time, and ran out the door without bothering to clean off the smears of pink and green and yellow covering my palms and fingers. That happened a lot. Callie was an artist too—mixed media collage mostly—but she was much neater about it.

Without a word Tor got out of the car, opened Callie's door, and held out his hand. "Come with me. I want to show you something."

She eyed his open palm. "What?"

"You'll see. It'll be good, I promise." To me and Lydia he said, "You guys come too. Leave the car running, Rem."

He led us out the garage's rear door and through the trees that separated my backyard from his. Callie complained loudly as she picked her way through the snow in her cork wedges and miniskirt. She was just as impractical a dresser as Tor.

Her choice of swearwords got more creative when he plunged into the woods at the back of his yard. The snow was harder to navigate here, but at least we didn't have to go far. Twenty feet in, Tor stopped at the base of a huge maple.

Callie's face softened when she realized where we were. Tor grinned at her and nodded.

The trunk of the maple grew at a low angle, extending over a ravine where a creek ran during the summer, so you didn't have to climb the tree so much as walk out onto it. Still, it would be a challenge in wedges. Callie didn't protest anymore, though.

She followed Tor in silence, taking his outstretched hand for support. Lydia and I stayed close behind.

Just before the place where the trunk split off into branches, we all dropped to a crouch and peered over the side.

"They're still here," Callie whispered.

Below us, a family of red foxes played in the snow-choked ravine. Three or four little kits dove into the snow and exploded out again over and over, while their mother kept an eye on them from a comfortable branch a few feet off. Years ago, when we were all eight or so, Tor had discovered the foxes and started taking us here to watch them. It had become one of the Boreal Five's first secrets: we'd never told anyone about them, not even after a neighbor's pet rabbit had gotten mauled and we'd all known who must've done it.

At some point we'd fallen out of the habit of coming here. We probably hadn't paid our foxes a visit since middle school.

"Hi, little guys," Callie said in an uncharacteristically sweet coo.

Tor set his big hand on her shoulder. "We've all been friends for how long, Callie?"

"Forever, pretty much," she mumbled.

"Exactly. A year ago, something horrific happened, and everything changed. But we're still here, just like they are. The four of us, at least. Still together, still driving to school in Rem's rust bucket every morning. Now Lydia and I are dating, and things have changed again. That's what life is, though. Things will always be changing. We'll get through this change too."

Tor could come off as cocky and insensitive sometimes, but every once in a while, when you least expected it, he'd shift into this gentle voice and say something kind and sweet and wise that left your insides feeling like warm oatmeal.

Callie remained unmoved, though. Her face darkened again. She turned away from the foxes and hoisted herself to her feet. "Whatever. We should get going. We'll be late for school." Once we'd all piled into the car and I'd backed out of the garage onto Boreal Street, she added in a low mutter, "You've got some fucking nerve comparing what happened to Pete to your little thing with Lydia, Tor."

Our eyes all veered toward the way back, like we could still see Pete's huge body crammed in there, his head propped against the window while he took his morning snooze.

Beyond that, through the Saab's rear window, the blue house at the very end of Boreal Street had shifted into view—much smaller and older and shabbier than the others, its front walk unshoveled, its driveway dug out just enough to let through a tiny compact, its porch hung with dozens of old and tangled wind chimes that murmured in the breeze.

Franklin Kettle's grandmother lived there. Up until a year ago, so had Franklin.

The whole way to school, Callie didn't say another word. I parked in the school lot, and we all shuffled up the front steps. In the hall Lydia held up her stack of posters. "We still have some time before class. Would you guys mind giving me a hand with these?"

"You got it, Strawberry." Tor hooked a thumb over his shoulder. "Rem and I can take this side of the building. You two take the other."

Lydia split the stack in two and gave half to me. Callie snatched the other half and took off down the hall, banging the floor with her wedges, her heap of black hair bobbing and listing and threatening to avalanche any second.

"Seriously, Lydia, don't mind her," I said. "I think the anniversary has us all on edge."

"Yeah." Tor gave her another kiss. "You know Elvira. She can figure out how to be in a bad mood even at the best of times." He grabbed one of the rolls of tape from around her wrist and tapped it against the posters in my hands. "We'll get right to work on these."

Lydia grinned, showing the freckly blush that had inspired the nickname Tor had given her. She hurried after Callie, her auburn ponytail bobbing as she went.

Tor and I started off in the opposite direction. We didn't talk as we turned a corner and headed toward one of the building's back exits, Pete Lund smiling at us over and over from the posters lining the walls. The cold walloped us in the face the second we stepped outside. Tor led the way along the rear of the building until we reached a place where concrete steps crusted with grimy snow led down to the basement. He glanced from side to side to make sure no one had spotted us before heading down.

At the base of the stairs Tor grabbed the padlock that held

the banged-up metal door shut, twisted it, and yanked down hard. It released, and he heaved the door open. We stepped into darkness. After pulling a cord to turn on a naked lightbulb hanging from the ceiling, Tor stomped down another staircase, this one long and narrow and made of wood. His boots shed crumbs of melting snow. At the bottom a corridor stretched off in both directions, and sweaty, searing-hot pipes ran along one wall. The air felt hot and soupy down here. Tor grabbed the posters from me and dumped them on the floor. I unwound the long blue scarf I wore around my neck.

Then we turned to each other in the dark and crashed together like cars in a head-on collision.

3

Tor buried his face in the curve of my neck. I pressed my chest against his, like we were still outside in the cold and I might freeze to death if I didn't.

"Are you sniffing me?" he whispered.

"You smell like chlorine."

"Well, you smell like turpentine."

"Is that bad?"

"Stop talking, Rem."

We grappled some more. His sweatshirt came off. So did my wool coat. Not my paint-spattered long-sleeve T-shirt, though. I didn't have the same superhuman level of body confidence Tor did. Not even down here, where he could barely see me. I put my arms around him, and he felt gigantic, his muscles hard and hot like the pipes on the wall behind us.

Then, because I'm pathetic, and even though I knew exactly how he'd react, I went in for a kiss on the mouth.

He turned his head to the side, and my lips landed in the short hair behind his ear. The chemicals in the school swimming pool had turned it wispy and soft, like stuffed-animal fur. We stumbled a few steps, our feet splashing in the puddle of melted snow that had already formed around us.

Normally I'd consider myself sufficiently humiliated and let it go at that, but something got into me today. I grabbed his chin and tried to turn his face toward mine.

Tor tilted his head back and slipped out of my grip. "What are you doing?" he said, pushing me away. He was laughing, his straight white teeth flashing in the low light.

"I guess I'm trying to kiss you."

"You're so weird."

"Why is that weird? Don't most people kiss in this situation?"

"Come on, Nice Guy. You know I'm not into that. You know I'm not really gay."

I took a few steps backward and bit my lip. Behind me the heat radiating from the pipes pressed against my back. Dozens of retorts rose up in my throat. Dozens of visits to these steam tunnels I could offer as evidence.

Dozens of not very nice things I could say.

"Look," he went on, "I think it's great that you're gay and out of the closet and all that, but I'm not like you. See, for me it's like this: girls are all bends and curves, guys are straight lines."

He gestured to illustrate his point, undulating his hands for the girls, slashing them downward for the guys. I listened in silence, even though I'd heard variations on this speech from him before.

"Girls are hot, but they're so high maintenance. Sometimes I just want to get a little play without dealing with their shit. You know, without it having to *mean* anything. With guys, it's simple. No complications. Am I right?"

He smacked my chest with the back of his hand. I stared at his snow boots and my sneakers swimming in the small, dirty puddle we'd created. I wanted to say yes, match his bro tone, maybe even come out with an off-the-cuff joke, but my mouth wasn't cooperating.

"Nice Guy? You okay?"

I raised my hands and noticed a streak of acrylic paint on the side of my right thumb that was still wet. I couldn't make out the color in the darkness. For a second I imagined myself melting into the puddle at my feet, leaving only a multicolored paint swirl floating on the surface of the water. Apparently whatever had gotten into me today was intent on disproving Tor's "guys are straight lines" theory.

I should never have tried to kiss him. I knew perfectly well how unbending he could be when he'd made up his mind about something, and although I guess you could call what we did in the steam tunnels making out, he never allowed his lips to touch mine. They went plenty of other places. My neck. My ears. Once he spent probably a full minute sucking on my nose, which was weird. But no mouth-to-mouth kissing. That was his rule.

And nothing beyond hand jobs. That was mine. If we weren't going to kiss like normal people, I'd decided, we weren't doing any inserting of things into places either. At least I had *that* much self-respect. So between his rule and my rule, we'd fumble and grope and slobber over each other for a while, and then we'd unzip and finish each other off without looking down. Like a handshake at the end of a business meeting. For two years, that had been our ritual.

Except today Tor said, "Listen, maybe we shouldn't hang out down here anymore."

I looked up. "Why not?"

"Because I think this might not mean the same thing to you as it does to me."

"What are you talking about? Of course it does. I'm all about no complications." Although the complicated way I'd started waving my hands around as I talked probably told a different story.

A dubious smirk flickered across his face. "Really? You're acting weird today, Rem."

I looked down again and stirred the puddle with the toe of my sneaker. "What about Lydia? You must be finding things pretty complicated with her."

"You mean because she won't put out?"

"Well, yeah."

He shrugged. "I'm starting to realize there are more important things in a relationship. I mean it, Rem, I've never felt like this about anyone before. I don't know why it took me so long to see how special she is."

Now it was my turn to smirk. *But you're still down here with me,* the smirk said, and I saw him read it on my face. He grabbed his sweatshirt from the pipe he'd tossed it over earlier and pulled it over his head.

"So how about we take a break from the tunnels for a while?"

The smirk wilted and dropped off my face. I picked up my coat and long blue scarf from where they lay on the floor. "Sure. We can do that. No problem." I wound the scarf around my neck, wishing I could hang myself with it.

"I think it's for the best," Tor said. He turned to head up the stairs, but he stopped with one boot on the bottom step and looked back at me. "Hey, I know I don't even need to ask this, but you haven't told anyone about what we do down here, right?"

"Of course not."

"Nobody?"

"Not a soul."

"Good." He grabbed the end of my scarf and gave it a tug. "It's not that I have anything against being gay. You understand that, right?"

"Sure."

"It's just that I'm not, like I said, and if this got around, people wouldn't understand. Especially Lydia. She's the sweetest person I know. I don't want to confuse her."

"Yeah, I get it."

"And it would probably be weird for you too if people found out."

I couldn't see his face. The lightbulb glowing behind him at the top of the stairs had turned him into a hulking black shape.

He still hadn't let go of my scarf. I wanted to ask what he meant. How would it be weird for me too? I'd come out of the closet three years ago, and Tor was the most popular kid at school. It wasn't like *my* stock would suffer if people found out what we'd been doing.

Or did he mean it another way? As a threat or something?

Tor started to turn away again and his face caught the light. On his chin where I'd grabbed it earlier was a smear of bright pink acrylic paint. I thought about not saying anything, imagining him fumbling to explain the smear to whoever pointed it out to him later.

Instead I touched his shoulder. Tapping my chin, I said, "You've got something right there."

I watched as he licked his fingers and rubbed, coaching him until he'd made the mark disappear.

Because that was what I did. I was the Nice Guy.

4

I spent the rest of the day and most of that night replaying the scene from the steam tunnels in my head. Thoughts of Tor even preempted my usual nightmares involving people having their brains blasted out through the backs of their skulls. (I'd been having those even more often lately, probably because of the upcoming anniversary.) After a while I stopped trying to sleep, turned onto my back, and did what I always did when my mind went into a tailspin: I worked on a new design for my Tattoo Atlas.

By the time pale light started to show through the blinds, I'd mapped out the image in my head enough to try putting it on paper. I crawled out of bed and, on the way to my desk, pushed one of the blinds aside to check the weather.

During the night more snow had fallen. Boreal Street ran along the side of a steep ridge, and our house stood on the uphill side of the street, so from my window I could see the whole city of Duluth spread out beyond the homes opposite ours, all the way down to frozen Lake Superior. A fresh layer of white covered everything. No one else seemed to have woken yet. I couldn't hear a sound except for Mrs. Kettle's wind chimes.

I sat down at my desk—a real artists' table, the kind professionals used. Mom had bought it for me three years ago as a coming-out present. She was one of those cool, progressive, supportive parents who thought coming out of the closet was "something to celebrate," and if that meant getting presents, I certainly wasn't going to argue. Now smears and drips of ink, acrylic, and pale watercolor covered the desk's angled white surface. My pencils and pens and brushes stood in mason jars lining the shelf above, along with a framed photo of my brother, Ethan, and a few stacked paperbacks: *Frankenstein*, *Dr. Jekyll and Mr. Hyde*, *The Picture of Dorian Gray*. All around, on the marked-up carpet, lay stacks and stacks of the sketches and paintings I'd done on paper. Some canvases leaned against the walls too. I reached under the bottom of the stack closest to my desk and pulled out the sketchbook I'd hidden there.

My Tattoo Atlas didn't look like anything much from the outside. It had a plain black cover, just like most of my other sketchbooks, but to distinguish this one from the rest I'd glued to the front a drawing of one of the little winged creatures I called imps. They looked sort of like creepy, huge-eyed, hairless kittens with bat wings, and I'd also incorporated them into most of the drawings inside the Tattoo Atlas. I flipped through the pages, some of them crinkly where I'd used watercolors, until I found a blank one. I spread the book out on my desk.

It didn't take me long to sketch the image in pencil: a knife cutting a straight diagonal line across the page, with trickles of blood seeping from it. Two imps held the knife aloft, and below that, two more supported a banner with *TOR* written on it. On the knife's blade, in neat, loopy cursive, were the words *Guys are straight lines.*

I grabbed a brush and roughed in some color: bright red for the blood, brown for the knife handle, various shades of blue and green and purple for the imps. Then I sat back to look at the image. The watercolors would have to dry before I could ink in the design, but it was already half past seven anyway. I jotted in a lower corner *left upper arm* and got up to take a shower.

5

"I'm running out the door," Mom said. "I put out the breakfast things for you."

I hadn't seen her last night. She'd been working even longer hours than usual lately, getting ready for the whole "putting a hole in Franklin Kettle's head" thing. She looked tired today, with dark circles under her eyes, but even with everything else she had to do, she'd still taken the time to style her gray-and-white hair. It made a neat sphere around her head, like an iron helmet.

"Thanks." I poured myself a cup of coffee, and it slopped out of the pot like syrup. Mom had made it extra strong this morning.

She paused with her metal travel mug halfway to her lips. "Are you okay, Rem?"

I looked away and shrugged. "I guess I'm feeling a little run-down. Abigail's keeping us all really busy with the prep for the Big Bang memorial."

Just because I'd come out to Mom and she was cool and progressive and supportive didn't mean I had to let her in on all the messed-up minutiae of my love life. Anyway, she didn't press. With her brain so full of brain-related thoughts these days, she probably didn't have room for much else.

"What about you?" I said. "Are you holding up all right?"

She gave an impatient wave. Mom didn't like it when I implied she was anything less than invulnerable. "It's been a busy week, but exciting, too. We're so close."

"When's the procedure happening?"

"Tomorrow, if all goes well."

I shook some cereal into the bowl Mom had set out. "And how's Franklin?"

She let out a humorless snort. "A handful. He's refusing to cooperate. Won't even talk. Which is making data-gathering difficult."

"He won't talk to anyone?"

Mom shook her head. Then her eyes dropped to her mug. She'd started prodding the pad of her thumb with her fingernail. "Rem, I've been trying to decide whether I should even tell you this."

"Tell me what?"

She peered into the murk of her coffee, hesitating. "Franklin did say there was one person he'd talk with." Her eyes flicked up to meet mine. "You."

The back of my neck went cold. "Why?"

"He said if I brought you in, he'd feel comfortable talking to you. I know you two weren't exactly friends, but you've lived down the street from each other since you both were tiny. And he told me you were one of the few kids at Duluth Central who was ever nice to him. Does that sound right, Rem?"

Did it? I dodged her eyes, grabbing my bowl from the counter and sitting down at the kitchen table. "I'm not sure."

She twisted the cap onto her travel mug. "I've been thinking if we did put the two of you together in a room, just for a short time, and saw how he interacted with you, it might yield a lot of valuable data. But I wouldn't want you to do it if it made you uncomfortable."

"When?"

"It would have to be this afternoon."

I stirred my cereal. The back of my neck still felt cold and tingly. Like one of my creepy little imps had landed there.

"I realize it might sound unorthodox," Mom pressed. She set down her mug and crossed over to where her coat hung from a hook on the wall. "He killed one of your closest friends right in front of you, and here I am asking you to meet with him face-to-face. But just hear me out on this. I think you might actually find it therapeutic to—"

"I'll do it," I said.

She stopped, looked over her shoulder at me, studied my face. "Are you sure? I do want to warn you, honey, even if he's positively disposed toward you, he may be . . . unpleasant. At least at school and around the neighborhood he kept himself reasonably in check." She grabbed her coat and thrust her arms through the sleeves. "I mean, until he didn't."

"Mom, I can handle it."

She nodded as she buttoned herself up. “I know you can. You’re like me: tough when you need to be. That’s why I don’t worry about you.”

Of course, she might’ve had a different opinion if she’d seen me yesterday with Tor.

On the wall next to Mom hung another photo of Ethan, this time in formal military dress, grinning at the camera from under the brim of a sleek black-and-white hat. She shot a glance at the picture. Her nail dug into her thumb. “Anyway, Franklin will be in restraints,” she said. “And we’ll have guards in there with you. And I’ll be watching the whole time. You’ll be completely safe. Nothing will happen to you.”

“There you go. No reason to worry.”

“But don’t let any of your friends at school know you’re doing this. Not even Callie or Lydia or Tor, okay? There’s a lot of controversy surrounding this project. I don’t want to put you in the middle of that. At least not any more than you already are.”

“I know, Mom. I’ve seen the news.”

To one side of Ethan’s photo hung one of my paintings—Mom’s favorite, even though it wasn’t the kind of thing I usually liked to paint. I’d done it for her a few months ago. A garden-variety watercolor of the Lake Superior shoreline in summertime, it had the bright greens and blues and pinks that looked so alien here in the middle of winter. She nodded at it now.

“Art. That’s something you two can talk about.”

“Franklin Kettle’s into *art*? Where did you get *that* idea?”

"Listen, we'll go over all that at the lab." She grabbed her mug from the counter and leaned over the table to plant a kiss on the top of my head. "Thank you, Rem. This is a big favor. I know you have your doubts about what we're trying to do, but—"

"What are you talking about?" I got up from the table so I could look her in the eyes. "Usually when there's a school shooting, everybody acts all shocked and outraged, but then nothing changes. You're actually trying to do something. I think that's huge. I'm proud of you, Mom."

Which was the truth.

Mostly.

6

Lydia hadn't seemed to notice that Tor and I hadn't put up any posters yesterday, but I felt guilty anyhow, so after we all got to school I took Callie aside and convinced her to help me do the job before class. That also gave me a chance to catch her up on the latest chapter in the saga of the steam tunnels.

Because of course I'd lied to Tor about keeping the tunnels a *total* secret. Callie was my best friend, and I was pretty certain if I couldn't talk to at least one person about the whole Tor drama, I'd go psycho. Maybe not Franklin Kettle psycho, but close. Anyway, she knew how to keep a secret—although yesterday morning in the Saab I'd seen how much effort it was costing her. That was the real reason Tor and Lydia's new coupledom was getting her all worked up.

"So he just drops you the second he suspects you might want more out of him than a quick knuckle shuffle." Her wedges pounded down the hall. "Jesus Christ, that guy can be such an asshole. I understand how you must be feeling, but if you want to know what I think, it's for the best. That thing you two had going was so fucking dysfunctional. It was just making you miserable, wasn't it?"

"Not *totally* miserable," I mumbled.

"Well, it should've been. He was treating you like fucking garbage, Rem. One of you had to put a stop to it. I just wish it had been you. Plus, things have changed now that Lydia's involved. I couldn't have cared less about those other pinheads he cheated on, but to do it to her was just *wrong.* And you're not entirely blameless yourself."

"What are you talking about?" I shot back, the posters under my arm flapping as I hustled to keep up with her. "I was with Tor first, wasn't I? Lydia's the interloper here, not me."

"She can't interlope if she doesn't even know the situation *exists.* I'm sure she thinks I'm a major bitch right now, but the truth is, I feel more sorry for her than I do for you. Tor knew perfectly well she'd been in love with him for years, and then he went and started something with her just so he could keep up his pathetic charade of straightness." She shook her head in disgust, her complicated arrangement of black hair rustling. "So why didn't you call me and tell me about this last night?"

"I didn't feel like talking about it. Look, it's true Tor's been acting like a jerk, but he's probably just feeling really confused. I know what it's like being in the closet."

"Stop making excuses for him. *You* wouldn't have behaved like this before you came out. What's he so scared of anyway? You did the Big Gay Reveal freshman year, and a week later you were runner-up for Freshman Homecoming Prince."

"Maybe it's harder for him because he's such a guy-guy. I was always the sensitive artist type. When I came out, can you honestly say anybody was surprised?"

Callie wasn't buying it. "Someone should just out him already."

"Don't even joke about that, Callie." I shot my eyes around the hall, suddenly paranoid. "The two of us are the only ones who know. He has no idea I told you. If we let it slip . . ."

"What?" she said, her wedges hammering the wood floor so hard they were probably leaving dents. "What would he do?"

"I don't know. Get mad. Look, if Tor's such an asshole, then how come you're still friends with him?"

"Good question," Callie muttered, her scowl deepening.

I knew the reason, even if she wouldn't come out and say it. It wasn't just that he was charismatic and good-looking and smart (second only to Lydia in our class, gradewise). Tor Agnarson was also the most exciting person we knew. At least once a week he'd get this glint in his eye and say, "Ladies and gentlemen, I have an idea." Whenever he said that, you knew something outrageously fun or hilarious or magical would happen. Maybe on the first really warm day of spring we'd all skip class so we could go swimming in Lester River. Or maybe we'd end up on his roof at midnight, watching the aurora borealis. Or maybe he'd take us to spy on a family of wild red foxes.

Tor was the gravitational center of the Boreal Five, the star the other four of us orbited around. I think in our own ways we were *all* a little in love with him. Even straight-as-an-arrow

Pete, who'd done pretty much whatever Tor had told him to do, including joining the swim team despite the fact that his chunky body had really made him better suited for football. Even prickly Callie, who, though she probably would've denied it, seemed to get a weird enjoyment out of constantly butting heads with him.

By then Callie and I had barreled all the way across school. Duluth Central was a sprawling behemoth of a building, built about a hundred years ago out of red brick and limestone and added onto many times after that. The hallways had almost as many twists and turns as the steam tunnels did. It took me a second to figure out where we were. I realized if we took one more turn, we'd reach Ms. Utter's former classroom. I'd made it almost a year without passing by that door, and I didn't feel like starting today. "Slow down. We're supposed to be putting up posters, remember?" I took one from the stack. "Hold it up so I can put on the tape."

While I went to work, she cocked her head to one side and scrutinized the poster. "God, this thing is tacky. Was all this glitter really necessary? Like Pete's headlining a show in Vegas or something. It fucking terrifies me to imagine what Abigail has cooked up for the memorial." She smacked the poster on an empty piece of wall, where it stuck at a haphazard angle, and then she went quiet. She was still studying the glittery image of Pete, but the grimace had left her face. "Maybe because we're the Boreal Five," she murmured.

"What?"

"Maybe that's why I'm still friends with Tor. The five of us grew up together. Now that Pete's gone and there are only four of us left, and we're all about to graduate and go off to different colleges and stuff, it would make me sad if we stopped being friends."

"So underneath it all, Callie Minwalla's really just a softie. I had no idea."

She smacked my arm. "It's just that we're sort of like a family. A seriously fucked-up family, but still." Her face lapsed back into an expression of disgust. "And that's yet another reason why Tor and Lydia shouldn't be together. It's like incest or something." She turned away. "Come on. That's enough for today."

"Callie, we put up *one poster.*"

The hall was thick with students now. Their voices glanced off the walls and floors. A locker slam drew my eye, and I spotted Nil Bergstrom—Nell really, but everyone called her Nil—about to shoulder her mysteriously massive backpack. She and Franklin Kettle had been best friends. Safety-pinned to Nil's pack, and staring me in the face, was a red patch with an image of a black military mask embroidered on it. The mask incorporated a helmet that covered the head, high-tech goggles over the eyes, and a gas mask over the nose and mouth. It was the insignia for that video game they played, Son of War. Franklin had hauled around a backpack just as massive as Nil's, with that same patch safety-pinned to that same spot. I couldn't believe Nil hadn't removed her patch or the principal hadn't forced her to do it. Glimpsing that mask always caused my breath to stop, and I knew it must make other students feel uncomfortable too.

Seeing it now, I wondered if I was really as ready to meet with Franklin as I'd claimed earlier. Maybe I should just bail.

But no. I needed to do it. And not just because I was being the Nice Guy and trying to make Mom happy. For myself, too. Seeing Franklin in the flesh somehow seemed like a more meaningful way to come to terms with the Big Bang than the endless parade of assemblies and rap sessions and candlelight vigils people like Abigail Lansing got so excited about.

Or maybe the reason wasn't as idealistic as that. Maybe I wanted to come face-to-face with Franklin Kettle for the same reason I'd been reading all those classic horror novels lately. Maybe I wanted to see a true monster. Talk to him. Understand him.

And find out why *he* really wanted to see *me*. Because one thing I knew for sure: it wasn't because I'd been nice to him at school.

Nil froze. She'd caught me staring at her. Her eyes narrowed and held mine for a second before she spun around and slouched off. The mask on her backpack seemed to glare at me with an equal amount of menace as she dodged away through the crowd.

7

That afternoon I told the others I needed to do something for Mom and couldn't give them a ride home. I headed to the lab, driving three miles northeast along the Lake Superior shoreline on Highway 61, turning off at a small sign imprinted only with the institute's initials, and crawling down a narrow road with snow banked high on either side. After a mile's worth of twists and turns, the pine trees opened up and the glass behemoth appeared in front of me. Hulking and glittering and ultramodern, the lab stood there all by itself on the edge of the lake like it had dropped from the sky. The Mother Ship, Tor had once called it. Like all his nicknames, that one fit perfectly.

I gripped the cold metal steering wheel and stared at the colorless, cloud-choked sky reflecting on the lab's glass surface. The whiteness of one of the glass panels made me think of the whiteboard in Ms. Utter's classroom last year. She'd hung a banner above it that read *"History, despite its wrenching pain, cannot be unlived, but if faced with courage, need not be lived again."—Maya Angelou.*

I could still picture everything else too. All of us sitting at our usual desks. To our left, narrow windows looking out on bare, black trees loaded with snow. To our right, a map of Europe on the wall, with red arrows pinned on it to show the movement of troops during some war or other. Tiny Ms. Utter, dwarfed by the big metal desk she sat behind. Pete Lund standing at the front of the class, giving a presentation about the Manhattan Project.

I'd stayed up late the night before helping Pete prep the presentation over Skype. Or, to be more accurate, I'd pretty much put together the PowerPoint myself and just made sure he knew how to pronounce all the big words. I never mentioned that to anyone. I didn't like to think of people knowing one of Pete's last acts on earth had been to cheat on his schoolwork. He hadn't been the brightest guy, but he'd been a good friend. Totally cool about the gay thing from day one. Sometimes, when Pete was still alive, I'd wish I could've fallen for him instead of Tor. True, he'd been 100 percent heterosexual, but at least he hadn't had a million issues like Tor did. Pete really *had* been a straight line.

He'd just finished the presentation, having pronounced Hiroshima and Nagasaki perfectly, but I still felt nervous for him, because now he had to get through the mandatory Q and A. As Ms. Utter switched the classroom lights on, I heard a noise behind me and turned. At the back of the class, Franklin Kettle had pulled on a mask. I recognized it right away. I saw it all the time in TV ads, on billboards, on Franklin's backpack and Nil's. There were also mass-produced Halloween versions, but this one he'd made himself. As I'd learn from news reports later, its gas mask and infrared goggles actually worked, and it even had prescription lenses so he could see clearly while wearing it.

Franklin's right fist rose, with a Beretta M9 tucked into the palm. Its muzzle was like a black hole that sucked up all the sound and breath in the room.

"Say 'I didn't know Napoleon was that small,'" Franklin ordered Pete, his low, level voice flattened out even more by the mask.

Nobody else made a noise.

"Say the words, Pete," Franklin repeated. "'I didn't know Napoleon was that small.'"

Pete never said them. Instead a dark stain spread over the crotch of his jeans. Then *BANG*, and the inside of his head splattered the blank whiteboard behind him, like a bouquet of red flowers dropped on the snow.

Thinking about it now, I felt dizzy, the same way I always did when my mind jumped back to that day. I clamped my hands hard on the steering wheel to keep from keeling over and spent a few seconds inhaling and exhaling until the woozy feeling passed. The grief counselor the school had brought in last year taught us to do that. The way the woman talked, nodding and overenunciating like a kindergarten teacher, had driven me crazy, but her technique actually worked.

She hadn't had any bright ideas about how to stop the nightmares, though.

I shook my head, wrapped my long blue scarf around my neck, and headed into the Mother Ship.

The main hall, with its sleek lines and high ceiling and concrete floor, didn't feel much warmer than outside. The building had only gone up a little over a year ago—thanks in large part to Mom's dogged efforts—and it still smelled like fresh paint.

"You must be Jeremy," the receptionist behind the white swooping desk said. "I'll let your mom know you're here."

He spoke a few words into a phone, handed me a visitor badge, and nodded me toward the elevator, which whooshed me to the top floor.

The elevator opened on Mom. She planted a firm kiss on my cheek. "Let's talk a bit in my office first." She walked me down the hall, touched her badge to a reader, and opened a door. Some kind of weird music blasted out at us. It sounded like a bunch of tone-deaf guys chanting in gibberish while banging arrhythmically on an assortment of pots and pans.

"Gertie!" Mom called over the din. "Would you turn down that goddamn noise?"

We entered the main lab, a big room with rows of white tables in the center and desks lining the periphery. Half a dozen scientists looked up from their computers. Gertie tapped her keyboard, and the music disappeared. "Sorry, Dr. Braithwaite. I was just playing this new piece I discovered. I thought it might help us stay awake."

"Try coffee. It's quieter." Mom steered me toward her office at the back of the room and shut the door. "Gertie thinks she's an avant-garde music connoisseur," she said. "Speaking of coffee, would you like some?" She grabbed her metal mug from her desk and topped it off from a pot on a side table.

"That's okay." I peeled off my coat and scarf and dropped onto the couch. On the other side of the floor-to-ceiling window, Lake Superior had darkened to gunmetal gray. Four o'clock in the afternoon, and the sun had already started to set.

Mom sat down next to me. "I just went to visit Franklin. He knows you're coming, but before we start, I want to tell you a little about what's going to happen. He'll have chains on, like I told you this morning, and guards will stay in the room with you at all times. He won't be able to do anything to you physically. But you may find this encounter difficult. You watched him kill someone in cold blood, so seeing him again is bound to raise feelings in you. And he can be disturbing to talk to."

An afterimage of the whiteboard splattered in red lingered behind my eyes, but I blinked it away. "Come on, Mom, he's just some kid who's lived on my block since kindergarten."

"He's also very sick and very intelligent. He knows how to get under a person's skin. That's why I want you to do your best to keep the conversation neutral. Don't bring up anything connected to the shooting, is that clear?"

"What does that leave? I know zero about computers, and I hate video games."

"I already said: art."

I scrunched my nose.

"According to his caseworker," Mom said, "it was the only

thing he took any interest in at the detention center, since he didn't have access to a computer. She told me he spent hours every day with a notebook and a piece of charcoal, just drawing."

"Drawing what? Dismembered human bodies?"

Mom sipped her coffee. "She didn't know. Apparently he wouldn't let anyone see the pictures. He'd tear them up and flush them down the toilet immediately after finishing them."

An image flashed in my head: Franklin sitting at the back of the class, his head down, his hair, dyed blue-black then, falling over his face, a notebook open on the desk in front of him, one arm bent around it to conceal the pages from prying eyes, his pen scratching away. I'd seen him carry that notebook around all the time. He'd decorated the cover with a Son of War sticker—of course—and written his name in red ink down the side, on the edges of the pages. I'd never gotten a look inside, but it had always seemed incongruous to me, a computer expert like Franklin using an old-fashioned paper notebook instead of an iPad or something.

"Okay," I said. "I'll ask him about his art."

"Thanks, Rem. It doesn't even matter that much what you two talk about. We just want to observe how he interacts with someone who was peripherally involved in the shooting."

"And then see if his behavior changes after the procedure?"

"Exactly. The conversation will only last five minutes. We'll cut it even shorter if things don't go well. And, Rem,"—she grabbed my forearm and gave it a squeeze—"thank you for doing this, honey. I know it can't be easy having a mad scientist like me for a mother."

8

Back in the main lab, Mom introduced me to two of the guards who'd come along with Franklin from the detention center to watch over him. One man, one woman, both built like football players, they wore crisp gray shirts and walkie-talkies on their hips that let out occasional burps of static. They gave me a nod and headed out to get their prisoner.

"You'll meet with him in here." Mom unlocked a door with her badge and held it open for me.

"Good luck, Rem," Gertie called from her desk.

Mom gave me another hard kiss on the cheek. "I love you," she said. "You know that, don't you?"

I nodded and stepped through the door. The room I entered, though about the same size as the one I'd just left, contained almost no furniture. A white table and two metal chairs stood near the window, and that was it. Like Mom's office, this room looked out on the lake. Outside, the sky had darkened even more, the clouds turning purple and black. I sat down in the chair across from the window.

A door to my left swung open. Right away, my fingers clamped onto the armrests. My forehead and cheeks felt cold, like they did whenever I woke up from one of my nightmares. It took me by surprise how fast the feeling crashed over me. I tried to remember all the reasons I shouldn't feel this way—Franklin would have chains on, he wouldn't have a weapon, the guards would stay the whole time—but my nervous system wasn't convinced. My heart seemed to bang at the same volume as that "music" Gertie had been playing out in the main lab.

Franklin Kettle slunk in, with the two guards close behind him. One of them, the lady, escorted him to the chair across from mine and sat him down. He looked pretty much the same as I remembered. He had on his bulky black glasses, and his hair fell down over his face in spikes. He hadn't managed to keep it dyed, though. It had faded from that startling blue-black to regular dark brown. And he didn't have on the old black denim jacket, tattered and held together with safety pins, that he'd worn all the time over a black T-shirt and a pair of narrow black jeans. Instead he wore a new but cheap-looking outfit I figured one of the lab techs must've bought for him at Target so he wouldn't have to wear his detention center jumpsuit. This wasn't much better, though: gray sweatpants and a hoodie the blinding orange shade of traffic cones.

He also had on his chains. They clanked with every tiny movement he made, as if they didn't want you to forget they were there.

I willed my fingers to uncurl from the armrests. "Hi." My

voice sounded thin in my ears. "Um. My mom said you asked to talk to me?"

Franklin shot his eyes toward one of the cameras hanging from the ceiling. "I just didn't feel like talking to *them*. I figured talking to you would at least be a slight improvement. And I figured your mom would jump at the chance to watch me interact with one of my peers."

"I guess you figured right."

The chains rattled as he shifted in his chair. "It's kind of ironic, though, isn't it? In real life, we wouldn't be interacting at all. Sure, we know each other, but it's not like we really *know* each other. Have we ever even had a conversation before?"

He didn't say it with any apparent anger. As always, he spoke in a quiet, empty voice. Still, ten seconds in, the conversation already felt like it had left neutral territory. I glanced at the guards. They stood on either side of Franklin, several feet back, in front of the glass wall. Each of them wore a small earpiece, which Mom would use to tell them to call the meeting off if things went south. For now the guards didn't move.

"Probably not," I said.

"At least you were never an asshole to me, like everybody else at school."

Behind his hair and his glasses, his eyes narrowed just the littlest bit. My chest tightened. I blinked and fumbled for something to say. "I don't—"

"I guess we never had many interests in common. That might be the reason we didn't socialize more."

I was pretty sure he'd meant that sarcastically, but the tonelessness of his voice and the expressionlessness of his face made it hard to tell. "Maybe," I said. "But my mom told me you're into art. That's cool. I actually do a lot of drawing my—"

The chains clattered some more while he settled into a deeper slouch. "Nope. Not really into art. There was just nothing else to do at the detention center. They didn't let us near any computers. That's what I'm really into. Computers. Video games."

"Son of War."

The second the words jumped out of my mouth, I wished I could stuff them back in. A tiny smile curled the corners of Franklin's mouth. "You play? Because *that* would be something we have in common."

Again I suspected sarcasm. I shook my head.

"I didn't think so. Mr. Nice Guy—isn't that what everybody calls you? Way too nice to play a game like Son of War."

On the other side of the window snow had started to fall. The flakes made a whispering sound as they tumbled against the glass.

"You're probably right," I said. "I don't know much about that game. Why don't you tell me?"

"It's not too complicated. You just kill stuff."

"You're a soldier or something?"

"Yep."

"And you shoot at things?"

"Yep."

He studied his fingernails as we spoke, as usual not so much avoiding eye contact as seeming indifferent to the whole concept. I glanced around, hunting for a clock. Our five minutes had to end soon, right? "But you must have a mission. I mean, there must be something you're trying to accomplish other than just shooting things up."

"Yeah, but mostly you're just killing stuff."

"And you get points? Like, for killing bad guys?"

"For killing anyone."

My sneakers settled flat on the smooth concrete floor. I glanced down and realized I'd gone back to clutching the armrests again. My knuckles had turned white. "For killing anyone?"

His eyes stayed on his fingernails, but his grin widened. "Sure."

"Even innocent people?"

"Depends on what you call innocent, I guess. Maybe there *is* no innocent, really."

Tendrils of nausea snaked through my belly. I couldn't look at him anymore. Outside, the snow had thickened. The huge window looked like a TV screen on static. "I think that's disgusting."

"It's how war works. Kill or be killed. The game's just teaching you how to be a real soldier. Did you know Son of War is used in military training programs all over the world to prepare soldiers for combat? And I still have one of the all-time high scores, which means—"

"Real soldiers don't shoot civilians," I said.

"Don't they? Have you watched the news lately?"

"I mean good soldiers. They try not to."

"You mean your brother. The one that got himself popped."

One of the guards put his hand to his earpiece and listened. I pictured Mom watching us on the monitor back in the main lab, hearing Franklin bring up her oldest son. I waited for her to call the whole thing off.

The guard's hand fell away from his ear. He didn't make a move.

I closed my eyes and commanded myself to breathe. *Don't take the bait. Keep the conversation neutral.* But that word he'd used—"popped"—had snagged in my brain. Like Ethan had been a balloon, or a grape. "Well, congratulations." I could hear how brittle my voice sounded, like thin, fractured ice. "It must feel good to be such a master player."

Franklin lifted his shoulders and dropped them. "It's okay." He sank even further down in his chair, looking bored, and threw his head back to peer at the lights hanging from the ceiling. They flashed in the lenses of his glasses. "Did your brother ever play?"

My fingers bit into the cold metal of the chair. "I don't think so."

"Maybe he should've. Maybe things would've played out differently if he had. He was probably like you, too nice for all that fighting."

I shot another glance at the guard. Why hadn't Mom intervened? Hadn't this gone far enough? "I don't think you should be talking about my brother."

"I'm curious, though: did you ever find out if he pissed his pants just before it happened, like Pete Lund did?"

The next instant I was on my feet and slamming my hands on the table. Behind me, something banged: I'd knocked my metal chair to the floor. "Fuck you," I said. "You're disgusting."

The guards had already landed on us. The lady had clapped her hands on Franklin's shoulders, even though he was still just slouching in his chair, and the guy, big as he was, had managed to pelt all the way around the table and grab me from behind in less than a second.

"Okay, buddy," he said. "I think we're done for today."

Franklin just smiled. When the female guard took him by the arm, he stood without resistance and walked with her to the door. "Bye, Rem," he called over his shoulder, like we'd just finished a pleasant conversation. The guard pushed the door open, and Franklin's chains jingled down the hall.

9

Long after Mom had guided me into her office and onto her couch, my heart went on pounding against my rib cage like it wanted to bust free of my chest. Outside, in the darkness, the snow continued its frantic dance. In my head I heard the grief counselor's singsongy kindergarten teacher's voice: *Iiiiinhale, eeeeexhale, iiiiinhale, eeeeexhale.*

Mom switched on the electric kettle on the side table to make me tea. "I promise you, honey," she said, "if I'd known he'd pull something like that, I never would've sent you in there."

I hadn't uttered a syllable since leaving the meeting room. When I spoke, the words came out soft and scratchy. "Then how come you didn't do something sooner?"

She stopped, an empty mug in her right hand, and blinked at me. Her left index finger jabbed the numb pad of her thumb. "The encounter was producing valuable data."

I sagged into the couch a little deeper. "Right."

"Plus, things escalated quickly."

"Did you even hear the stuff he said about Ethan?"

Her face hardened. "Of course I did, Rem. I hope you're not implying—"

I waved my hand to stop her. "It's okay. I'm okay. Never mind."

The kettle started to whistle. She wiped back her white lock of hair, took a breath, and turned away, busying herself with fixing my tea.

Maybe it shouldn't have surprised me. Over the past couple years Mom had been constantly losing herself in her work, and this current project especially obsessed her. I understood the reason too. Ever since Ethan's death, she'd needed something to focus on. So had I. That probably explained why I was always losing track of time and forgetting to wash my hands when I did my painting.

Mom sat down next to me and passed me the warm mug. "You can't take what Franklin says personally. Remember, he's a sociopath. From a neurological perspective, that means the parts of his brain that should allow him to experience empathy, to put himself in the place of other human beings, don't function like they should. That's why he could shoot Pete without feeling any remorse. That's why he could say those awful things to you."

I nodded and took a sip of tea. My heart had slowed a little. As usual, the inhaling and exhaling had helped. "But what caused his brain to be like that? Was he abused? Because that can affect brain development, right?"

"It can," Mom answered, "but in Franklin's case, we haven't turned up any evidence of abuse."

"What about his parents? Maybe they did something horrible to him before he moved in with his grandma."

Franklin had appeared on our block when we all were five or so, after his mom and dad died in a car crash. His grandmother seemed harmless enough—if a little reclusive and not all there—but I'd always wondered, especially after the shooting, if something had happened to him in those early years to make him the way he was.

Mom was shaking her head, though. "By all accounts, Franklin's parents were decent people. And our testing doesn't lead us to suspect he was a victim of early trauma."

"So why is he like this?"

She turned up her hands. "I don't know, Rem. The wrong combination of genes, maybe. Or something could've gone awry in utero. There are dozens of possible causes."

"That doesn't make what he did okay. Killing Pete."

"Of course it doesn't."

"I mean, people who have less empathy or whatever can still use common sense, can't they? Even if Franklin doesn't *feel* bad about the Big Bang, at least he can still *understand* that what he did was wrong, right?"

"Not necessarily. We humans like to think of ourselves as more rational than we are. We imagine we navigate through life using pure logic, but far more than we realize, we do things for illogical reasons and then bend our perception of reality to make our actions *seem* logical, at least to ourselves. It's a trick of the brain, something we all do. With sociopaths like Franklin, this phenomenon's often amplified. I'm sure he has it all worked out in his head why Pete deserved what happened to him."

I sipped my tea and looked out the window at the big black space where Lake Superior lay. "Okay, but if Franklin's like he is because he just happens to have a brain that's wired a certain way, then what about evil? Does evil just not exist?"

"I'm not sure. Maybe it does. But I don't think that word's particularly useful when it's used to label individual people."

"So you don't think Hitler was evil?"

She smirked. I'd pulled the Hitler card on her before. "I think Hitler was a person who did reprehensible things, but I also think labeling him as evil, or a demon, or a monster, makes it too easy for us to think of him as belonging to a category apart from the rest of us, when the truth is, he was still just a person."

I clasped the mug with both hands and let the heat radiate into my palms. They still smarted from when I'd slammed them on the table. "What about the guy who killed Ethan?" I asked. "You don't think he was evil either?"

I heard Mom's breath snag in her throat. I didn't bring up Ethan often. "No," she said. "Not even him. We don't know anything about Ethan's killer, except that he was in a war zone with a gun in his hand and a gun aimed straight at him. He did what any number of people would've done in that situation."

"That's generous of you, Mom."

"Not really." She brushed my cheek with the backs of her fingers. "It doesn't mean I don't wish every day that Ethan had pulled the trigger first and blown that other person's head open instead."

10

I drove home with my mind still in overdrive. Thinking about Franklin. Thinking about Ethan.

Maybe the real reason Franklin's comments had set me off was because he'd been right about my brother: Ethan *hadn't* been a killer. He'd always been too busy working on his Saab and reading poetry and running the crisis hotline at Duluth Central to play shoot-'em-up video games.

Not that he'd been some kind of wimp. Far from it. Ethan had exuded a quiet strength, so his gentleness had never come off as weakness. The younger kids on Boreal Street had all looked up to him, Tor and Pete included, which probably explains how I ever got to be friends with those two. Under other circumstances, as an arty, skinny, nonathletic proto-homosexual, I'd have been a natural target for a couple big, rough boys like Tor and Pete. I'd have been . . . someone like Franklin, maybe. Not a sociopath—at least I hope not—but an outcast. Ethan didn't let that happen. He set a tone for the block by being kind and friendly with everyone, and other kids naturally followed his lead. (Except maybe when it came to Franklin himself, although . . . I could just be making excuses, but Franklin didn't seem much interested in our friendship anyway.)

I never fully understood why Ethan enlisted, but I always suspected he did it because he thought he could somehow stop the fighting *there.*

But Afghanistan wasn't Boreal Street.

Mom and I found out Ethan had died at the beginning of my sophomore year, on the same day Tor took me down to the steam tunnels for the first time. During lunch that day, my phone buzzed with a Skype call from Ethan, but Tor grabbed it out of my hand. I tried to explain that Ethan and I had made a plan beforehand, that it was hard for us to get our schedules to sync up because of the time difference, but in the end Tor convinced me to blow Ethan off and go with him instead.

At that point I'd come out of the closet a year earlier, but I still hadn't touched another boy in a PG-13 kind of way. It surprised the hell out of me when Tor, a guy I'd always thought of as the pinnacle of heterosexual guyness, grabbed me in the dark of the tunnels and put his mouth on my neck. I arrived home that evening feeling excited and ashamed and incredibly flattered all at once. Mom was in the kitchen making dinner, and I hoped my cheeks didn't look as flushed as they felt. She glanced up from the cutting board to say hello, and her face turned as white as the streak in her gray hair. I thought for sure she could tell exactly what had happened just from the expression on my face, but it turned out she wasn't looking at me at all.

A black sedan bearing a military license plate had pulled up in the driveway. The car was shiny in spite of the winter weather, like someone had just washed it five minutes ago. A guy in formal military dress stepped out.

Mom let out a scream and I probably jumped three feet. I'd never heard a sound like that come out of her mouth before. She was usually so controlled, so pulled together. When I turned again, the tip of her left thumb lay in the center of her white plastic cutting board, along with a spattering of blood. The soldier ended up taking us to the hospital so she could have her thumb tip sewn back on.

I never found out all the details of Ethan's death and didn't want to, but I heard enough. Ethan and a few other troops had been clearing a house. He'd entered a room, and an enemy combatant had jumped up from behind a couch with a gun in his hand. "Get back!" Ethan had yelled to the soldier behind him. Always thinking about others, right up to the end.

But that meant he should've had enough time to fire. He didn't. The other guy did. And that was it.

Game over.

11

After I got home from the lab, I microwaved a pizza for dinner but couldn't bring myself to eat it. I went to my room to do my homework but just ended up staring at the same page in my biology textbook. So I spent the rest of the evening inking in the knife picture I'd drawn that morning. By the time I finished, it was late, but I still didn't feel sleepy, so I turned to a fresh page in my Tattoo Atlas and started reworking an image I'd played with before.

First I penciled in a simple rectangle that could've been a classroom whiteboard or could've been a white kitchen cutting board. In the center, I drew a big severed thumb tip spattered with blood. Below that, near the bottom of the rectangle, a headless body slumped, wearing Pete Lund's letterman jacket. Above the rectangle hung a banner, held aloft by two imps, that read, in neat cursive, *History, despite its wrenching pain, cannot be unlived, but if faced with courage, need not be lived again.* Another banner underneath the image bore the words, in all capitals, *THE BIG BANG.*

12

The Big Bang. Tor had thought of the name, of course, although he hadn't had the usual mischievous spark in his eye when he first said it. Pretty soon that was what all the students at Duluth Central called it. Teachers and parents and news reporters used other designations, like the Tragic Shooting, or the Appalling Incident, or the Senseless Murder, but we preferred the Big Bang. We needed a code name, a way to talk about what had happened, but not too directly. Anyway, that particular code name fit well. Like the actual Big Bang scientists always went on and on about, our Big Bang had been an explosion and also a beginning. It had created the universe we lived in now.

Although for me personally, the Big Bang had really come a year before that. By the time Pete Lund died, I already knew the people you cared about could get taken from you in horrible ways. I'd just never seen it happen firsthand.

Mom sometimes said I'd seen too much death for someone so young, and maybe she was right. (She was probably thinking not just of Ethan and Pete, but of Dad, too. He died of a brain tumor when I was a toddler.) While Abigail Lansing bawled and wailed and wondered how a tragedy like the Big Bang could possibly happen, I just wanted to know how long we had until the next one.

13

The day after my visit to the Mother Ship, Lydia, Callie, Tor, and I got to skip first period to attend rehearsal for the memorial assembly. Abigail Lansing had insisted we come, even though it seemed like she'd already planned everything out herself. In fairness, she *had* asked if one of us would like to give a speech—and to everyone's surprise, Callie had raised her hand first. She'd admitted she didn't normally go in for "fucking sentimental shit like that," but she'd wanted to make an exception for Pete.

When we arrived at the gym, the school choir members, all of them dressed in white robes, had assembled on the basketball court. Abigail stood off to the side, conferring with Mrs. Chen, the principal, and Mr. Larsen, the choral director. When she noticed us, she waved and jogged over.

"I'm so happy you guys could make it," she said, furrowing her forehead in the earnest way she always did whenever she talked about anything even slightly related to Pete's death. Mascara clung to her eyelashes in clumps. I was pretty certain she put it on so thick specifically so it would make dramatic track marks when she cried, which seemed to happen on an hourly basis since the Big Bang. "It would've made Pete so happy to see all of us here together honoring him. Why don't you have a seat on the bleachers? I can't wait to hear what you think."

"I have a bad feeling about this," Callie muttered as she teetered up the bleacher steps in her wedges.

"Shouldn't we sit closer?" I asked.

She shook her head, already at the top. "I need a buffer zone."

My phone buzzed, and I pulled it out as I sat down next to Callie. A message had just come through from Mom. *Heading into OR. We'll begin procedure soon. Keep your fingers crossed.*

You'll do great! I texted back. *No empty superstitious gestures like crossing fingers necessary! But I'll keep them crossed anyway just in case!!!*

I hadn't wished Mom good luck that morning. She'd had to leave early, and she'd probably figured I hadn't gotten up yet, but I had. After waking from the usual nightmare in the usual cold sweat, I'd spent the hours before dawn inking my latest Tattoo Atlas drawing. I heard her moving around in the kitchen and knew I should go out there and say a few words of support and encouragement. Maybe it had something to do with the nightmare, though, or my doubts about the procedure, or the way she'd left me in that room with Franklin so long yesterday, but I couldn't bring myself to do it. I felt bad about it after. Even though I tried to be a good son, and most of the time succeeded, sometimes I suspected it didn't come naturally to me the way I knew it had to Ethan.

I hoped my liberal use of exclamation points now would make up for it.

Lydia and Tor were sitting in the row just below mine and Callie's. "Abigail told me yesterday how the assembly's supposed to go," Lydia said. "They're going to sing one song at the beginning. Then come the speeches. Then they sing again. The whole thing will be pretty short."

"Thank God," Callie said, readjusting the chopsticks that held her black hair in place.

The overhead lights went down, and a couple spotlights bathed the chorus in an angelic glow. Mr. Larsen put up his hands. The chorus started to sing.

"I see trees of green, red roses too. I see them bloom for me and you. And I think to myself, What a wonderful world."

"Oh Christ," Callie said much too loudly.

Lydia spun around and put her finger to her lips imploringly.

Lowering her voice a fraction of a decibel, Callie said, "I get that the song's supposed to be sweetly hopeful in spite of all the horror in the world that the Big Bang represents, but I mean, come on. It just comes off as deluded and pathetic."

"I see friends shaking hands, sayin', 'How do you do?' They're really sayin', 'I love you.'"

"Take it down a notch," I whispered into Callie's ear. "Abigail's going to hear you."

"Well, she should know!" she hissed back.

Lydia put her face in her hands, mortified.

"Strawberry," Tor said, tapping her shoulder. "Don't mind her. I got something for you."

He kissed her. On the mouth.

Just seeing it made me want to hurl myself off the bleachers that very second, but Mom texted again just in time. *Thanks, honey.*

No prob!!!!! I texted back.

The chorus scooped into their final *"Oh yeah."* Abigail trotted up the bleacher steps, a stack of brightly colored index cards in her fist. "What did you think?"

"Very moving," Lydia blurted before anyone else had a chance to speak.

"I'm supposed to give my speech next." Abigail flipped through her cards, frowning. "I wanted to have it memorized, but I'm not sure I do. Lydia, could you come down to the front and follow along on these cards and help me if I forget something?"

Abigail thrust the cards at Lydia and hurried back down. Lydia squinted at Abigail's loopy handwriting.

"I'll go with you," Tor said, standing up behind her and giving her shoulders a squeeze. "Moral support." He saluted Callie and me, and the two of them headed down the steps after Abigail.

Callie noticed me watching them and patted my forearm. "Between their gooeyness and that gooey fucking song, I was about to spill my breakfast a second ago. How are you holding up?"

"Oh, you know, just feeling like used toilet paper over here."

"Have you and Tor talked? About your new relationship status, I mean. 'Friends without benefits,' apparently."

"Not since the last time we went down to the steam tunnels."

Tor and I never talked about anything connected to the steam tunnels outside of the steam tunnels. Usually when he wanted to go down there with me, most often toward the end of lunch, he'd suggest we step outside for a smoke. Lydia and Callie both found smoking disgusting—Callie called it a "fucking filthy habit"—so we never had to worry about them wanting to join us. The funny thing was, Tor and I both found smoking disgusting too. The one time I tried it, it made me want to puke, and Tor would never in a million years jeopardize his swimming career that way. He'd used the same box of cigarettes as a prop for over a year now.

He hadn't suggested we go out for a smoke yesterday.

"I'm starting to wonder if he was telling the truth all those times he claimed he wasn't gay," I said. "He always made such a big deal of not kissing me, but apparently he doesn't have any problem kissing *her*."

Tor and Lydia had settled themselves on the bottom row of bleachers. She rested her head against his shoulder while she went through Abigail's cards.

"You have to admit, Callie, he's being extra sweet with her. Maybe we've been wrong about him. Maybe he really does prefer girls. Maybe he just likes the convenience of . . ."

"Your right hand?" Callie shook her head. "It doesn't matter,

Rem. Whether he's gay and just pretending he likes Lydia or an actual bisexual who's dropped you now that he's found someone else, either way, he's a douche bag. He's got to know how seeing him with her is making you feel, but he doesn't care. I'm telling you, you're better off without him."

"Maybe." I sat forward, resting my elbows on my knees, and watched the two of them lean into each other. "I still say he's just a jerk sometimes because he's got a lot going on inside."

"That's no excuse. We're all fucking confused and terrified and miserable. Every single person on this goddamn planet, with the possible exception of Lydia. Does that mean we all get to act like assholes?"

"Shh," I said. "Abigail's getting ready to speak."

"Oh joy."

I glanced at her. "What about you? Where are *your* index cards?"

"I've got it all up here." She tapped her temple. "Get ready, Remmy. I'm going to make you weep like a fucking baby."

14

She pretty much did. Unlike Abigail, Callie didn't talk about how Pete had gone to a better place or read excerpts from Robert Frost poems or expertly make her chin quiver and summon pretty, sparkly tears to her eyes at the exact right moment. She just told stories about the Boreal Five. The one that really got me was from sophomore year, not long after my brother's death.

I'd barely set foot outside my room for three weeks. Mom knocked on the door one evening and said, "There's something in the backyard I think you should see." I followed her to the kitchen and peered out through the sliding glass doors.

Just before he'd left to join the military, Ethan had spent a summer building a simple wood gazebo behind our house, so we could sit outside on summer afternoons and drink iced tea. During the winter it mostly just sat there under piles of snow. But that day the rest of the Boreal Five had turned it into a tiny palace of ice and light. Tor's idea, naturally. They'd filled up all the open spaces in the walls with blocks of snow, making the walls solid. Then they'd poured bucketfuls of water down the outsides until a smooth shell of ice covered the structure. To light up the crystalline house they'd created, they'd carved niches into the insides of the walls in dozens of random spots and placed a votive candle in each one. The flickering candles made the gazebo pulse and glow like a living thing.

I bundled myself up, and when I stepped into the gazebo, I found Tor, Pete, Lydia, and Callie waiting for me. The five of us hung out there until late, telling stories about Ethan and drinking Fat Tire, Ethan's favorite beer.

That night was the Boreal Five at its best. At one point, because somebody had to, Pete jumped up and danced around the ice palace singing "Let It Go." Considering he weighed two hundred plus and danced like, well, a straight jock with zero rhythm, it was quite a sight. Under pressure from Tor, Lydia tried her very first sip of beer. "But only in honor of Ethan," she said. Callie, in an uncharacteristically sentimental outburst, declared, "Guys, I fucking love us," and right then I knew everyone else felt the exact same way.

At one point, after we'd spent an hour in the gazebo and our fingers had started going numb, I left to get some blankets from the house, and Tor ducked out after me. He grabbed my hand and drew me back behind the gazebo. "When we lose people we care about," he said in that gentle voice he only used every once in a while, "we have to hold even tighter to the ones who are still with us." Then, with the ice wall pulsating next to us, he gave me a hug—a long, tender one, not the kind of insistent tackle he'd surprised me with in the steam tunnels a few weeks earlier.

No kiss, but at least a real hug.

Part of me had thought he might also apologize for making me miss my chance to talk to Ethan one last time, but maybe that had been too much to expect. Maybe he hadn't even put it together that Ethan had died on the same day he'd shown me the tunnels. Still, sometimes I'd spin out fantasies in my head, imagining that if Tor hadn't yanked my phone away from me, I would've kept Ethan on the line long enough for things to play out differently. I knew it was a stretch. I knew any reasonable person would say Ethan's death couldn't have been Tor's fault. But sometimes, like a cockroach you couldn't get rid of, the thought would scuttle through my brain anyway.

As we stood there behind the gazebo, though, the way Tor was holding me and looking into my eyes, I would've forgiven him anything.

At that point we'd only gone down to the tunnels that one time. A few weeks later, once I'd returned to school and started trying to go through life like a normal person, I was the one who suggested, in my most casual voice, that we "check out those tunnels again." I felt especially crappy that day. I hoped if we went back down there, Tor might give me something that would make me feel better. Maybe a repeat of the hug. Maybe even a kiss.

No such luck. But at least the robotic fumbling took my mind off other stuff.

15

The rehearsal didn't finish until the end of first period, so the four of us went straight to Ms. Utter's second-period history class. We had her again this year, although she'd moved to a different classroom. The one where the shooting had taken place, down on the first floor, had been permanently locked.

Ms. Utter stopped me on the way to my desk and drew me into a corner. "I have a question for you, Rem."

The alcohol on her breath wafted toward me as she spoke. Ever since the Big Bang, she'd carried the scent of liquor around with her the same way I did turpentine and Tor did chlorine. I understood: like Mom with her work, like me with my art, she needed something to help her deal with all the messed-up thoughts death left behind. It made me sad, though, and worried, too. Ms. Utter was one of my favorite teachers. So far her drinking hadn't gotten in the way of her teaching, but I dreaded the day it did.

"I know your mom's performing her procedure on Franklin Kettle today," she said, "and I'm betting the other kids in class do too. It was all over the news last night. I think people might like to talk about it, but I wanted to check with you first to make sure it wouldn't make you uncomfortable. If it would, we can skip it, or I can send you to the library for a few minutes."

"No, it's okay. It doesn't bother me."

I got why she wanted to take some time during class to talk. Like me, most of the other kids in this class had taken Ms. Utter's first-period history class last year. They'd witnessed the shooting firsthand. More than any other students at Duluth Central, they had a personal interest in what was happening to Franklin today.

"People may want to ask you questions," she said.

"That's fine. I mean, I'm not really a science person, so I probably won't be able to explain what my mom's doing very well, but I can try."

She nodded. "Thanks, Rem."

I dropped into my regular spot in front of Callie. Ms. Utter called the class to order and, with her small hands folded on her massive desk, explained that she wanted to take a few minutes to discuss the news coverage concerning Franklin Kettle and "any feelings it may have brought up in you." A few students gave weary nods. Since the Big Bang, it sometimes felt like all we did was talk about feelings.

A girl named Anna raised her hand. She'd been sitting in the front row the day Pete had gotten shot. I could still picture the blood speckling her pale, frizzy hair. Now she always sat near the back of the class. Outside the Splash Zone, I guess.

"I want to know what's supposed to happen to him after," Anna said. "They stick some gizmo in his brain, and then what? He's cured? They just release him?"

"I don't believe that's the plan," Ms. Utter said. "The way I understand it, the treatment's experimental, so it won't have any effect on Franklin's sentence. Is that right, Rem?"

"I think so," I said.

"Rem, maybe you'd like to explain to the others exactly what your mother and her team are doing with Franklin."

I rubbed my palms together, the skin dry and probably smelling of turpentine. I tried to remember how Mom had explained it to me. "Basically, she's using energy to change the way Franklin's brain works. Which is nothing new—shock therapy would probably be the earliest example—except over time scientists have made better and better maps of the brain and learned how to target more and more specific areas. The technology my mom's developed is the most advanced yet. Before now, nobody's been able to treat anything nearly as complicated as—"

"Being a psycho killer," Callie supplied.

A few desks squeaked as kids shifted in their chairs. Uncomfortable looks bounced around the room.

"Franklin Kettle's a sociopath," I said. "My mom and her team figured that was a brain disorder, just like any other. They created an implant—this super-high-tech capsule thingy—that's supposed to send targeted pulses of energy to malfunctioning neurons located in different parts of Franklin's brain to make them work like they should. Today they're opening a hole in the back of his head, and . . ."

I spaced out for a second, wondering if Mom was bent over Franklin's exposed brain at that very moment. An image jumped into my mind of the whole team standing in a tight huddle around Franklin, who lay facedown on an operating table, the back of his head open, the rest of his body hidden under blue paper, the scientists digging into his red, jiggling brain with their flashing tools like a bunch of fork-wielding diners chowing down on a shared bowl of spaghetti.

"Rem?" Ms. Utter said.

I blinked a few times to pull my mind back into the classroom. *Iiiiinhale. Eeeeexhale.* "So they're opening a hole in Franklin's skull and inserting the capsule. It's supposed to be a pretty simple procedure actually. The capsule does the rest on its own."

"And then when he wakes up he's suddenly going to be a model citizen?" Callie said.

"I guess that's the idea."

She crossed her arms and shook her head. "It's just so god-damn weird. The idea that you can change who a person is just by sticking some gadget in his brain."

"Language, Callie," Ms. Utter said.

"What about security at the lab?" a guy called Mike asked. He'd sat all the way on the far side of the room on the day of the Big Bang and later said he'd found a piece of bone lodged in his ear. "That lab wasn't built to contain prisoners, was it? What if he tries to escape?"

I'd heard others making similar arguments on the news lately. After Franklin's arrest journalists had turned up comments he'd left on a Son of War subreddit. In them he seemed to talk, in a sort of coded way, about the shooting he was planning. He claimed if he got arrested no prison on earth could hold him, and he referenced his hacking expertise and all the experience playing the game had given him. A lot of people probably had those boasts on their minds right now, and I couldn't blame them.

"The detention center sent six guards to watch Franklin," I told Mike. "He'll have constant supervision. And my mom had a special high-security room built for him. I don't think he's going anywhere."

"If this is the first time they're trying a procedure like this, why would they do it on a *kid*?" blurted a girl named Denise who almost never talked in class. A half hour after the Big Bang, once we'd all evacuated the school, no one had been able to find her. Then the police had stumbled across her back in the classroom passed out cold underneath her desk.

"I guess it just sort of happened that way," I said. "Franklin had actually gone to my mom's lab to have some tests done way back before the Big Bang, so after everything happened, her team had all this data about his brain and realized he'd be a perfect candidate for the procedure. I think they were also hoping the capsule might work better with Franklin because teenage brains are more malleable than adult ones."

In the very back row a hand went up.

"You have a question, Nell?" Ms. Utter said.

The room went quiet. A few people glanced over their shoulders.

"That's not what I heard," Nil Bergstrom said.

I sometimes thought of Nil as a girl version of Franklin. She wore tattered black T-shirts with the names of obscure punk bands on them. She had chaotic hair that fell over her eyes, though she dyed hers acid green instead of blue-black. And of course she carried around a gigantic backpack with a Son of War patch on it. The police had never determined she'd had any involvement in or prior knowledge of the Big Bang, but people had treated her like she had a disease ever since anyway—steering clear of her in hallways, talking to her only when necessary, and then only in clipped, careful sentences. Of course, they'd treated her a lot like that before the Big Bang too. They'd started calling her Nil all the way back in sixth grade. By eighth grade she'd started calling herself the same thing. The other kids' increased wariness of her after the Big Bang didn't seem to bother her any more than her nickname did.

Anyway, judging from how Nil had looked the second after Franklin's gunshot had jolted the room, I was pretty sure he hadn't told her a thing. She'd been the first to break the silence: "Holy shit, Kettle, what the hell did you do?"

"I heard the reason they chose him," Nil continued now, "was because they couldn't find an adult sociopath who would give consent. But since he's a minor, they could get consent from his grandmother, who's basically senile and clueless."

My stomach did a flip-flop. That rumor I hadn't heard before. "No way. My mom would never agree to something like that."

"So you're saying he *wants* the procedure done?" Nil said.

"Nell, I don't think this discussion's going in an appropriate direction," Ms. Utter said.

Lydia spun around in her desk. "But if Franklin isn't in his right mind anyway, how meaningful would his consent be? How can he know what's best for him?"

"What does that even mean? 'In his right mind.' It's the mind he was born with, isn't it?" Nil tossed her green hair out of her face so she could glare at Lydia better. "What gives us the right to change who he is just because he doesn't fit in? Locking him up because he broke the law, fine, that's one thing, but this is something else. And where do we draw the line? All of us have some crazy in us, don't we?" She swiveled her head toward me, and her fierce, direct gaze felt like a snowball in the face. "What's your mom's plan, Rem? Make *everyone* perfectly empathic and compliant? Except for the people in charge, because you can bet your ass they won't be doing the surgery on themselves. And while they're at it, they can fix people's other mental deviances too. Maybe you should watch your back. The gays might be next."

Ms. Utter stood up, furious. "Nell. Quiet."

Nil gripped the sides of her desk like she still had a lot more to say, but her eyes sagged away from mine. Little by little she sank back in her chair. Ms. Utter may have been small, and probably under the influence most of the time, but we generally did what she said. I think we were all a little in awe of her, especially since the Big Bang.

That day, after the gunshot, after the silence, after Nil's murmured "Holy shit, Kettle," not one of us had done a thing. Not Tor, the captain of the swim team, the biggest guy in the room now that Pete was dead. Not Lydia, the junior class president. Not me. Franklin had just started to wheel his Beretta around, and for a long second, I felt certain I'd be the next one to have the back of his head blasted open.

Then he slammed to the floor.

I couldn't tell what had happened at first. The back row of desks blocked my view. I lurched to my feet, apparently more curious than terrified, to find Franklin subdued by our over-fifty-years-old, under-five-feet-tall history teacher. She'd made it all the way across the room before the rest of us had even thought to move.

Only then did Tor and I and a few others rush forward to help. We held Franklin down, leaving the mask on because none of us wanted to look at his face, and waited for the cops to come. The matte black Beretta lay a few feet away. Nobody touched it. I pulled his right arm behind his back and held it there, watching his fingers writhe and twitch.

I later found out I'd been right to think Franklin had planned to take out more targets that day. Those comments he'd left on the Son of War subreddit also seemed to refer to multiple intended victims. "Those assholes will pay," one of them said. "A bullet for each one." Which left all of us in that class with one question lodged in our brains like a splinter, though nobody'd had the courage to ask it out loud in any of our sharing sessions so far: had Franklin Kettle meant one of his bullets for me, too?

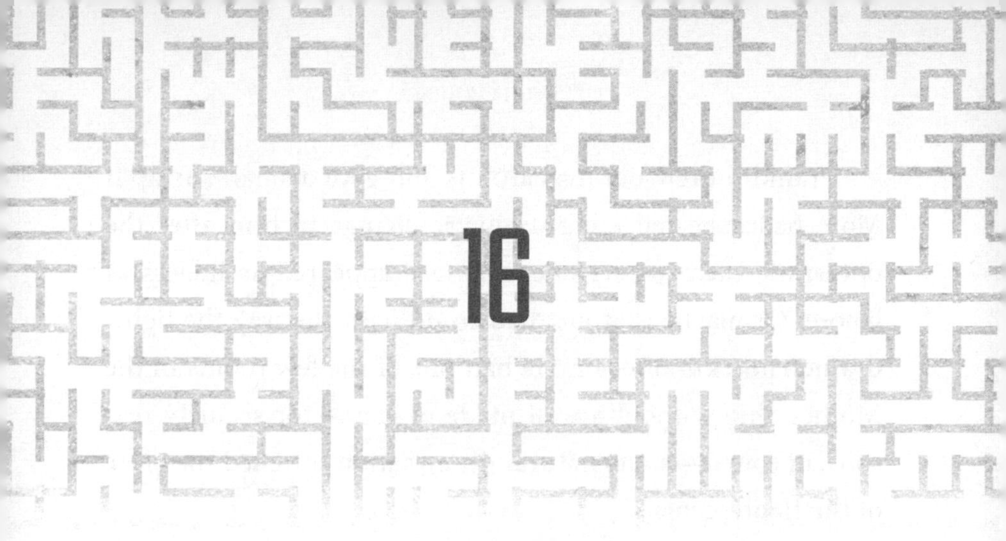

16

At the lab, a couple hours after the procedure, Mom gave a nod to the guard standing outside Franklin Kettle's door, touched her badge to the reader, and pushed the door open. Franklin lay on his bed, listening to music on an old iPod touch. His dark brown hair had disappeared. Mom had told him they'd need to shave it off in back for the procedure, and he'd said they might as well take the rest of it too. Gertie was perched on the edge of the mattress next to him, talking and pointing at the iPod's screen. She stood when Mom came in.

"Sorry, we were just discussing music, Dr. Braithwaite."

Mom motioned Gertie over. She spoke in a lower voice, so Franklin couldn't hear, but I could still make her words out later, when I watched the surveillance footage. "What's he doing with an iPod?"

"His grandma brought it in for him. I checked it out myself. I didn't think it would be a problem."

Mom pursed her lips and turned to her patient. "How do you feel, Franklin? Still groggy?"

Franklin drew out his earbuds and gave a small shrug. If Mom had expected a big dramatic change in him after the operation, there wasn't one. His face appeared as lifeless as before. Or maybe that just had to do with the way the lights drained his skin of color. He had one of the few rooms in the Mother Ship without a wall made of glass—for security reasons, of course—so no natural illumination softened the blaze of the fluorescents.

"Does your head hurt?"

He nodded. "A little." His voice sounded thick and dry.

"We can give you more painkillers, if you'd like."

"No more. I don't like the way they make me feel. All floaty." He blinked, and his eyelids moved lazily, the two just slightly out of sync.

Mom sat down on the chair next to his bed and made a note on her clipboard. "And how do you feel otherwise?"

"What do you mean, Madame Doctor? Am I still a psycho?"

"That's not what I meant."

"Because I don't feel any different. So I guess I must still be a psycho." Behind his glasses, his eyes had regained a little of their alertness. He gazed at the ceiling—apparently the capsule hadn't cured him of his indifference to eye contact, either—and that private smile of his appeared at the corners of his mouth. Even on the footage from the lab cameras, you could see it.

Mom sat back and smoothed the iron-gray hair on either side of her face. "I have something for you, Franklin."

She nodded to Gertie, who went to the door, lifted something from the floor just outside, and passed it to her. Franklin's smile faded. Mom set it on his nightstand: the Plexiglas cage, with only five mice in it now. They all pressed to the side of the cage farthest away from him, climbing over each other and scratching at the walls, like they remembered what he'd done to their friend.

Something shifted in Franklin's face. His cheeks filled with color. His chin started to shake. "Take them away," he whispered. The heart rate monitor next to him had started beeping faster. He edged sideways in his bed, away from the mice. "This isn't cool, Dr. Braithwaite."

"I don't think they're—"

"Take them away," he repeated, more loudly this time. He clutched at his headboard the same way the mice were clawing at the Plexiglas. His chains clanged against the bed's metal frame, which only made the mice more frantic. "GET THEM THE FUCK AWAY FROM ME!"

"All right, Franklin." Mom picked up the cage and passed it back to Gertie. "We'll leave you alone for a while."

His panting slowed little by little, but he stayed in a tight ball jammed against the headboard. He grabbed the earbuds and started to nestle them back into his ears one by one.

"We'll need to take the music player too," Mom said.

"Please don't," Franklin whispered between pants. "The music helps."

"It's not connected to the network," Gertie put in. "I don't see what harm it can do."

Mom nodded. "We'll be back in a while, Franklin. I apologize for upsetting you."

Gertie started to follow her, but then she lifted the iPod from Franklin's hands and gave the screen a few taps. "Listen to that one," she said in a gentle voice. "It's my favorite."

17

By lunchtime I still hadn't received an update from Mom, but I couldn't stop thinking about the procedure, wondering how it had gone. I ducked out of the cafeteria and into the hall to call her. I figured she probably wouldn't answer, so it surprised me when she picked up on the first ring.

"Did it work?" I said. "Can you tell yet?"

"It's looking promising."

I knew enough scientist-speak to understand "promising" meant *we're pretty sure we totally nailed it but still want to sound scientific and professional*. "Mom, that's fantastic."

"I was just going to text you, actually. Can you come to the lab after school tomorrow?" She sounded keyed up, like she'd had even more coffee than usual.

A few guys in snow boots clomped down the hall. I turned into a corner and clapped a hand over my other ear so I could hear better. "Why?"

"I'd like you to interact with Franklin again. He was asking about you, and I think another encounter between you two might—"

"Yield valuable data. I know."

"Don't worry," Mom said, "it won't be like last time. I promise you."

My fingers tensed like they wanted an armrest or a steering wheel to clamp onto. *How can you promise something like that?* a voice in my brain asked. But I gave my head a shake to silence it. "Sure, Mom. I can do that."

"Four o'clock tomorrow?"

"I'll be there."

When I got back to our table, Lydia said, "Where'd you disappear to? Out for a cigarette?"

"No, I just wanted to call Mom to see how the procedure went."

"And?" Callie asked. "Did it work?"

"Promising. That's what she said. But it's too early to really tell."

"I don't know." Tor grabbed a fistful of fries from his tray. "No matter what your mom does to him, he'll still always be the motherfucker who killed Pete."

"Tor." Lydia put a hand on his arm. I half-expected her to say something sweet and naive about how we needed to show forgiveness, but she changed the subject instead. "So you didn't go out to smoke, Rem? I haven't seen either of you doing that lately. What's going on?"

My eyes skipped to Tor. I couldn't think of anything to say. Usually when we slipped off together during lunch I'd let him do the lying.

"We quit," Tor said, managing to flash Lydia a dazzling grin despite the french fries jamming his mouth. He finished chewing and swallowed. "We finally realized what we were doing was dirty and disgusting, so we made an agreement to stop. Isn't that right, Nice Guy?"

His grin hardened a little as he turned it toward me. I nodded, while in my head I was picturing myself dissolving into a puddle again.

Lydia gave Tor's forearm a squeeze. "I had a feeling. Callie, isn't that great?"

"Peachy," Callie muttered, stealing a fry from my tray and nibbling the end.

"Congratulations. I'm very proud of you guys."

"I did it for you," Tor said.

He gave her a kiss. So I wouldn't have to watch, I grabbed a fry and used it to dab the ketchup on my white styrofoam tray until it resembled the splattering of blood in my latest Tattoo Atlas drawing.

18

On the way back to Boreal Street in the Saab, we passed Nil Bergstrom trudging through the snow, bent nearly double under her massive, mysterious load. The sun would go down soon. Indigo and purple seeped across the sky like watercolors. Nil's words in Ms. Utter's class earlier that day still echoed in my head. *Had* Franklin wanted the procedure done? I had no idea. And the crazy thing was, it had never even occurred to me to ask myself that question. But on the other hand, maybe Lydia was right. Maybe his thoughts on the procedure didn't even matter, because *his thoughts* were the very problem the procedure was meant to fix.

Anyway, as far as I knew, the explanation I'd given in class for why Mom had chosen Franklin was true. Apparently it had all started with Franklin's grandmother. Before the Big Bang, a little while after Mom's sleek new lab had gone up, Mrs. Kettle had read an article about the Mother Ship in the local paper. Franklin's strange behavior had been troubling her, and the shrinks she'd sent him to hadn't helped, so late one evening she'd made one of her rare excursions out of her house, crept down the street to our front door, and begged Mom to take a look at him. I'd eavesdropped on the encounter from the hall and heard her say in her small, fragile-sounding voice, "I just don't know what to *do* with him anymore." Mom had agreed to help.

I parked the Saab in the garage, said a quick good-bye to the others, and went into the house. Feeling restless, I grabbed a water from the fridge and prowled around for a while, searching for a place to settle. I finally dropped into a rolling desk chair in a corner of the living area, where we kept a big-screen computer for random Internet browsing. My water bottle jostled the mouse as I set it on the table, and the desktop sprang up on the computer screen. In the lower left-hand corner, the Son of War mask, in icon form, scowled at me. Mom had downloaded the game a few weeks ago in preparation for Franklin's arrival. Research, she'd called it, so she could understand him better, although as far as I could tell she'd only played the game once and then walked away in disgust. The icon had sat there on the desktop ever since, unclicked.

I clicked it now.

The screen went black while the game loaded. Then SON OF WAR appeared in big red letters. I slid forward in the chair and gripped the mouse.

The game started with a cinematic opening sequence showing the backstory of the main character, a US Marine named Jim Colby. In the first few seconds, as propulsive orchestral music played and lots of stuff exploded, Colby lost his leg in an IED strike. He then had it replaced, *Six Million Dollar Man* style, with a bionic limb that made him even stronger. The montage that followed showed Colby repeatedly going back into battle and performing feats of bravery and skill, only to lose another limb and have another mechanical version attached in its place. As the coup de grâce, a piece of shrapnel from an exploding Humvee sheared off his face and the front of his skull, missing his brain by millimeters. This was shown in graphic detail, of course. His special team of doctor-engineers now had to come up with a replacement for *that*. The last shot of the opener showed, in close-up, the iconic Son of War mask sliding into place over what remained of Colby's head, which meant it wasn't a mask at all, but the guy's actual face.

The scene shifted to a shadowy briefing room, where a general with a white crew cut and ice-blue eyes gave Colby a rundown of his next mission. A helicopter would air-drop him into a small occupied town in Afghanistan. He'd have to infiltrate a terrorist stronghold, steal important documents containing information about the terrorists' next target, and blow the place up. "But no one can know the US military is involved in this operation," the general growled, speaking straight through the screen at me. "Which means you'll be on your own in there. You must take any measure necessary. Kill anyone who gets in your way. *Anyone*. Is that understood?"

My stomach twisted. The nerves in my fingers as I clutched the mouse had started to tingle.

The music swelled again while the helicopter flew Colby into Afghanistan. Panoramic views of the landscape stretched across the screen. Dusty yellow mountains baking under a sinking red sun. A river cutting toward the horizon, with a narrow border of grass and trees on either side. The hot colors burned into our chilly living room, a jolting contrast to the unbroken white outside the window.

Colby jumped from the chopper. His black parachute deployed, and for a second the red sun, just now touching the mountains, framed him as he descended. I had to say, the game's imagery impressed me. The compositions of the shots. The radiant color palette. And it all looked so *real*. I wondered if Ethan had seen something similar when he'd flown into Afghanistan. I thought back to the conversations we'd had over Skype but couldn't remember anything specific he'd said about the place. Had he found it beautiful?

The soldier landed on the outskirts of a blasted, smoking town. Now I had control of him. I was seeing the town from his perspective. The edges of the screen had darkened to suggest I was peering through the Son of War mask. A bunch of numbers appeared along the screen's bottom edge, indicating my score, my time, how much ammo I had, other things I didn't understand.

The game started off slowly. Hints popped up explaining how to make Colby move, pick up objects, remove tools and weapons from his pack. Even with their help, I had a hard time at first. As I steered him into the town, I kept making him walk into walls and fall off ledges, and it took me forever to figure out how to get him to open doors.

The screen flickered red, and another hint materialized. DANGER: ENEMY NEARBY. READY YOUR WEAPON.

Colby seemed to have several, but I managed to make him

pull out some kind of automatic rifle. A guy in a ragged green T-shirt sprang out from behind an oil drum, a gun in each of his hands. I gave a shout, jumped up from my chair, and started hammering at the keyboard with one hand and madly clicking the mouse with the other. I must've done something right, because Colby ducked to the side and fired. The guy's chest opened up. He went flying against a wall, his arms spread wide, the blood spattering the graffiti-covered concrete rendered in photorealistic detail. The little box on the screen marked SCORE ticked up from 0 to 732. I wondered what had gone into the calculation of that score. How did the game figure out the worth of each life in points? Or did it have something to do with the way I'd killed him? Or had the game just randomly generated the number?

Colby kept going, killing more enemy soldiers under my direction. He hadn't run across any civilians yet, or at least I didn't think he had. It was confusing: everyone he encountered had a gun, but no one wore a uniform that clearly identified him as a soldier.

The town sank into twilight. The bright colors faded, replaced by sinister blues and blacks. The music grew more ominous too. The bad guys got harder to bring down. Colby took a few hits himself. But we pushed on.

I'd never played this kind of game before. The thought of shooting things up had never appealed to me, and my lack of hand-eye coordination whenever I was forced to play sports during gym class had made me think I'd probably suck at video games too. I hadn't realized they felt this good. My body buzzed, like the electricity traveling from the computer to the mouse and keyboard was continuing into my hands and up my arms. Like *I* had cybernetic appendages too.

And I didn't suck. As I pounded on the keys, a monologue started in my head. *See?* the monologue went. *I can totally do this. Not bad for an arty, uncoordinated gay kid.*

I barely even noticed when I started speaking the monologue out loud.

"See? Bam! You're dead, asshole!"

Colby blasted a bad guy through the heart. Then he rounded a corner, where a whole gang waited for him. I didn't hesitate, I just charged Colby forward. The electricity coursing through me felt stronger. More aggressive.

"This isn't hard."

He mowed down a couple more thugs.

"You just have to pull the trigger. What's so hard about that?"

Colby's bullets ripped apart the crowd, slathering the concrete walls in red. It was like a whole new approach to painting.

"Like this, Ethan, see?" I shouted. "Why couldn't you just fucking do it? Why couldn't you just pull the goddamn trigger? Like this!"

The garage door rumbled open. I stopped, breathing hard. Outside, night had fallen, just like it had in the game. The lights had come on in the city below, and the lake had turned into a big black hole, the same way it did every evening. The house was dark too. I glanced at the clock. Three hours had gone by. My fingers ached. So did my legs. Only now did I realize I'd never even sat back down after jumping to my feet that first time. Through the whole game, I'd hunched over the desk while dancing back and forth in my socks, leaving a puddle of footprints on the rug around me, like some kind of deadly altercation had taken place right here in this room.

19

I quit the game and put the computer to sleep, for some reason moving at a frantic pace. I didn't even know why. It wasn't like Mom had ever told me she didn't want me playing Son of War.

By the time she came in, I'd flicked on some lights and started pulling stuff out of the fridge for dinner. "I didn't think you'd be home so early."

She shrugged off her coat. "Franklin needs sleep, and the rest of the team's tired too, so I gave everyone the evening off."

Mom looked exhausted herself, not that she'd ever have admitted it. She opened a cupboard to take down some plates, but I said, "Just have a seat, Mom. I'll get dinner tonight."

Without protesting she lowered herself into a chair at the kitchen table, mopped back her hair, and glanced around the house frowning. "When I drove up all the lights were off. Were you sitting here in the dark?"

"I just got sucked into watching a movie and lost track of time."

Maybe I sounded nervous, because she turned her frown

toward me, like she didn't quite believe me. But then she thought of something else and groaned. "The garage door opener's making that funny sound. We should probably have it looked at before it goes kaput again."

"Don't worry, I'll take care of it. Want a glass of wine?"

"God yes."

I pulled an open bottle from the fridge. Mom had a nightly ritual of pouring herself exactly one half glass of red wine each evening before bed. She probably needed it just to come down from all the caffeine she ingested during the day. I set the glass in front of her.

"How was your day?" she asked.

"Okay." I opened a box of week-old Thai and sniffed. "We had rehearsal for the memorial assembly."

"And?"

"It's going to be a schmaltzfest. Abigail Lansing's basically running the show."

"That's a shame."

I shrugged. "Maybe schmaltz is what the school needs right now. Callie gave a good speech, though. She told the story about the ice gazebo."

Mom's eyes slipped to the backyard, where Ethan's gazebo stood under a heap of snow. She took a sip from her glass. "Did anyone at school ask about the procedure? It's been getting a lot of news coverage."

I shoved a couple boxes of the Thai food into the microwave. "Yeah. We talked about it in Ms. Utter's class."

"Are people concerned?"

"A few are." I pushed some buttons. The microwave beeped and started to whir. I shot a glance over my shoulder. I could tell Mom was in no mood to answer hard questions, but I had to ask. "Someone said the reason you chose Franklin for the procedure was because you couldn't find any adult convicts who'd give their consent. Since he's a minor, you could get consent from his grandma instead. Is that true?"

Mom took another long sip of red wine. She pulled herself up straight in her chair and folded her hands together on the table, like she was getting ready to speak at a press conference. "You have to understand something, Rem. Making science happen is hard. Sometimes you have to get creative. We did try to find an adult subject, with no success. Then I thought of Franklin. We'd performed an exhaustive analysis of his brain, and when I went back and looked at the results of the tests we'd run, I realized he'd make a perfect candidate. And yes, the consent issue was easier to manage in his case."

She glanced up from her glass to check my reaction. Maybe she saw some lingering doubt there, because she added, "I wouldn't be doing this if I didn't sincerely believe I was helping him, with minimal risk to his health. I know it's not a perfect answer, Rem, but we don't live in a perfect world."

20

Over the phone later that night I told Callie about my conversation with Mom. Callie's house stood across the street, and her bedroom faced front, like mine did. I could see her pacing back and forth while she kneaded her pile of long black hair into its nighttime configuration.

"Makes sense to me," she said. "Franklin Kettle's a minor, a murderer, and a fucking psycho. Why should they have to get his permission to fix his brain? I mean, doesn't it make sense to you?"

"I guess. To be honest, that isn't even the part of this whole thing that really bothers me."

"Oh yeah? What is?"

I sank into the chair in front of my desk. All the smudges of ink and paint covering the white surface had almost become a painting themselves. "I guess I'm not sure I believe in what my mom's doing. Not whether it's right, but whether it'll even *work*. I know *she* believes, and I try to be supportive, but . . ."

"But what? Spit it out, Remmy."

I propped an elbow on the desk and pressed my forehead

into my palm. "Look, if I tell you something, do you promise you won't repeat it?"

"Come on, you know I can keep a secret."

I glanced at the door, even though Mom's bedroom stood all the way on the other side of the house. "I visited Franklin at the lab yesterday. My mom asked me to do it, so she could observe how he interacted with me."

Callie stopped pacing and stared straight at me through her window. "Are you fucking kidding me? So you saw him? You talked to him?"

"Uh-huh."

"And your mom *asked* you to do it? Isn't that a little fucked up?"

"This project's important to her. You know how she is about her work."

"But she didn't even stop to think it might retraumatize you to see him?"

"It didn't, Callie," I snapped. "I was in there for five minutes. Less."

Across the street she shook her head and went back to pacing. "So what the hell was he like?"

"He was a monster, Callie. He said stuff about my brother. That maybe he wouldn't have died if he'd played Son of War. And other stuff too."

"That's fucking sick."

I stared at the smears of color on my desk, trying to make a picture emerge from the random markings. "Here's what I can't stop thinking: even if Mom's procedure succeeds, even if Franklin suddenly starts acting completely different, Pete's killer will still be in there, won't he? Like Tor said at lunch today, Franklin's always going to be the guy who shot Pete. I mean, I'm no brain scientist, I'm not even *good* at science—"

"I can confirm that."

"But something inside me says whatever made Franklin Kettle the way he is, capable of doing the things he's done, you can't just fix it with a little cerebral rewiring."

"What do you mean? You think there's something wrong with his *soul*?"

On the shelf above my desk, on the top of my stack of gothic horror novels, lay my copy of *Dr. Jekyll and Mr. Hyde*. Like the other old paperbacks on that shelf, this one had a lurid cover from the sixties or something. Half the reason I'd bought the books in the first place was for their covers. Painted with crude strokes in garish colors, they had a weirdness that had inspired some of the images in my Tattoo Atlas. The *Jekyll and Hyde* cover depicted a man's face split in two, one half handsome and respectable-looking and brightly lit, the other twisted and menacing and shrouded in shadow. On that side a bunch of demons—the original inspirations for my imps—hovered around him.

"Maybe," I said. "I just don't think I believe evil is some disease you can treat, like malaria."

When I glanced across Boreal Street, Callie had stopped pacing again. She leaned her shoulder against the window frame and peered across at me. "I understand how you feel, Rem. I do. I've told you about my mom, right?"

"A little." I knew Callie's mother suffered from clinical depression, and I knew that had made life tough for Callie sometimes, although to me Mrs. Minwalla had always been this friendly neighborhood mom who invited us all over every year on Callie's birthday for a huge Indian feast she cooked herself.

"For a long time," Callie said, "when my mom would have one of her sad spells and start crying constantly, I'd get so fucking furious at her. I'd take it personally, almost. I'd want to shake her and say, 'We have a good life, there's nothing to be sad about, so why can't you just be fucking happy?' It took me a long time to understand she had an illness. She wasn't sad because we had a bad life, she was sad because there was something wrong with her brain. Maybe evil's the same way. Maybe evil *is* a disease."

I set my copy of *Jekyll and Hyde* back on the shelf. "But if we start thinking of evil like that, then what happens to the whole idea of personal responsibility? Just because my mom tweaked Franklin's brain a little, does that suddenly mean we don't hold him accountable for the horrible thing he did? Does that make him innocent somehow?"

"I don't know," Callie said. "Believe me, I get what you're saying. I'm pretty sure I hate Franklin just as much as you do. How could we not? But do you think—and I'm just playing devil's advocate here—do you think that has more to do with us than with Franklin? Like to *us* he'll always be Pete's killer?"

I didn't answer.

Callie went quiet too. She turned away from the window, so I couldn't see her face anymore. "Hey, Rem," she said in a lower voice, "you want to know a secret? Like, a really twisted one?"

"Sure."

"Before the Big Bang, I thought there was something sort of hot about him."

"Franklin Kettle? Really?"

"In a weird, weird way. I mean, weird can be hot, can't it? The way he walked around school all quiet and moody in that black hair and black denim jacket of his . . . you have to admit, it was kind of sexy. Plus, have you ever really looked at his face under all that hair and those glasses?"

"I'm not sure." I hoped my voice hadn't gone funny, or if it had, that she didn't notice. "But Callie—"

She groaned. "I know. Thinking about it now, it makes me fucking nauseous knowing my brain even went there. But back then he wasn't a killer. Just the odd kid who lived at the end of our block." Across the street she turned around to peek at me. "It's late. I should go."

"Hey, before you do." I stood and touched my fingers to the cold glass of my window. "I meant what I said earlier. Your speech today totally got me, just like you told me it would. Everything else about that stupid assembly was a joke, but what you said was the real thing. You did Pete proud, Callie."

She put her fingers against her window too. "Thanks. Sleep well, Rem. No nightmares, okay?"

"Fingers crossed."

She reached for the string on her blinds and disappeared.

It was almost eleven. I still didn't feel tired, so I pulled my Tattoo Atlas from its hiding place. I already knew what I wanted to draw. Another story Callie had told about Pete in her speech had given me the idea. Each morning when he rode to school in the way back of the Saab, with his gigantic bulk draped across the bench seat, he'd almost always fall back to sleep for a while. Once we forgot all about him and left him there, and he slept clear through the first two periods. After that he'd always say to us as he climbed in through the rear door, "Now, don't forget I'm back here, okay?"

I grabbed a pencil and turned to a blank page in the sketchbook. From memory I drew my Saab as seen from the back. Pete sat in his regular spot on the rear-facing bench seat, his knees and round face visible through the window, a small bloody bullet hole in the center of his forehead. I sketched the neck and shoulders and upper back of a person sprouting from the bottom of the car, like the Saab was actually someone's head. Over the top of the drawing, following the line of the car's roof, I wrote in cursive, *Now, don't forget I'm back here, okay?* Then I drew a little banner below, held up by two imps, that read *PETE*.

I'd just started to reach for my watercolors when my phone buzzed with a text from Lydia.

Can you come outside? I'm on your back porch. I need to talk.

I squeezed my bottom lip between my forefinger and thumb while I stared at the screen. It was cold outside. If she needed to talk, why didn't she ask if she could come in, or invite me over to her place? And what did she need to talk to *me* about? Of all the other members of the Boreal Five, I'd always felt least close to her. Her goodness sometimes got on my nerves. Ironic, maybe, considering everybody knew me as Mr. Nice Guy. These days, for obvious reasons, I felt like talking to her even less.

Be there in a sec, I texted back.

21

Mom was still up when I left my room, still sitting at the kitchen table with her back very straight, still cradling the same glass of wine. Or maybe she'd broken her rule tonight and poured herself another. "Shouldn't you get some sleep?" I asked.

"Can't. Brain's too busy." She wiggled her fingers next to her head. "Neurons firing all over the place." Pushing back her gray hair with its thick lock of white, she peered at me. "You're sure you're okay with talking to Franklin again tomorrow? Because you know you can change your mind. I don't want you to feel pressured."

"It's not a problem, Mom."

There, you see? I told Callie in my head. *My mom* does *worry about how seeing Franklin will affect me.*

Grabbing my coat, I said, "I'm just going over to Lydia's for a bit. I'll be back soon."

I went out through the front door, but then I circled around the house and found Lydia sitting on a bench on the back porch.

"What's up, Lydia? Why did you want to talk out here? It's freezing."

She shrugged. Her eyes flicked toward Tor's house. His bedroom window was visible from here, and light still glowed from it.

"Why don't you come inside?"

She shook her head. Even in the darkness I could make out tear marks on her freckly cheeks.

I cleared more snow off the bench and sat next to her. "Tell me."

"I didn't know who else to talk to," she said in a choked voice.

"What about?"

She bit her lip and gave her head another shake, like she couldn't decide how to begin. "Rem, do you have a cigarette?"

"You mean, like, to smoke?"

She pulled off her gloves, rifled around in her purse, and pulled out a pack. "Never mind. I have one."

I gaped at her. "Okay, I feel like I've just jumped into an alternate reality."

She had a lighter, too. The flame sprang up, the light flashing in her wet eyes. The cigarette crackled as it caught. She exhaled.

"Seriously, Lydia, you're freaking me out. You hate smoking. It goes against everything you stand for."

"Which is why I don't tell anyone I do it, and I hope you won't either. This doesn't happen very often. Only when I'm feeling reeeally pooey."

She smoked, but she still couldn't bring herself to say the word "shitty." That, at least, I found reassuring.

"How long have you been smoking? Since . . . ?"

"The Big Bang. Yeah. A few weeks after it happened, I had this weird urge to do something really bad, so I stole three cigarettes from the pack Tor keeps in his coat and smoked them when I got home. That was it. I was hooked."

I smirked at her. "Yeah, that's *really* bad."

She held the cigarette out to me.

Uh-oh, I thought. I'd only ever taken about one and a half puffs, and lots of coughing and retching had ensued. How was I going to fake this?

"Oops," she said. "You quit. Sorry, I forgot."

"Right."

She took another drag and stared at the gazebo. The sight of her smoking was still blowing my mind. Like Callie, I'd always sort of assumed Lydia was the most psychologically healthy person on earth. But I supposed it stood to reason that Pete's death had left its mark on her, too.

"Would you answer a question for me, Rem?" she finally said. "And be honest. Do you know of any reason why Tor might be faking his feelings for me?"

My cheeks turned hot in spite of the cold. "Not that I can think of. Why?"

"Is there something wrong with me? You can tell me. I can take it."

"Of course not. What's going on, Lydia?"

She studied the red glowing tip of her cigarette. "I told you how the two of us got together, right?"

"You were lab partners, you'd been working together in the bio lab after school, the sight of cat intestines and the smell of formaldehyde got you in the mood. It makes perfect—"

"He had a panic attack."

I looked at her. "Tor?"

"At least I think that's what it was. We were working on the cat, and all of a sudden he stumbled back from the table and sat down on the floor like he was dizzy. His face was all pale and sweaty. I ran over and put my arm around him and asked him if he was thinking about Pete. He nodded yes. It made sense to me, with that dead cat laid out in front of us and the posters with Pete's picture all over the lab walls. They'd only gone up that morning. So I just sat there and held him.

"After a while, he seemed to feel better. Then he grinned and said, 'So this is what it takes to get you to put your hands on me.' The next thing I knew, we were kissing. Even at the time, I almost wondered if he was just trying to cover up for his freak-out. And ever since then, he's been . . . odd. He acts all affectionate in public, but when we're alone, there's suddenly a game on TV he has to watch, or he decides he needs to do a million push-ups right then. We've been going out for three weeks, and already it's like we're an old married couple. That's weird, right?"

I nodded. It *was* weird. I'd never heard any rumors about Tor having trouble getting physical with other girls he'd dated. Then again, I hadn't been close to any of his previous girlfriends. There had been a lot of them, but none had lasted very long. Had he been like that with them too, or was Lydia the exception?

Not that I was complaining either way. I couldn't help it: a warm flush of pleasure spread through me as I imagined the two of them sitting awkwardly side by side, not touching, while in his mind he was creeping back down to the steam tunnels with me.

I wondered if that made me an asshole, but then I reminded myself of what I'd told Callie: I'd been with Tor first. Lydia was the interloper here, even if she didn't know it.

She sniffled, scrunching her freckle-covered nose. "I was always worried I'd be too much of a prude for Tor, but evidently *that's* not an issue." With a glance at me, she added, "I thought maybe you'd have some idea what's going on. You know him as well as anyone."

"Nobody *really* knows Tor," I said. "The guy's a mystery."

"Do you think he might just be going out with me to please his parents?"

Tor's parents did love Lydia. Why wouldn't they? She was kind, smart, pretty, polite—the perfect girl next door, who actually *did* happen to live next door. "I don't know," I said. "I'm sorry."

She flicked her cigarette, and a smattering of dark ash dusted the white snow at her feet. "I've had a crush on Tor since I was seven. It never even mattered that he could be a jerk sometimes. I swear, he's my kryptonite."

Mine too, I could've said.

She took another drag and flashed her eyes in my direction. "Any more news about Franklin?"

"Not really."

"So they still don't know if the procedure was a success?"

"Uh-uh. They have to do lots of tests."

"I have to admit, sometimes I wonder how it would even be possible to fix someone like him." She shook her head. "I guess that's not very nice of me to say."

"Don't worry, I feel the exact same way. I was just trying to explain it to Callie. Like, you know that game he's obsessed with, Son of War? My mom downloaded it for her research, and earlier today I got curious and tried playing it. I felt so gross afterward I felt like I should take a shower. I'm pretty sure *anyone* who likes playing that game must be completely sick. I guess that says a lot about the general population of our country."

Lydia got quiet. She pulled her auburn ponytail over her shoulder and played with it, her face caught in a wince. "Rem? I think I need to make another confession."

"You don't."

She buried her face in her hand. "I do. I downloaded Son of War the same day I smoked my first cigarette, and now I love playing that awful game. Blowing those bad guys' guts out just feels so good. It takes my mind off things when I'm having a bad day." She brushed her ponytail back over her shoulder. "Which probably explains why I've been playing it so much lately."

"I guess I can understand that. To be totally honest, part of *me* liked playing it too. But it really doesn't bother you, all the violence? Even after the Big Bang and everything?"

"Not really. Maybe there's something wrong with *my* brain."

She dunked the tip of her cigarette in some snow banked on the side of the bench. "I should go."

I gave her coat sleeve a tug. "Will you be okay? I wish I could've helped more."

"Just give me an hour in my room with Son of War and I'll be good as new." She stood. "You won't repeat what I told you about me and Tor, will you?"

"Of course not."

Lydia glanced again at the gazebo. A sad smile crossed her face, and I knew she was thinking of the five of us hanging out in the ice palace. From there her eyes went one more time to Tor's window. Then she turned away, still carrying the cigarette so she could dispose of it responsibly in a trash can.

22

I waited to hear the distant clunk of Lydia's front door closing before cutting across my backyard and through the trees that separated the Agnarsons' property from ours. On the way I texted Tor. *Coming to your kitchen door. Need to talk.*

Tor opened the door and waved me in. His parents had gone to Europe for their twentieth anniversary, and he didn't have any siblings, so I'd figured I'd find him there alone. I followed him down the hall and up the stairs. Tor's mom kept the place immaculate, with bouquets of fresh flowers and tasteful arrangements of *objets* everywhere you looked.

"What's up?" Tor said, pushing his bedroom door shut behind him. His room was neat too, but instead of flowers and *objets*, military-straight rows of swimming trophies covered every available surface.

I leaned back against his desk, folded my arms across my chest, and tried to figure out what I wanted to say. It felt strange being alone with him in his room. I hardly ever found myself in Tor's house without Lydia and Callie here too, and we'd certainly never messed around here before. Another of Tor's unspoken rules, besides the no-kissing thing, was that his house and mine were off-limits.

"I was just talking to Lydia."

"Really?" For no apparent reason, he peeled off his T-shirt and tossed it in a corner. I was used to that—he did it in front of Callie and Lydia too—but it still got harder to form coherent sentences with all those muscles bulging and rippling in my field of vision.

"She was upset, Tor."

"What about?"

"You. She said you're all over her in public, but you ignore her whenever you two are alone." I arched my eyebrow. "What's wrong? Don't you like her bends and curves anymore?"

"They're nice," he said, ignoring the sarcasm in my voice. He pitched backward onto his bed and tucked his hands behind his head.

"She asked me if I knew of any reason why you might be faking your feelings for her."

That got his attention. He picked his head up to look at me.

"Don't worry, I didn't say a word. But, Tor, if you don't really like her, you have to end it. She's not just some random girl. She's one of your best friends, and one of mine, too. You can't lead her on."

"It's none of your business, Nice Guy." His voice had turned serious now. "Leave it."

I slumped back against the desk and bit my lip. If Tor didn't want to discuss something, no power on the planet could get him to talk.

"What's the latest on Franklin Kettle?" he asked.

"That's what everyone wants to know."

"Oh yeah?"

"Lydia was just asking the same thing." I glanced over my shoulder. From here the roof of Ethan's gazebo, covered in snow, looked like a perfect white upside-down bowl.

"So?" Tor said. "Did your mom turn him good or whatever?"

"Unclear. Still testing."

"Ah."

I turned back to where he lay staring at the ceiling. My teeth pressed into the flesh of my lower lip again. "Tor, do you ever think about the way we treated him?"

"Franklin? No. What do you mean?"

"You have to admit, we were sort of jerks."

"So was the entire Duluth Central student body."

"Yeah, but he lived on *our* block. He was our neighbor pretty much all our lives, and most of the time we just acted like he was invisible. And when we didn't . . . we could be pretty vicious, Tor." In a lower voice, I added, "Especially you."

He raised his head again and squinted at me. "What do you mean, 'especially me'?"

"Didn't you make up his nickname? Kettlebot? And Nil, didn't you think of that one too?"

"They're just nicknames. I like making up nicknames. That's my thing. Plus, you four messed with him plenty."

"But you were usually the one who had the idea in the first place."

"Bullshit. What about that time Lydia tore him a new one at the Halloween dance?"

It had happened junior year. Lydia, as the class president and the dance's head organizer, had been working the door that night. She stopped Franklin and Nil when they tried to enter carrying toy rifles. I wasn't there to see it all happen, but apparently things got pretty heated. When Lydia told them it was against the rules to have fake weapons on school grounds, Franklin pushed back in that quiet, creepy way of his, talking about freedom of expression or the right to bear arms or something stupid like that. Finally she lost it and said, "Why don't you just leave? Nobody wants you here anyway." Probably the most scathing words that had ever fallen from Lydia's lips.

"And I had nothing to do with it," Tor said.

"I know. She felt horrible afterward. I think she even wrote Franklin a letter of apology."

"Of course she did," he said, chuckling.

"But remember what happened after that?"

Franklin and Nil had come back to the dance entrance a few minutes later claiming they'd ditched their rifles, and Lydia let them in. When I first noticed them circulating through the crowd, the sight of them made me do a double take. Franklin had on a vintage slim-cut tux with a bandolier slung over each shoulder, and Nil a ball gown made of dark camouflage fabric. Both of them wore Son of War masks, the off-the-shelf variety.

The effect was both disturbing and weirdly cool. But then they hauled out their rifles, which it turned out Nil had hidden under her dress, and their outfits became just plain disturbing.

By then word had gotten around about Franklin and Lydia's altercation, and it outraged Callie when she saw what Franklin and Nil had done. More than anything, she saw it as an insult to Lydia. She was just about to rat on them to one of the chaperones, but Tor stopped her. "I have a better idea." He bent close, eyes glittering, and whispered into her ear.

Moments later, he threw down one of the firecrackers he'd brought with him as part of his (shirtless) magician's costume. Callie splashed a cup of bloodred punch across the front of her white snow-princess dress. Tor's firecracker went *BANG*, and Callie let out a bloodcurdling scream. Thrusting a finger at Franklin, she yelled, "He shot me! Kettlebot shot me!"

Mayhem ensued. Everybody stampeded for the cafeteria exits and threw themselves behind tables, leaving Franklin standing alone in the middle of the dance floor.

Callie later told Principal Chen it had all been a misunderstanding. Someone had let off a firecracker, someone else had spilled the punch on her dress, she'd seen Franklin's gun and, in her fright and confusion, jumped to a conclusion. She ended up getting off without punishment. Franklin and Nil got a week's suspension each.

After Pete's death, the thought would sometimes weave into my head that maybe that prank had given Franklin the idea for the Big Bang in the first place. Maybe he'd discovered he enjoyed seeing all his classmates running from him in terror.

Tor might've had the same thought now, because the grin faded from his face. He shook his head and propped himself on his elbows so he could get a better look at me. His eyes narrowed. "What about you? That day in the locker room. Mr. Nice Guy wasn't so nice."

My stomach tightened. Instead of answering, I lifted my hands and studied the ink marks and paint smears on my palms like they were a Rorschach test with the power to reveal something deep and important about me.

"Rem," Tor said, "why are we talking about this? I really hope you're not about to spew some bullshit about how we're the ones who turned Franklin Kettle into a monster. About how Pete deserved what happened to him."

I looked up. "What? Of course not."

"Your mother seems to think it has more to do with the fact that the guy has a fucked-up brain."

"Look, I didn't come here to talk about that."

He shrugged his huge shoulders. "You brought it up."

"I came here to talk about Lydia."

"Right. You're standing up for your friend. So selfless of you. So noble."

"I'm not being noble, I'm just—"

He sat all the way up and raised one hand to silence me. "Come on, Nice Guy. Fess up. Why did you *really* come here?"

"I don't know what you're talking about." I hated how weak my voice sounded.

"It doesn't have *anything* to do with the fact that we haven't been going down to the steam tunnels? And maybe you're missing it? And maybe you're wondering if I am too?"

I looked down at my hands again. He scooted forward on his bed and knocked my leg with his bare foot to get my attention.

"Because maybe I am."

23

I did a face-plant a half hour later on my way back to my house from Tor's. I'd been sneaking through the trees between our yards, paranoid Lydia might see me while out walking her dog or something, when my boots flew out from under me and I landed on my belly deep in a snowdrift. I must've jostled a tree, too, because a few chunks of snow punched me in the back. Within seconds snowmelt had soaked my jeans and found its way under my coat and down my boots. Somehow it felt like an appropriate ending to my visit at Tor's, during which he'd broken his "our houses are off-limits" rule but not the one about no kissing.

It took some flailing before I managed to get back on my feet. I trudged the rest of the way home. Mom had gone to bed by then, so at least I didn't have to bother concealing the wretchedness most likely painted all over my face. I took a hot shower, balled myself up in my bed, and called Callie for the second time that night.

This time she didn't pull up her blinds.

"What the hell, Rem? I was asleep."

"I know, I'm sorry, Callie. I wouldn't be calling right now if I didn't really need to talk."

As usual I told her about my most recent encounter with Tor, and also about my conversation with Lydia beforehand. True, I'd promised Lydia I wouldn't talk about that, but I felt pathetic enough having to keep my nonrelationship with Tor, and all the drama surrounding it, a secret from the rest of the school. I couldn't keep it from my best friend, too.

"What an asshole," Callie fumed. "Thinks he can have his cake and get a hand job too. So when he got all sexy, you just went along with it?"

"Well, yeah," I said. "I missed him."

"Jesus, Rem, do you have *any* willpower? Or self-respect?"

"I know, I know, you win, Callie. I was hoping it would make me feel better and it just made me feel like shit, okay? For three weeks I've had to watch him acting all romantic with Lydia, even if it *has* just been a show. Meanwhile what he does with me he treats like something necessary but gross, like going to the toilet. And to top it off, he refuses to admit how bizarre and fucked-up it all is."

"*Now* will you listen to me and just stay away from him? If you can't do it for yourself, at least do it for Lydia. She's your friend, remember?"

"I *know* she's my friend. I *do* feel bad for her. That's the whole reason I went over to Tor's place just now: for Lydia. To speak up for her. To get him to treat her better."

"Stop kidding yourself, Rem. It was a booty call, plain and

simple." Across the street, Callie's bedroom light had snapped on, and I could see her in silhouette pacing back and forth behind her blinds. "Lydia needs to know about this. That's all there is to it."

"Are you kidding? Tor would freak! Plus, how do you think it'll make her feel to know her boyfriend and one of her best friends have been fooling around behind her back?"

"She can handle it. She's a plucky girl."

"Not as plucky as she lets on. You didn't see how she was tonight. Obviously I agree Tor needs to end it with her, but in a nice way."

"Nice." Callie spoke the word with maximum contempt. Then she heaved a sigh. "So what are you going to do?"

"I'm going to try talking to him again."

"Because that approach worked so well tonight."

"Look," I said. "He's in a difficult position. I wasn't sure before, but now it seems pretty clear he's gay and in the closet and not really into Lydia. I want to try to help him. He must really be confused."

"Whatever you're doing with him right now, I don't think it's helping. At least not in the way you mean. Man up, Rem. Tell Lydia. Being a nice person isn't the same as being a good person, you know."

My phone chimed. I glanced at the screen and saw I'd received a photo from a number my phone didn't recognize. I couldn't make it out clearly from the thumbnail.

"Hold on, Callie."

I tapped to bring up the picture and froze.

Someone had created the image using some kind of art software. It depicted a face. Mine. No body or background to give context. Just me from the neck up, staring at some spot in the distance with a thoughtful expression.

I told Callie I had to go, feeling too startled even to tell her why, and stared at the digital painting some more.

My first pathetic thought was that it had come from Tor. That he'd meant it as a sign that he'd enjoyed tonight and was thinking about me. But that made no sense. I'd never known him to have any interest in art, let alone talent, and whoever had made this knew how to paint. The image had life, and also detail. The artist had captured the cowlick in my short strong-willed hair, the way I tended to scrunch my mouth to one side when I was concentrating on something, even a stray smear of green paint on my left cheek by my ear.

I thought of that gangly junior in art class, Spencer something—one of the five other out gay boys I knew of at Duluth Central. He was always painting tacky pictures of rainbow flags blowing in the wind, or big equal signs, or two boys in silhouette holding hands. I'd never known him to do anything like this. Or this good. But sometimes I caught him staring at me across the art classroom. Had *he* sent this?

Then Franklin Kettle jumped into my head. He'd admitted he drew sometimes, though he'd denied having any real interest in it. But that was crazy. He was locked up, without access to a computer or a phone. How could he have sent this? And why?

No, it had to be Spencer. Too bad the guy did nothing for me.

24

That same night back at the lab a security camera fixed to the ceiling in Franklin Kettle's room captured him sprawled on his bed and propped up on his elbows. His iPod and a few comic books lay scattered in front of him, illuminated by the small lamp clipped to his headboard. On the back of his head a white wad of gauze, held in place by medical tape, covered the place where Mom had put a hole in his skull. On either side of that white earbuds nestled in his ears. His feet, hanging over the edge of the bed, clad in white socks, knocked rhythmically together.

Security personnel monitoring the camera feed that night wouldn't have noticed anything unusual, but when I watched the footage later, I saw it: Franklin tapping on the screen of his iPod. Franklin glancing at the badge reader on the wall next to the door, where a small light changed from red to green. Franklin smiling a tiny, secret smile.

25

While I warmed up the Saab the next morning, I watched Lydia cross Boreal Street in my rearview mirror. Her eyes were cast down, her hands buried in her coat pockets. Maybe it was my imagination, but her ponytail didn't look as neat and shiny as usual. She went to Tor, who stood on the sidewalk waiting for her. He slung his big arm around her neck, and they continued to the wagon without saying a word to each other.

Just like last night when Lydia had told me about how busy she and Tor weren't getting behind closed doors, a warm, pleased feeling slithered through my body as I watched them now.

They scooted into the backseat.

"Morning," I said, my voice brighter than I'd intended.

"What's up, Nice Guy?"

"Hi, Rem," Lydia added in a low murmur.

That was when I noticed: Lydia looked *happy*. Not "putting on a brave face even though I think my boyfriend might not actually be into me" happy. Really, truly happy. She nestled herself against Tor's shoulder and shut her eyes, her freckly cheeks pink, a drowsy smile on her face. Now that I could see her close up, I realized what I'd taken for misery was actually exhaustion.

Callie noticed it too. She dropped into the passenger seat, glanced back at the two of them squashed against each other with their eyes closed, and raised an eyebrow at me as she hooked her thumb at them. I shrugged and put the car in reverse. While I backed the Saab down the driveway, I had to turn around in my seat to see out the back window, so I found myself staring straight at them. Tor had taken Lydia's head in his hands and started to kiss her. A deep, full, passionate kiss. And Lydia didn't pull away blushing, like she usually would've done. She seemed to have forgotten Callie and I were even there.

"What the fuck is with you two this morning?" Callie said. "Lydia, I thought you were waiting to kiss with tongue until after marriage."

Now Lydia blushed. She broke the kiss, gave a self-conscious laugh, and buried her face in the curve of Tor's neck. I could imagine exactly what she smelled there: soap and sweat and chlorine.

"We had a late night," Tor said.

Callie squinted. "Both of you? Lydia, don't your parents have you on lockdown by eleven on weeknights?"

Too shy to look up, she stared at Tor's hand holding hers. "Yes, but a sort of crazy thing happened. I woke up at one o'clock in the morning to find someone tapping on my window."

"Who?" Callie thrust a finger at Tor. "Him?"

"He'd climbed up the trellis," Lydia said. "He could've broken his neck."

"I just couldn't stay away," Tor put in.

"I tried to explain to him what my dad would do if he found him there."

"I believe it involved the removal of one of my testicles."

Lydia knocked his chest with the back of her hand. "No, it didn't." Her eyes met mine in the rearview mirror, and she gave a little nod. After showing up on my doorstep in such a wrecked state last night, she probably thought it would make me happy to know her relationship with Tor had some spark left in it after all.

"Wait a second." Callie's voice had become a growl. She jabbed her finger at Tor again like it was a switchblade. "You mean you went over to Lydia's last night to jump her right after—"

My heart nearly hurled itself out of my chest and onto the dash, but Callie caught herself just in time.

"After what?" Lydia asked.

Callie's face had turned red. She looked ready to climb into the backseat and rip out Tor's intestines with her bare hands. "You're such a fucking pig, Tor."

The car went silent, and it made me think of the silence in Ms. Utter's class that had followed the Big Bang.

"That's a horrible thing to say," Lydia whispered. "I know things are different, Callie, but you're just going to have to accept it: Tor and I are together now."

She didn't have a clue what was going on.

But Tor did. I glanced at him in the rearview mirror, and his eyes burned as they held mine.

26

Tor kept it together, though. He looked away and forced out a chuckle. "Jesus, Elvira, get a grip."

I faked a laugh too. "Yeah, relax. They didn't get caught. Tor didn't lose a testicle."

"Too bad," Callie muttered, under her breath but still loud enough for all of us to hear. "It might solve a lot of problems if Lydia's dad just chopped off both the fuckers." She slumped down in her seat with her arms crossed and settled into an angry silence. The rest of us didn't say much after that either.

When we got to school, once Callie and Lydia had peeled off to head to their first-period classes, Tor grabbed me by the collar and steered me all the way down the winding first floor hallway to the far end of the building, where the locked door to Ms. Utter's former classroom stood. He turned me around and slammed me against the door. A shock of pain went through me. I'd never seen him like this. Even when angry, he usually did a lot more with a sneer and a cutting remark than with his fists. Right now, though, as he crushed me against the door with one arm and started to raise the other, I felt absolutely sure he was about to punch my head clear through the little papered-over window in the door behind me.

Instead he stuck a finger in my face and snarled, "You fucking told Callie. About the steam tunnels. About what you and I did last night. *That's* why she was so pissed in the car."

I shook my head while I struggled for breath to speak. "She hasn't told anyone, Tor. And she won't. We can trust her. Please don't be mad. I've just been feeling really confused about everything that's been happening, and I needed to talk to someone about it."

"You had no fucking right to tell her, Rem. That stuff we did, it's *private*." He leaned in until our noses almost touched, and his eyes looked straight into mine like they never did down in the steam tunnels. In a weird way, this felt more intimate than anything we'd ever done down there.

"I'm sorry," I stammered. "I'm telling you, it's okay."

"It better be." He banged me against the door one more time and turned on his heel. "Otherwise you'll both regret it," he muttered before disappearing around the corner.

27

"This is Franklin Kettle's brain immediately prior to the procedure."

Mom had brought up the black-and-white image on the huge flat-screen fixed to the wall in the main lab. It showed a human head in profile, with the brain coiled inside the skull like a clump of those extra-thick Japanese noodles. Everything looked normal enough, at least to a nonscientist like me. Except I did notice a few white dots, very small, located in various places among the doughy coils. "What are those spots?"

"They're cerebral nanodrones. The day Franklin arrived here, we injected them into his brain through his nose, and they navigated to sites we suspected were underperforming. The drones monitored Franklin's neuronal activity at those sites, and we used the data to help us configure the capsule."

"Those are nanodrones? You told me about them. I didn't know you were already using them on actual people."

Her eyes shunted away from mine in a weird way. "We just started. Franklin's our first subject."

She punched a few keys on the keyboard in front of her,

and the image began to move. A drill appeared—disturbingly similar to the kind we had hanging on the wall in the garage at home—and positioned itself against the back of Franklin's skull. A jolt, and the drill started to bore through bone. I winced and turned my head a little to one side but didn't look away.

Dr. Hult chuckled. I hadn't heard him come in. He stood near the door with his arms crossed and his comb-over draping across his head in thick, greasy tendrils. "At least it gives you a sense of how hard the human head really is."

"I'm fast-forwarding through the footage of the operation now," Mom said.

The video sped up. The drill withdrew and the capsule appeared, smooth, egg-shaped, and about the size of an acorn, held by a delicate pair of forceps. The capsule slid through the hole in Franklin's skull and nestled at the back of his brain.

"Now watch this."

From the pointed end of the egg, around a dozen slender threads deployed, snaking their way through Franklin's cerebral matter. The sight was oddly beautiful, like a time-lapse video of a growing plant, or the undulating tentacles of a squid. Eventually the end of each thread settled near one of the nanodrones.

"They're specially designed electrodes," Mom said. "We have thirteen of them positioned at various sites, mostly in the amygdala and orbitofrontal cortex. They send out tiny energy pulsations that target specific neurons and stimulate them to function like they're supposed to."

Dr. Hult wagged his finger at the screen. "That's a very sophisticated piece of equipment we've put inside Mr. Kettle's head, constantly tracking his brain activity and adjusting itself accordingly. It's connected to our wireless network too, so we're able to monitor and control it at all times."

"What about the nanodrones? What happened to them?"

"Watch," Mom answered.

The tiny white dots began to move, all of them flowing toward the place where the scientists had inserted the capsule.

"We extracted them through the burr hole at the end of the procedure."

I sat back in my chair and folded my arms across my chest. "I still don't understand how you're going to know, *really* know, if the capsule's working, though. This isn't like fixing a broken bone, where you can just glance at an X-ray and see if it's healing. With mental stuff, it's a lot harder to tell, isn't it? What if the capsule doesn't work, but Franklin decides to . . ."

"Fake it?" Dr. Hult asked, his face splitting into a grin.

"Exactly. If he's still a sociopath, he might enjoy screwing with you like that, right? And would it really be that hard to do? You said yourself, Mom, he's a smart guy."

"It's certainly possible." Mom grabbed her mug of coffee. "That's why we're administering a wide range of tests and watching him carefully. If nothing else, he's become more cooperative since the procedure, which is making testing easier. We're measuring his heart rate, pupil dilation, other involuntary responses that are almost impossible to fake. He could try to put one over on us, but I'm confident something would give him away eventually." Mom's phone chimed. She glanced at it and said, "They're ready to bring him up. Now listen, Rem: I already told you I don't think he'll behave like he did last time, but I still need you to keep the conversation as neutral as you can."

"I tried before," I said, "but he didn't want to talk about art."

"So talk about the weather. You can't go wrong with the weather, right? We'll limit the conversation to five minutes, just like before. It'll be over before you know it."

I nodded. "Five minutes."

"You're sure you want to do this?"

"Absolutely."

And I meant it. I couldn't have told her why, I didn't even know if I understood the reason myself, but I wanted to see Franklin again.

Mom kissed me on the cheek, and a few seconds later I found myself sitting at the big white table again.

28

When Franklin came in and slouched over to the chair in front of the window, his appearance took me by surprise, but not in the way I'd expected. I'd been all ready to search his face for some sign that the procedure had transformed him, but instead, the second I set eyes on him, I thought, *Holy shit, Callie was right.* Now that his hair had disappeared, I could actually see his face, and it was definitely striking. Not handsome in Tor's conventional, Nordic god sort of way. But intriguing, sculptural, with jutting cheekbones and a nose that zigzagged like a twisty mountain range. He must've broken it at some point, but I didn't know when or how. The look suited him, though. I wondered what he'd look like if he also got rid of the glasses.

I squirmed in my chair. Catching myself thinking thoughts like that about Franklin made me feel even grosser than catching myself enjoying Son of War had yesterday.

Apart from the hair, I couldn't detect much change in Franklin. Mostly he just looked tired. His skin seemed grayer, and if anything his pebble eyes had grown even duller behind his glasses. He still wore the same bright-orange hoodie. The same chains bound his wrists and ankles. The same two guards stood on either side of him like unenthusiastic backup singers.

"Hi," he said.

"Hi." I nodded toward the window behind him and hoped my voice sounded casual. "It's been cold, huh?"

He glanced over his shoulder, his chains clanking. "I wouldn't know. I haven't been outside since I got here."

Brilliant idea, Mom.

"I don't have windows in my room either, so I've barely even seen what it looks like."

Another thing that apparently hadn't changed: Franklin's determination to make our conversations as awkward as possible. I turned to one of the guards. "Is it okay if we switch?"

"I didn't mean—" Franklin began.

"No, you should have the view this time."

"Really, I don't—"

"It's only fair."

We changed places, the guard keeping a hand on Franklin's shoulder as she walked him around the table.

He slumped into his new seat. "Thanks," he muttered. His eyes wandered over the lake behind me. His chains clinked as he raised his hands and pointed. "It's pretty."

I looked back at the view. "Yeah."

"Sort of frozen and empty and dead, but in a nice way."

"Uh-huh." I nodded like he'd just said something completely normal. "Bleak, I guess you'd call it."

"Bleak," he repeated, firing the final *k* off the back of his tongue.

I stole another look at Franklin and noticed something. That morning, I'd thought Lydia was miserable, but it had turned out she was just exhausted. In the same way, now that I could see Franklin better with the fading daylight landing on his face, I realized he wasn't exhausted. He was miserable. Behind his glasses, red rimmed his dull eyes, and his eyelashes stuck together in clumps. Maybe that explained why he'd resisted when I'd proposed we change places. Maybe he hadn't wanted me to see. He must've felt my eyes on him now, because his face wriggled, like an insect was crawling over his cheek. As if to redirect my attention, he said, "How's school?"

"Same as usual, I guess." I racked my brain for news to share, but everything I came up with seemed inappropriate. Preparations for the Big Bang anniversary assembly? Concerns among Duluth Central students about Franklin's procedure? Of course, I could always tell him about how Tor had taken up with one of our mutual best friends, ended our clandestine nonrelationship, and threatened to do horrible things to me if anyone found out about it.

"What about Tor? How's he?"

I jumped. His eyes were still resting on the lake. Had that capsule in his brain given him the power to read minds? If so, mine must've blared with thoughts of Tor. He hadn't left my head for more than a second all day. My back still felt sore from when he'd slammed me against that door.

I hoped none of that showed on my face while I said, "He's the same as usual too. Why do you ask?"

Franklin shrugged. "He's your friend, isn't he?"

I nodded but didn't say anything. He shifted his sneakers on the floor, and his chains made noise. The conversation wasn't coming easily, but at least we hadn't started yelling at each other yet, and at least he was making an effort now too.

More than anything, I wanted to ask him if he felt different, if *he* thought the procedure had worked, but Mom wouldn't consider that neutral conversation. Anyway, he could always lie.

He pointed out the window again. "Is that the kind of thing you like to draw?"

I cast another glance over my shoulder. Outside, the wind had blown up, scraping loose sheets of snow across the surface of the lake. "Sure, sometimes I do landscapes. Once I did a view of the lake really similar to this, except in summer."

"So not as bleak."

I laughed. "Yeah. Not as bleak."

He nodded as he considered the view. The wind moaned behind me. Pulling himself out of his slouch a little, he said, "Listen, I should probably set the record straight about something I told you last time."

"What's that?"

"When I said I didn't like art, I was just messing with you. I do. Not landscapes, though. Portraits. So maybe we share an interest after all."

I could've sworn his eyes glanced off mine for a split second as he said it, like actual eye contact, but it happened so fast I couldn't be sure. That image I'd received last night sprang to the front of my mind, along with the crazy theory that Franklin might've somehow sent it. My neck tingling, I watched his face, waiting for another sign, something more definitive. I even opened my mouth to speak, but I caught myself just in time. What could I possibly say? *Excuse me, just wondering: while you've been busy recovering from your brain surgery, did you happen to get onto a computer, paint a painstakingly detailed picture of my face, and anonymously send it to me?*

Instead I said, "Maybe more than one. I tried playing Son of War yesterday, just to see what it was like."

His eyebrows scrunched a little. "Really?"

"Uh-huh. I did okay, but I'm not a master soldier like you or anything." I rubbed my palms together and felt some residual paint crumble from my skin. "I liked playing it though. I didn't think I would."

I waited for him to come out with a smug remark about my change of heart, but he stayed quiet.

"You were probably right that my brother should've played that game. If he had, maybe he wouldn't have gotten killed." Now I was the one who couldn't make eye contact. I stared at my paint-flecked hands.

Franklin resettled himself in his chair. His chains rustled. "I've told you I'm one of the top-ranked players in the world, right?"

Jesus, not that again. "Yeah, you might've mentioned it."

"And that includes some of the finest soldiers on the planet, because the game's actually used in mil—"

"Military training programs around the world. Right."

"So in a way, you could say I'm better trained than most soldiers."

"Okay, I get it, Franklin."

His chains made more noise as he shifted around again. He seemed to be having trouble getting comfortable. When he next spoke, his voice had dropped nearly to a whisper. "But I used to die too. All the time."

The light from the window behind me had almost disappeared. The glow falling over Franklin's face had turned bluish.

"Sometimes within the first five minutes," he said. "The way Son of War's designed, it's a little different every game, so no matter how many times you play, you can still get surprised. No matter how good you are, once in a while you just die. Like in real life."

His face was still nearly expressionless, but in some subtle way I couldn't put my finger on, it had shifted. Maybe it was just my imagination, or maybe it had something to do with the light, but his eyes didn't look dull and dead anymore. At least to me, at least right then, they appeared to have depth and feeling.

"I wanted to set the record straight about that, too. What I said about your brother last time wasn't accurate. Just because he got popped . . . got *killed*, doesn't mean he wasn't a superior soldier. Even a highly skilled player can have bad luck and get taken out of the game."

He dropped his hands into his lap with a clank.

"And your brother only got to play once."

He went still and stared, like the speech had drained him of energy.

Neither of us spoke for a while.

One of the guards coughed.

I shook my head. "I don't know. My mom once said Ethan just wasn't a killer. I think she meant it like it was a good thing, but the truth is, I wish he *had* been. I wish it every day. Or better yet, I wish I'd been there myself, so I could've pulled the trigger for him."

His gaze lifted. This time our eyes really did connect. He looked straight at me, and in that moment, I understood why these conversations with Franklin kept circling back to my brother. Ethan hadn't pulled the trigger when he'd had the chance, and Franklin had. Maybe Franklin and I both wanted to understand why.

I glanced at one of the cameras attached to the ceiling, only then remembering Mom. I never talked like this about Ethan's death around her. It must've come as a shock to hear me just now, even though she'd said almost the same thing herself a couple days ago. But maybe all the valuable data our conversation was yielding would soften the blow. And by the way, hadn't it been five minutes yet?

Franklin's head sagged forward. He reached up and to one side with his chained-together hands so he could touch the bandage on the back of his skull.

"I guess you know what it feels like to be angry like that," I said.

He kept probing his wound with his fingertips. I started to think maybe I'd made him uncomfortable or even offended him, but then he said, "I was angry all the time. I woke up angry, and I went to bed angry. At school I was angriest of all. The only time I didn't feel angry was when I was playing Son of War and killing things. It relaxed me. I always thought that was kind of funny."

He looked up, out the window behind me, and I glanced back too. The daylight had drained away altogether now. The window had become an indigo rectangle.

"That was why I thought up my mission," he said. "It felt good to imagine going into school with a plan and a weapon and targets, just like in the game."

My belly sucked in a little at his mention of targets. The question that had stuck in my brain for a year screamed for an answer. *Was I one of them?*

The overhead lights had automatically brightened now that the sun had gone down. They covered Franklin's face in bland light, but the subtle change I'd noticed in his eyes lingered.

"My mission even had a name," he went on. "Son of War High. For a long time I just liked picturing exactly how I'd do it, but then one day that wasn't enough anymore. I realized if I could play all the way through my mission for real, at the end I might stay relaxed permanently."

By "stay relaxed permanently," he meant he'd planned to kill himself. That much I understood. *Those assholes will pay,* that comment he'd left on the Son of War subreddit said. *A bullet for each one. And then a bullet for me.*

"I really did feel that way when I put on my mask in class and fired my gun. Relaxed, like I was playing Son of War." He paused to take a slow breath. "But then I was stopped."

A grimace smeared across his face. His head dropped forward again. His hands went back to his skull. His shoulders shook. I shifted in my chair, wondering if I should say something, or pat him on the back maybe. But that probably wasn't allowed, and even if it was, the thought of giving the person responsible for the Big Bang comforting pats didn't exactly appeal to me.

Then, when he looked up again, I could see it.

He was *laughing.*

"By Ms. Utter," he cackled, barely able to get out the words. "She tackled me. Tiny Ms. Utter."

I eased back in my chair. My hands caught each other and squeezed. Christ, what had Mom done to him?

"The lady comes up to my armpit," Franklin panted, "she has half a century on me, and she took me *down.* End of mission. Maybe *she'd* been playing Son of War."

He buried his face in his palms, and his shoulders rocked some more. He didn't say anything else for a while. He just went right on laughing. For a second, a chuckle started to rise in my throat too, because it *was* sort of funny, Franklin getting taken down by our child-sized middle-aged history teacher. But then I realized this was the guy who'd killed my friend

Pete and now I was about to *laugh* with him about it. How fucked up was that?

Franklin kept on, though. His face, still clutched in his hands, slid to the table. A weird sound seeped from him, something between a groan and a hiccup. Then he turned his head to the side, his face contorted, his cheeks wet. He opened his lips wide, and the sound coming out of his mouth changed into a scream.

I grabbed the armrests and looked at the guards. They both put fingers to their ears as they listened to their earpieces, and then they didn't make a move. One raised his hand, telling me I should wait. Mom wanted to see how this would play out. By now I knew five minutes must've come and gone long ago. *Jesus, Mom, what the hell?*

Franklin stopped screaming and went still, his head on the table, his face twisted up like a wet rag. I cleared my throat but still couldn't think of anything to say. He wiped his cheeks with the heels of his palms and, with a jingle of chains, sat up in his chair. His face, though still red and puffy and damp, had melted back into expressionlessness.

"I've been having nightmares," he said. "Since the operation."

I forced myself to let go of the armrests and once again try to act like this was a regular conversation. "About what?"

"You know. That day. The Big Bang. That's what you all call it at school, right?"

I gave a small nod.

"Nil told me. She came to visit at the detention center a few times." He sniffed. "In my nightmares, I'm back in the classroom, just about to put on the mask, except I'm also outside myself watching it happen. All the anger's there, but it feels like somebody else's anger." He reached up to scratch his crooked mountain-range nose. "Do you remember that time in Ms. Utter's class when I had to give a talk in front of everybody and Pete messed with the projector?"

"Yeah."

Like I could ever forget. Last year Ms. Utter had made all of us give PowerPoint presentations. In September she'd assigned everybody a subject and a date, and Franklin's presentation had come months before Pete's, close to the beginning of the year. I could still picture Franklin standing in front of the class in his tattered black jean jacket, his blue-black hair screening his face as he stared down at the crinkled papers in his hands. He mumbled something about how the subject of his speech, Napoleon, was known for being "a small man but a masterful military leader." Then he nodded at Ms. Utter to turn off the classroom lights and punched the projector remote to start the slide show.

But instead of an image of Napoleon, a short video playing on a loop appeared on the whiteboard next to Franklin. Over and over, the video showed Franklin standing in the boys' locker room wearing nothing but a towel around his hips and a seething expression on his usually expressionless face as he stared at something or someone outside the frame. A circle of boys surrounded him, all of them laughing. A kid named Eric snatched off the towel. Franklin hurried to cover himself, his anger replaced by surprise. Then the video started again.

Gasps filled the classroom, followed by a rush of laughter.

"Wait, is that him?" Pete said. "I didn't know Napoleon was *that* small." He lifted up his pinky finger. "He's, like, *tiny*." Really, though, everything happened so fast in the video you couldn't see a thing.

Ms. Utter got the class back under control fast. She stormed across the room, yanked out the projector's plug, yelled at us all to quiet down. It turned out Pete, sitting at the desk next to the one where Ms. Utter had set up the projector, had unplugged the classroom laptop and plugged in his phone instead.

In the end, he got a week's detention for that prank.

"Pete wasn't a bad guy," I said now. "He only did stuff like that when Tor got him going. I'm pretty sure Tor gave him the idea."

"That's no excuse," Franklin said, his quiet voice sharpening a fraction. Then he shrugged. "So maybe I do still feel angry. In my nightmares, though, my presentation and Pete's get all mixed up. I'm at the back of the classroom, but I'm also at the front." He grimaced again. "And when I raise the gun, I'm aiming at myself."

He put his hands to his skull and released another yell, as if from physical pain, though not as loud this time. His fingers curled back toward the hole in his head and clawed at it.

"Sometimes I wish I could dig it out."

My eyes darted to the guards and then to Franklin again. Would he actually try it? Right here? "You can't. They put it in too deep."

"I know." His fingers relaxed.

Without realizing it, I'd inched all the way to the edge of my seat. My body felt like a compressed spring. "You think that's why you're having the nightmares? Because of the capsule? You think it's working?"

He studied his palms. "I do feel different. Like I want to cry all the time. Yesterday I agreed to start doing the scientists' stupid tests. And you know why? Because I didn't want to hurt their feelings. That's crazy, isn't it? They put a hole in my head, and *I* didn't want to hurt *their* feelings."

"What are they making you do?" I asked.

"Mostly just watch old episodes of *Friends*."

"Are you serious? So in other words they're torturing you."

He let out a soft snort. "Pretty much. They keep stopping the video at random points and asking me questions. 'What do you think this character is feeling?' 'What would you say to that character?' Stuff like that. The worst part is, the show's been making me cry too. So I sit there blubbering while I answer their questions. 'Phoebe is confused.' 'Joey is jealous.'"

Empathy. Just like Mom had talked about. So did that mean he had it now? Or was he faking?

"Then, when I finish the test," Franklin continued, "I look around at the scientists and the guards and I keep playing the game in my head. This person is happy. That person is bored. As soon as I came in here today, I thought, *Rem is sad*."

"Me?" My face heated up. I wondered how he'd even noticed my expression without ever seeming to look directly at me. "You thought I looked sad?"

He nodded. "Are you, Rem?"

My eyes darted to one of the cameras. There was no way in hell I was discussing my joke of a love life in front of Franklin *and* Mom *and* all her colleagues. Not even in the name of science. I shook my head. "I'm fine. Just a little tired."

He studied his chained hands some more. I waited, wondering if he'd press the issue.

"Philip Glass," he said.

"Excuse me?"

"Philip Glass. He's one of my interests too."

"Who's he?"

"A composer. He makes music that's really simple. Repetitive, but in a good way. Mathematical. Sometimes you hear music, and there's just too much going on. Drums and guitars and keyboards all banging away at once. Even when I played Son of War I had to turn the music off, because it made me too tense. But Philip Glass's stuff isn't like that. Not that it's relaxing, some of it's pretty dramatic, but it's all simple. One of his songs is basically just people counting numbers. Can you believe that?"

"Huh."

All the zigs and zags our conversation had taken today had made me dizzy, but at least it seemed like we'd gone back to more mundane subject matter for a while.

"One of the lab techs here, Gertie, she likes that type of music too," he said. "Yesterday she told me this one piano piece of his was her favorite. I already had it on my iPod, but I'd never listened to it much. When I heard it yesterday, for some reason it sounded completely different from how I remembered it. It did something to me. Made me cry. Made me think about things I didn't want to think about. And I didn't understand why."

"Sometimes music does the same thing to me."

His eyes settled on my paint-spattered shirt. "I'll play it for you sometime, if you want to hear it."

"Sure."

His mouth had creased into a tiny smile. In the same way his eyes had changed, his smile had changed too. It wasn't that same creepy smile from before, or at least I didn't think it was. But it still seemed to hold a secret.

"I think you might like Philip Glass's music," he said. "Maybe it'll be another interest we have in common."

29

You could've heard a pin drop back in the main lab. The scientists, about a dozen of them, had all rolled their chairs close to the big monitor. They stared at it, their faces stunned into slackness, even though the screen now just showed the empty meeting room. Dr. Hult stood a little behind the others, arms crossed, a wide grin on his face.

Mom had just brought me in from next door.

"That was way longer than five minutes," I told her.

She turned to me and gripped my shoulders. "I know that must've been intense, Rem, but the feelings he expressed, the things he told you about the shooting . . . they were astonishing."

So she'd already gone from "promising" to "astonishing." Red blotches of exhilaration colored her cheeks, and her wide-open eyes seemed to look not so much at me as through me.

"He got pretty worked up," Dr. Hult said. "Maybe we should send a couple electrodes to his median forebrain bundle to offset the depression brought on by his feelings of remorse."

Mom nodded. "That's a good thought. Not yet, though. We should do more testing first."

"But what about what I said before I went in there?" I protested. "He could be faking, couldn't he? I mean, the stuff he said about the Big Bang, it *sounded* like real remorse, but how do you know for sure?"

"That's true," Mom answered. "We don't. But the fact that he spoke about the shooting at all was highly significant."

Franklin's quiet voice sounded in the background. The scientists had already started replaying the session on the monitor. Gertie flashed a glance at me, biting her lip. She didn't look as thrilled as the others.

"I know he didn't testify at the trial," I said.

"No, Rem." The white streak in Mom's hair seemed to blaze with her excitement. "He's *never* spoken about the shooting. Not a word. Until today. With you."

30

Before I left, Mom took me aside. "*Are* you, Rem?" she asked, keeping her voice down so her colleagues couldn't hear. "Sad?"

"Maybe a little," I answered, turning away to grab my coat and scarf so she couldn't see my face. "I guess I've been thinking about Pete a lot lately, with the anniversary coming up and everything. I didn't think I should say that to Franklin, though."

"Of course. You thought right. I suppose we've had a lot to be sad about, you and I, but you know if you ever need to talk, you can always—"

Her eyes cut away as a tortured cry filled the room. On the opposite side of the lab, the other scientists traded handshakes and murmurs of congratulations as, on the monitor, Franklin had his meltdown one more time.

31

The temperature outside had plunged during my time in the Mother Ship. When I stepped through the sliding front doors, the cold wind whipped back the long tail of my blue scarf and snatched the oxygen out of my mouth. I wound the scarf around my neck a few more times, dug my hands into my pockets, and cut through the dark parking lot toward the Saab.

"Ethan Braithwaite?" someone said.

I spun around. A figure loomed up from between a couple cars like a ghost. I stumbled, my boots slipping on the icy pavement, and went flying backward, banging against the side of an SUV. I leaned against it, my heart jackhammering.

"I'm so sorry, Ethan. I didn't mean to scare you."

The figure stepped into the light, and I instantly felt like a total idiot. It was Franklin's grandmother, Mrs. Kettle. I recognized her right away, though I'd only seen her a handful of times on Boreal Street even before the Big Bang—the rumor on the block had always been that she was a shut-in and possibly a hoarder—and since then I didn't think I'd seen her once. I couldn't blame her for that, though. For weeks following the shooting, swarms of reporters had hovered on the sidewalk at the end of Boreal Street, using her little blue house as a backdrop while they'd shouted into their microphones, leaving squashed coffee cups strewn across her snowy yard at the end of the day. It came as a surprise to see her here now. A thin spray of white, almost translucent hair pushed out from under the hood of her worn coat, and the wrinkles covering her pale dry skin went every which way, giving her face a shattered appearance.

"No, it's my fault," I said between pants. "I guess I'm just jumpy. Hi, Mrs. Kettle. I'm not Ethan, though, I'm Jeremy, Ethan's brother."

Her wrinkles shifted and deepened, her forehead furrowing, her mouth puckering, as she squinted at me. "I'm so sorry, of course you are. I got mixed up. How's Ethan doing these days?"

I blinked. A few days after Ethan's death she'd left a mushroom casserole and a note of condolence on our doorstep. Maybe she wasn't an actual shut-in, but apparently Nil had been right when she'd called Mrs. Kettle senile. "He's fine," I said.

She smiled. "How nice. I have an appointment with your mother. She told me she had you come in and talk to Franklin. He asked for you specifically, she said, because you were kind to him at school. Or am I thinking of your brother again?"

My face turned hot. "No," I stammered. "That was me. I just saw him." I stood there for a few seconds nodding and blushing and trying to figure out what to say next. "Are you going to see Franklin too?" I ventured.

She shook her head and let out a thin laugh. "Just your mom. It seems Franklin's saying he doesn't want to see me right now, and your mom thinks it's best if we respect his wishes, at least for the time being. I can understand that. He's been through a lot, and I get on his nerves sometimes. Anyway, your mom has been giving me updates every day."

Franklin's grandmother glanced up at the lab, and I thought I might've caught a tiny flutter of guilty relief pass across her face.

"She's a wonderful woman, your mother," Mrs. Kettle added. "I'm so grateful to her for what she's doing for Franklin now, and for what she did for him before, too. I was so worried about him. He never left his room, barely ate, played that awful video game at all hours. She was the only one who really seemed to care. I just wish I'd had him come here a little sooner, so your mother could've finished her tests. Maybe if we'd known then how serious his problems were, we could've prevented what happened."

I opened my mouth to reassure her, say something about how she'd surely done everything she could've and no one could've predicted what he'd do, but then I stopped. "I thought my mom had already finished her testing on Franklin. I thought that was how she knew he'd be a good candidate for her project."

Mrs. Kettle's expression turned vague again. "I guess she must've finished some of it. All that science stuff goes right over my head." She kneaded her gloved hands together as she talked. "Your mother did her best to explain it all to me, the neurons and nanodrones and whatnot, but—"

"Nanodrones?"

"That's right. I still remember that word because it's so odd. She was using them to do some kind of test on Franklin's brain, and we were supposed to come back in a week to get the results. But four days before that . . ." Her voice trailed off, and the fingertips of one hand worried a little hole in the thin knit glove that covered the other.

Meanwhile, my stomach had clenched. The wind had kicked up, and it slanted through the gaps between my sleeves and my gloves, my collar and my scarf, biting into my skin. Mom had said she'd just put in the nanodrones a few days ago. Had she lied? Maybe Mom had discussed the nanodrones more recently and Mrs. Kettle was mixing things up.

Except now that I thought about it, Mom had been talking a lot about nanodrones a year ago. They'd been one of her most promising projects, one of the main reasons she'd won the funding to have her new lab built. Then she'd gone quiet about them. I'd always assumed the project just hadn't panned out, which was why it had surprised me earlier today when she said she'd used them on Franklin.

Plus, I'd never known he'd gone to the lab only a few *days* before the shooting.

"Anyway," Mrs. Kettle said, "I'm just so grateful to your mother. Of course, she hasn't gone into much detail about how Franklin's doing right now and whether the procedure was successful, but I can understand why. She wants to do all her tests first. She's a scientist. I know that's how scientists are."

"She's a scientist," I repeated, barely listening. My brain was still turning, struggling to make sense of this new information.

"She probably doesn't want me to get my hopes up," Mrs. Kettle babbled. She waved her hand and tried to make her voice sound light. "Not that I would, you understand. Get my hopes up. It's just that I'd like to know how he's doing. How he seems. If he's changed."

Franklin's grandmother stopped talking. She rubbed her gloved hands together and watched me, an expectant look on her fractured face. Only at that moment did it dawn on me why she'd called out to me in the first place, and why she'd steered our conversation down this particular path.

I glanced at the hulking glass structure behind me. Mom wouldn't want me to say anything. And I still had doubts about Franklin myself, didn't I? But maybe that didn't matter. She just wanted a bit of hope. What would it cost to give her that?

"He does seem different," I told her. "I had a rough day and wasn't feeling so good, and he was the only one who noticed."

32

My brain wouldn't settle down after I got home. I paced around and around the house, until finally I pulled on my heavy-duty cold-weather running gear and charged down Boreal Street. I didn't normally run after dark, or in weather this cold and windy, but tonight I felt a weird craving for the sensation of the wind scouring my face. Once I got down by the lake, the wind grew even wilder, but at least it tired me out and gave me something specific to struggle against, because the thoughts blowing around in my head felt a lot harder to grapple with.

What did it mean if Mom did lie about those nanodrones she put in Franklin's head? If they went in way back before the Big Bang, did that mean they had something to do with what happened? The idea of it made my insides churn.

Or was it all just a misunderstanding? That had to be it.

Didn't it?

I managed to push those thoughts out of my mind eventually, but the empty space only filled up with thoughts of Tor, and whether things between us would ever get back to where they'd been a few weeks ago, and whether they even should. And then there was Lydia. Was I betraying her, like Callie kept saying? Tor had never really been hers to begin with, had he? Sure he kissed her in public, but I was the one he wanted to be with when no one was looking.

I stopped on the running path that followed along the Lake Superior shoreline and looked out at the frozen-over lake, what little I could see of it in the darkness. Years ago Mom had sometimes taken me and Ethan down to the shore in winter and told us about how the lake never froze all the way to the bottom. "There's water under the ice," she'd said, "and fish still living in it."

The image came back to me now: all those fish down there weaving their slow way through the cold depths.

Inside my jacket my phone vibrated. I yanked it out and checked the screen. My heart seemed to stutter and lose its rhythm for a second: I'd received another picture from that same unknown phone number. I bit into the fingertips of my glove and dragged it off with my teeth, not even minding the freezing wind. I touched the screen to pull up the image.

A second digital painting of me. Similar to the first one, just my head again, but this time I had a different expression on my face.

Sad. I looked sad.

33

I stared at the image until my fingers turned numb and started to throb, at which point I thrust my phone into my pocket, pulled my glove on again, and raced back the way I'd come.

Mom needed to know about this. Right away. First thing when I got home, I'd ask her about what Mrs. Kettle had told me, find out if she'd lied (but she couldn't have, right?), and tell her about the pictures.

Because my wild hunch had been right: Franklin Kettle must have sent them. There was no way Mom or anyone else at the lab would've allowed him access to the Internet, so he must've done it on his own. Somehow he'd breached security, just like everybody had feared he would.

Other questions still nagged at me, though. Why would he put so much effort into making pictures of *me*? And why would he send them to me, when doing that would put him at serious risk? Had he meant them as some kind of threat? That didn't seem right, especially after the weird conversation we'd had today. It felt more like he wanted me to know he'd seen me. Seen my sadness. Further evidence of his developing empathy maybe?

All the more reason to tell Mom.

But then, what if we were all wrong? What if he *was* just faking his transformation? That would make him a dangerous sociopath with unobstructed access to the outside world.

I put on speed, the wind blowing me forward now. When I turned onto Boreal Street, I could see it straight ahead of me: the Kettles' little blue house, its windows dark, its wind chimes clanging like an alarm in the crazy wind.

Once I got close to home, though, I noticed something that made me slow down. It looked like Mom had returned and switched on the lights while I was out, and a car I didn't recognize stood parked in our driveway. The license plate bore a US flag and, across the bottom, the words PROUD TO BE A VETERAN. The muscles surrounding my rib cage tightened, squeezing my thudding heart and heaving lungs, while I thought of the car with the military plate that had pulled into our driveway two years ago. The cry Mom had let out when she'd seen it. Her severed thumb on the white cutting board. But that car had been black and freshly washed. This one was a silver compact crusted in dirty snow. Still, part of me wanted to turn and race back the way I'd come, into the scouring wind once again.

I clicked the garage door remote on my key chain and entered that way, thinking I'd slip straight through the kitchen to my room, but I walked in to find Mom sitting at the kitchen table with a stranger. He looked young, maybe in his early twenties.

He didn't have on a crisp military uniform like the man who'd come to tell us about Ethan had. Just a button-down and jeans. He stood when I came in.

Mom got up too. "Rem, this is Sergeant Sam Durham. He was in Ethan's unit."

"Not sergeant anymore," the guy said. "I'm a civilian now. 'Sam' is fine." He put out his hand for me to shake. Sam had a stringy body, with a long neck jutting at an angle from stooped shoulders. "I was at Ethan's funeral. You probably don't remember me."

I didn't. I could picture a pack of guys in military dress sitting near the back of the church, me having to shake their hands at one point, but their faces had become blurry in my mind, along with pretty much everything else connected with Ethan's funeral. He gripped my hand now with military firmness.

"He was in the area and decided to drop by." Mom spoke in her usual smooth voice, a composed smile on her face. But she'd started prodding her thumb with her index fingernail.

"I was out for a run," I said. "I should go change."

Sam waved his hands. "Don't trouble yourself, Rem. I need to head out anyway." He turned to Mom. "Thanks for your hospitality, Dr. Braithwaite." He nodded at the photo of Ethan on the wall. "I still miss your son. He was the heart of our unit."

A faint bell rang in my head. Now I remembered Sam. He'd said the same thing about Ethan when I'd shaken his hand at the funeral. Then, when we'd walked away, Mom had put her hand on my shoulder and told me who he was.

"You were there," I said now, without thinking. "You were right behind Ethan."

Now that the memory had come back to me, I imagined I could see Ethan's death printed on him—in the way his long body hunched forward, in the shadow his deep-set eyes seemed to contain. I noticed how his Adam's apple bulged from his jutting neck, like he had something permanently stuck in his throat.

He gave a nod. "That's correct. I'm the one who saw that child shoot your brother."

I blinked at him, not sure I'd heard right. "Child?"

Mom picked up a bottle of wine from the table. "Sam, are you sure you wouldn't like some—"

"I never heard he was a child." The floor seemed to slide sideways underneath me. "How old?"

He cut an inquiring glance at Mom, but she had her eyes on the table. "Ten or eleven."

"And you . . ."

He nodded again. "I shot the boy after he shot Ethan."

The curve of his spine, the shadow in his eyes—they made even more sense now. "I'm sorry," I said.

Without looking at either of us, Mom poured herself more than half a glass of wine.

"Why didn't you tell me?" I asked her.

"You were heartbroken after we got the news, Rem. You didn't need to hear details like that."

"Why not later then? We just talked about Ethan's killer a

couple days ago, and you said we didn't know anything about him. You lied to me."

"What good would it have done to tell you the truth?"

"Maybe it would've helped me understand."

She set down her glass, too hard. Some wine sloshed onto the table. "Understand what? That war is senseless and horrible?"

"No. Why Ethan didn't pull the trigger."

Sam looked miserable. His huge Adam's apple bobbed up and down as he swallowed. "I'm so sorry, Dr. Braithwaite. I didn't realize—"

"Neither did I," I said, my eyes still on Mom.

She smoothed her gray hair and took a slow breath to calm herself. "Can we talk about this later, Rem?"

"Why? Is there anything else you haven't told me?"

"Rem."

I turned away from the table. My running clothes felt cold and slimy against my skin. "I'm going to my room." To Sam, I said, "Thanks for coming by."

He extended his hand for another shake, but I was already cutting out of the kitchen and heading down the hall.

34

After showering and changing into clean sweats, I sat down at my desk. My chest still felt tight. My heart banged inside it. I pulled out my Tattoo Atlas but couldn't get myself to draw anything besides a few aimless lines. Outside, the wind was still blowing hard. Sam Durham's car had disappeared from our driveway. Mom knocked on my door and asked what I wanted for dinner. Without opening, I told her I wasn't hungry.

I couldn't say exactly why this new information about Ethan's death bothered me so much. It should've even helped to know the reason Ethan hadn't pulled the trigger. He hadn't wanted to shoot a child. Who could blame him for that?

Me. The truth was, I still wished Ethan had done it. Maybe *that* was what bothered me. For over two years I'd carried around a mental picture of Ethan's killer. I hadn't consciously tried to imagine what the guy looked like. The picture had just formed there all by itself. I'd even drawn it in my Tattoo Atlas a few times: a full-grown man with fierce eyes and, for some reason, a sweat-soaked black bandanna tied around his head.

The picture was a total cliché based on a mishmosh of various action movie villains and zero actual information, but it gave me something to hate. Now the picture had changed. In one second, it had become a frightened ten-year-old kid.

And with all my heart I still wished Ethan had blown his brains out.

Probably not a very nice thought for Mr. Nice Guy to have. But then again, Mom had said pretty much the same thing the other day. She'd told me she wished Ethan had managed to fire his weapon first, and she'd known his killer was a child. Did that make my illustrious humanitarian mother totally fucked up too?

Maybe. And it didn't even come as much of a surprise after some of the other stuff I'd seen her do lately. Like putting her own son in a room with the sociopath who'd shot one of his best friends (which, Callie would be happy to know, I could finally admit was *seriously* fucked up). And then leaving him in there even longer than she'd said she would. And lying to him about how his brother died.

Plus, there was still that other thing Mom might or might not have done.

A little after eleven, she came to my door again. "Are we going to talk about this, Rem?"

I dropped my pencil on my sketchbook and yanked open my door. "Actually, Mom, there's something else I want to talk to you about."

Her eyes flared in surprise. "What?"

"I ran into Mrs. Kettle when I was leaving the lab today."

She stiffened. At least I thought she did. "Really? What did she say?"

"I knew Franklin went to your lab for testing before the Big Bang, but I never knew it was *three days* before."

"Was it? I don't remember the exact timing."

"She also said you hadn't finished the testing when the Big Bang happened. So what made you think he'd be such a perfect candidate for your procedure?"

"It's true," she said smoothly, "we didn't have all of it done, but we had enough data to make an assessment."

"That's not how you made it sound when I asked you about it yesterday. You said you'd run an 'exhaustive analysis' of Franklin's brain. And another thing: according to Mrs. Kettle, you put nanodrones in Franklin's head during that first visit. Didn't you say you just put them in a few days ago?"

"We did. She must've been confused." I saw it, though: her index finger had slid toward the pad of her thumb.

"She told me you were using the nanodrones to monitor Franklin's brain activity, and he was supposed to come back in a week so you could get the readings. That's basically how the nanodrones work, isn't it?"

"Yes, but—"

"It doesn't seem like she was confused to me."

Mom crossed her arms. "What are you getting at, Rem? Just say it."

I gripped the doorframe. My throat had gone dry. "Just

for the sake of argument, say Mrs. Kettle wasn't confused. If Franklin had those drone things floating around in his head when he shot Pete, it makes me wonder . . ." I closed my eyes and pushed out the rest of the words. "Does that mean they made him do it somehow?"

"Of course not, Rem, that's—"

"For Christ's sake, Mom, stop lying. Just tell me."

She flinched at the sharpness in my voice. I never talked like that to her.

"Was it Dr. Hult? Did he talk you into covering it up?" I'd always thought that guy seemed shifty. Maybe because of the comb-over. "Come on, Mom. Tell me the truth."

Mom stood there, her fingernail driving into her thumb. Outside, the wind chimes on the Kettle house, together with the howling of the wind, made a frantic, eerie music, like something Gertie might listen to. Mom's eyes narrowed, as if she'd come to a decision. "All right then. You want the truth? Here it is. We did inject the nanodrones a year ago. They were an experimental technology, meant solely to monitor brain activity. We had no reason to believe they'd also alter it. But after the shooting, we did wonder if there was a connection, so we conducted more testing. The nanodrones measured the activity of neurons by sending out tiny targeted pulses of energy. It turned out those pulsations were somehow signaling the neurons to suppress their activity."

I tightened my grip on the doorframe. I thought I might topple over if I didn't. "And you didn't tell anyone?"

She wiped back her iron-gray hair with its stripe of white. Her voice stayed as steady as ever. "No, Rem, we didn't tell. Our tests also showed if we modulated the frequency of those pulsations just slightly, they would stimulate the neurons instead of suppressing them. It was a breakthrough, Rem. We'd stumbled on a discovery that would let us influence brain activity in a far more precise and nuanced way than ever before.

"We knew if we admitted our nanodrones had had anything to do with the shooting, our project would end right there. The media would go into an uproar. Our lab would get shut down. By keeping it a secret, we were able to build the capsule we believe will help Franklin, and potentially thousands of other people suffering from serious mental illness."

"Helping Franklin doesn't exactly count, though, does it? Considering you're the ones that made him that way."

"That's not true," she retorted. "Remember, he'd started leaving threatening comments on that Son of War subreddit months before we ever touched his brain. The whole reason his grandmother brought him to us in the first place was because she recognized he had serious problems."

"Are you saying he still would've killed Pete if you hadn't injected him with the nanodrones?"

"It's possible."

"You heard what he said today. He'd just liked *imagining* bringing a gun to school. Creating a revenge fantasy in his head, turning it into a game like Son of War, planning it all out—that was enough for him. But then, all of a sudden, it wasn't anymore.

After you put in those drones." My chest felt hot, like a furnace. "Admit it, Mom. He was just a garden-variety angry messed-up kid, and you made him a killer."

"No," she said, with a fierce shake of her head. "We don't know that for sure."

"Maybe you don't know for *sure*, but it seems pretty likely. And isn't that enough? You must've realized there'd be a risk putting those nanodrones in his head. You said yourself they were still experimental."

"There's *always* a risk. I told you before, we don't live in a perfect world. And if my team did cause what happened, I believe we're making up for it now."

"By lying." I took a step back. I couldn't even look at her anymore. "All you've been doing is lying, Mom. About Ethan's death. About Pete's. Is there anything you're *not* lying about?" She opened her mouth to reply, but I said, "You know what? Don't answer that. It'll probably just be another lie."

I slammed the door shut and leaned my back against it, breathing hard.

After a silence Mom said from the hall, "Listen, Rem. I'm not dismissing what Franklin did or our possible involvement in it. But do you realize what an important discovery the nano-drones led us to? We've quite possibly found a way to eradicate violent crime on our planet, and to offer redemption to the most seemingly irredeemable among us. Just imagine: if evil *does* exist, we've found the *cure*."

Across from me, on my angled desk, lay my vintage paperback

edition of *Frankenstein*. I'd pulled it out that morning to look at the cover: a portrait, in lurid colors, of Dr. Frankenstein bent over the slab where his monster lay. He looked like the classic mad scientist. White lab coat. Eyes big and maniacal. The streak of white blazing through his dark hair looked just like Mom's.

35

Outside my window the wind had finally blown itself out. Boreal Street was still. I let a few minutes pass after Mom went back to her room at the other end of the house, and then I tucked my Tattoo Atlas under my arm and padded down the hall. I couldn't handle staying inside the house another second. I needed to feel the cold air on my face one more time. I stepped into my sneakers, pulled on my coat, and wound my long blue scarf around my neck. From the couch I grabbed a folded-up blanket.

I went out through the sliding back door. The outdoors always seemed so much quieter in winter, with the snow sucking up all the sound. I crunched down the narrow path I'd shoveled last weekend to Ethan's gazebo and climbed the icy wood steps. Three simple benches stood in a U shape inside. I set the folded-up blanket on one of them and sat. Between the edge of the gazebo roof and the tops of the trees that separated our yard from the Agnarsons', a strip of night sky showed through, dusted with stars.

I opened my Tattoo Atlas and paged through it, hunting for one image in particular.

"Rem?"

Fright went through me like an electric shock. Before I could even think, I was on my feet, whirling around, hunting for the person who'd spoken. Near the back of our yard stood a figure in a bright-orange hoodie. Under the hood, a pair of glasses glinted in the low light.

I gave a shout, stumbled back, grabbed one of the gazebo's wood posts for support.

"It's just me," Franklin said.

As if that was supposed to make me feel any less terrified. "What the hell are you doing here?" I gasped, the words riding out of my mouth on a cloud of vapor.

He dug into his hoodie pocket. I dove behind the gazebo railing, covered my head with my arms, and waited for gunfire to rip through the wood.

Nothing happened.

I peeked through the railing's wood supports, my pulse throbbing in my throat.

Franklin held up an iPod touch and earbuds, a small grin on his face. My freak-out appeared to be amusing him. "I wanted you to hear that music I was telling you about. Remember I said I'd play it for you sometime?" He started toward me, holding the earbuds up as if he wanted to stick them in my ears right then.

"But now?" I panted. "Jesus, Franklin, how did you get out?"

He'd circled around to the steps leading up to the gazebo. I faced him, still in a crouch behind one of the benches, ready to jump the railing if I needed to. My eyes went to the house. If I yelled, would Mom hear me?

"Please don't call her," Franklin said.

I'd never told Mom about the messages Franklin had sent me. In my anger, I'd completely forgotten. Maybe if I'd remembered, Franklin wouldn't be standing here now.

"Please," he repeated.

Even if I did yell to her, how would she help? By calling the police? If Franklin wanted me dead, and if he still had a weapon hidden away somewhere, I'd already be a corpse by the time they got here.

He placed his foot on the bottom step.

"Don't come any closer," I told him, trying to sound commanding but probably failing miserably. "I won't call my mom. For now. But just stay where you are."

His eyebrows furrowed. "I'm not going to hurt you, Rem." He said it like that should've been obvious.

I stayed in my huddle at the back of the gazebo. "How did you escape from the lab?"

"My iPod." He held it up. "I used it to get on the lab's Wi-Fi network and hack into the security system. When the guard outside my room went to take a pee, I disarmed the door locks and put the security cameras on a loop, and then I just walked out."

"You're kidding. You did all that on an iPod?"

"Sure." He waggled the device in his hand. "What's an iPod? Just a little computer. You can do almost anything with this you can do on a laptop, as long as you have a Wi-Fi connection and the right software. I modded this one a long time ago, loaded it up with password-breaking and hacking programs and then buried them deep so no one would find them." The grin returned, wider this time. "Impressed?"

I was, I had to admit. That must've been how he'd made those portraits and messaged them to me.

"I told you computers are one of my interests," he said. "And I also have tons of experience breaking out of prisons."

"You mean you broke out of the detention center, too?"

"No. But I escaped from prisons all the time in Son of War."

"Oh. Right."

He must've heard skepticism in my voice, because he said, "You don't think virtual prisons count?"

"I wouldn't know. I've never been virtually incarcerated." I patted my sweats, pretending to wipe some snow off my hands while really checking my pockets for my phone. Maybe I could call for help that way. But no. I'd left it up in my room. I could picture it in its regular spot, propped on the nightstand next to my bed.

"What's that?"

He pointed at my Tattoo Atlas. It lay on the snow-dusted floor a few feet away from me. I grabbed it. "Nothing. What are you doing here, Franklin? You really just came here to play me some music?"

"No." He stuffed his hands into the pockets of his hoodie. "I wanted to find out why you looked so sad today. When I asked you at the lab, I saw you glance at the camera. I figured whatever the reason was, you probably didn't want to say it in front of your mom and the other scientists, but maybe you'd tell me in private."

"Well, you figured wrong. It's none of your business."

Down the block, Mrs. Kettle's chimes sounded, more softly now that the wind had died down.

"But thanks," I added. "For being concerned."

He nodded. I noticed his chin had started shaking. Only then did it register: in this insane bitter cold, he had on nothing but a thin orange hoodie. Not even Tor would come outside dressed like that in weather this frigid.

"Jesus, aren't you freezing?"

"I ran most of the way here, so that kept my body temperature up, but now that I've stopped—"

"Wait. You *ran* here? All the way from the lab?"

"Uh-huh."

"But you just had brain surgery yesterday! That can't be good for you."

He shrugged. "I'm young. My system's resilient. I feel okay."

I grabbed the blanket from the bench and threw it at him. "Well, at least take this."

Franklin wrapped the blanket around his shoulders, sank to the floor of the gazebo, and leaned his back against one of the posts. I still hadn't left my crouch behind the bench. Only ten feet or so separated us. I shifted to a more comfortable position but stayed down.

"What happens now, Franklin?"

He shrugged again.

"I still don't think you're telling the truth about why you're here."

"Both of those reasons I told you are true."

"Maybe so, but I don't think they're the only reasons. I'm going to ask you one more time. Why did you come here?"

Franklin stared at the snowy floor.

"Well?"

He exploded to his feet and launched himself at me. The blanket went flying. My body lurched backward, my back slamming into the wood railing. My feet flew out in front of me. I landed hard on my ass. Franklin grabbed me by my shoulders and, once again, looked me straight in the eyes. My pulse drummed so strong this time, I could feel it in every single part of my body. I knew for certain this was it. I'd lived on borrowed time ever since Ms. Utter had tackled him on the day of the Big Bang, but now I was about to die.

Franklin pressed his lips against mine. His fingers dug into my arms, holding me tight, but I didn't even try to push him away. Maybe I was too surprised. At first his lips felt hard, but then they softened, and I suppose mine did too. Our mouths melted together. Where they met felt so warm. The warmth spread through my body like a tranquilizer, making my limbs go heavy and loose.

Then he let go of me. I fell against the side of the gazebo. He staggered back and thunked down on the bench. His shoulders heaved up and down.

"I also wanted to do that," he panted.

When I finally recovered my ability to speak—and it took a while—I gasped out, "But why?"

He managed a smirk in spite of his breathlessness. "Why do you think?"

I threw my hands up. My lips still felt hot, and so did the whole rest of my face. "I don't know. So you're gay?"

"True."

"Since when?"

"Since always. Nobody ever asked."

I wiped the back of my hand across my forehead. I was pretty sure I felt actual beads of sweat forming there, which should've been pretty much impossible in weather like this. "And you have, like, feelings for me or something?"

"True again."

I pushed myself up to a seated position, my back leaning against the railing supports. My butt still felt sore where I'd landed on it, but apart from that, his attack, or whatever you'd call it, hadn't hurt me. I touched my mouth, as if his lips might've left some trace there, some tactile proof that what I thought had just happened had actually just happened.

I'd finally had my first kiss.

And it had been a good one. True, I didn't have anything to compare it to, but even so, I felt pretty confident this one had been *really* good.

And it had been with Franklin Kettle, the freak sociopath who'd shot one of my best friends. That was . . . I didn't even know. "Fucked up" didn't begin to cover it.

Franklin's hood had fallen back when he'd jumped me. He pulled it over his head again, picked up the blanket from the floor, and wrapped it around his shoulders.

"You can't have feelings for me, Franklin," I said.

"Why not?"

I tossed my hands in the air again while I fumbled for an answer. "Because you barely know me. You're just experiencing all these new emotions because of the capsule, and you've been seeing a lot of me lately, so you're probably connecting some of those emotions with me."

"That's not it. I had feelings for you before the procedure too."

"Really?" I got that crawly feeling on the back of my neck. "How long before?"

"Middle school maybe. Not in the same way I do now, but I did."

"What do you mean, 'not in the same way'?"

"The feelings I had for you before were different. More complicated."

"More complicated how?"

Franklin didn't answer. The smirk had left his face. He turned away, and I saw a flash of the white bandage on the back of his shaved head.

My fingers, moving on their own, fussed with the tail of my blue scarf. "Franklin? When you arrived at the lab, why did you tell my mom you wanted to talk to me? You did it before the operation. Why did you want me to come there?"

He shrugged.

"You said I was nice to you at school. We both know that isn't true."

"I don't remember why I wanted you to come."

"I think you're lying, Franklin."

He turned back around to face me, the moonlight flashing in his glasses. "Just leave it, okay?" he hissed through his teeth. "Right now I'm trying to be a good person. I'm really trying. You have to believe that."

"I do, Franklin. It's okay. You don't have to tell me."

He nodded. His breathing slowed. He scratched his twisty nose. "So do you still want to hear that music?"

"Are you serious?" Our conversation was doing that zigzagging thing that made my head spin again. I dragged my palm down my face and wondered when I was going to wake up. This was slightly less terrifying than my usual nightmares, but definitely much weirder. "Look, Franklin, it's incredibly cold, and you're *really* not supposed to be here. Why don't you just go back to the lab and play it for me the next time I see you there?"

"They won't let me. It has to be now." He pulled out the iPod and earbuds again. "Please."

I dropped my head back and peered at the roof of the gazebo, the rafters extending outward from the center like an asterisk. I sent a long breath up toward it. "Fine. One song. That's it." I pushed myself up and sat on the bench next to him while he tapped on the iPod's screen. "Hand them over."

He hesitated before placing the earbuds in my palm, like he felt shy all of a sudden.

"I hope you like it."

I fitted the earbuds into my ears. He pressed the play button.

"This is Philip Glass?"

He nodded. "The song I told you about before. 'Orphée's Return.'"

A piano had started to play. I didn't know anything about this kind of music. It sounded . . . nice, I supposed. Repetitive, like he'd said.

"How's the volume?" he asked, his eyes locked on the space on the bench right next to me.

"Fine."

Then it started: a sequence of high notes like an unspooling thread. While the lower part continued to play, that thread seemed to tie itself to something deep inside my chest and pull. An ache—that was what it felt like. The kind that hurt but felt good, too.

I glanced at Franklin, wondering if my reaction to the music showed. He was still staring at the bench, and I realized what he'd fastened his eyes on: my Tattoo Atlas. I'd set it next to me when I'd sat, the side with the imp drawing facing up.

He lowered the volume a little. "I used to have a notebook like that."

"I remember," I said. "It had a Son of War sticker on the cover, and you'd written your name down the side in red ink. It was always so mysterious the way you used to carry that thing around. What did you write in it?"

"What do you write in yours?"

I almost said, *I asked you first*, but then I changed my mind. My palm pressed flat against my Tattoo Atlas's black cover. I'd never shown it to anyone before. Not even Callie. "I don't write," I answered. "I draw."

I picked up the book and set it in his hands. He flipped through the pages, studying each image with care. When he reached one of the drawings I'd done of the Big Bang, with him in his Son of War mask wielding his Beretta, my stomach flipped, and I silently swore at myself for giving him my sketchbook without thinking about that. But he just paused for a second, peering at the picture the same way he'd peered at the others, and then kept on turning pages.

The music continued playing in my ears, the thread of sound still pulling at that place deep in my chest. I took out one of the earbuds and handed it to him. Without glancing up, without saying a word, he stopped his flipping long enough to take it from me and place it in his own ear.

I'd never known Franklin well. Like he'd said, we'd never even had a real conversation prior to the Big Bang. I wondered what he'd been like before Mom started tinkering with his brain. More like the Franklin who'd mocked my brother's death a couple days ago? Or more like this?

"What *are* these anyway?" he asked after a while. "They look sort of like designs for tattoos."

"Exactly. I call that book my Tattoo Atlas."

"So they're tattoos you're planning on getting?"

"Not really. It's sort of a long story. See, when I was in middle school, I decided I wanted to keep a journal, but I wasn't much of a words person, so I did one in drawings instead. Whenever something important happened to me, I'd draw in a series of sketchbooks I kept. I guess it was my way of processing my life. Then when Ethan died, the pictures started getting weirder and weirder. I was sad. Thinking about death a lot."

"Yes, these are strange." He said it with approval. "I always had a feeling you were secretly an oddball like me." He'd paused on a self-portrait I'd made in which my face had a smile so wide it literally split my head open. *Mr. Nice Guy*, a banner below my face read.

"At about the same time," I continued, "I got interested in tattoo art, and I incorporated a lot of that imagery into the drawings. I started imagining I was turning all the events and people that had left marks on me inside into tattoos for my outside. But I wasn't about to get actual tattoos, so I just kept them in the book. It was sort of like *The Picture of Dorian Gray*, but with body art."

"What's *The Picture of Dorian Gray*?"

"It's a book about this twisted guy who does all this stuff, like going to prostitutes and taking drugs and even killing a man, but none of his experiences leave a trace on his body. He doesn't even age, because he has this magical portrait someone made of him, and the image of him in the painting gets old and damaged and diseased instead of him. I think of this book the same way. My experiences go into the book instead of onto my skin. Except my experiences aren't as exciting as Dorian Gray's."

He scrunched his eyebrows behind his glasses, dubious. "Why couldn't you put these tattoos on your body, though?"

"Well, it's against the law, for one thing."

"Sure, but what about that place on West First Street? All you have to do is show a fake ID. They don't care. Nil and I went there once, and it was no big deal." He shrugged the blanket off his shoulders and hiked up his hoodie and T-shirt to show me his back, the skin pearly in the moonlight. On one side, just above the sharp corner of his shoulder blade, the Son of War mask glared at me. Franklin must have noticed the look on my face when I saw the image, because he let his T-shirt drop and tugged the blanket around his shoulders again. He resettled the earbud in his ear.

I'd heard about that place on West First Street. Abigail Lansing had gone there a few months after the Big Bang to get Pete's name tattooed on her wrist, along with a rose to represent the corsage he'd given her for that one dance he'd taken her to.

"Yeah," I admitted, "I know technically it's possible to get one. But if my mom saw—"

"Wear a shirt. My grandma never saw mine. She still doesn't know about it."

I shrugged. "Maybe I'm just too straitlaced or something. Plus I like being able to move the tattoos around and switch them out. There's no way I could fit all the designs in this book on my body."

"But isn't that sort of the whole point with tattoos? That you can't change them? That they're permanent? That you have to commit?"

I hadn't expected him to have such strong tattoo-related feelings. "Maybe," I mumbled.

He was studying the image I'd drawn a few days ago, the one dedicated to Tor, with the knife cutting a straight bleeding line across the page. He didn't ask me to explain it, but for some reason I felt like I should.

"'Guys are straight lines,'" I said. "It's just something Tor likes to say."

Admittedly, that didn't explain much. It was a good thing my Tattoo Atlas was so weird and cryptic, because I had other drawings involving Tor in there. Everyone knew he and I were good friends, though. I didn't think the images would make Franklin suspect the whole sick truth.

"I like these pictures," he said. "They're strange, but in a good way. You're a good drawer."

"So are you. I got those pictures you sent. That *was* you, wasn't it?"

Franklin nodded. "Yep."

"Weren't you afraid I might figure out who sent them and say something?"

"Nobody would be able to prove it was me. I covered my tracks. Anyway, at this point, what have I got to lose?"

He flipped through a few more pages.

"Why me, Franklin?" I asked. "What did you like about me back in middle school?"

He stopped turning pages and thought about it. "Well, for one thing, you're incredibly cute. Take your lips, for example. I used to stare at your picture in the yearbook all the time and just imagine what it would be like to kiss you. I thought your lips looked like they'd be really soft." He slanted a grin at me. "I was right about that, by the way. And then your ears—"

"Okay, Franklin," I said, my face sizzling. "I get the picture."

"Plus there was the whole art thing. I thought it was cool you were into art and I was too. And the way you always walked around with paint smears all over your skin and clothes and didn't even care. And the way you'd always look at everything so hard, like you were trying to memorize it for a painting. And then . . . like I said before, I thought you might secretly be more like me than you let on. I remember there was this one time in art class near the beginning of sophomore year . . ." He must've noticed my confusion, because he added, "It's okay if you don't remember I was there. It was a big class. I kept my head down."

"My brother died a few weeks after school started that year," I said, "so that whole period's pretty much a blur."

"Yeah, I think you'd just come back to class a few days before. Mr. Hampstead gave us this assignment to paint what joy looked like to us. You raised your hand and asked if you could paint something else. I figured it probably had something to do with your brother—you still looked pretty wrung out—but Mr. Hampstead got all red-faced, like he always did when he thought somebody was trying to undermine his authority, and he said, 'No, you have to paint joy, that's the assignment.'

"You did this still life with flowers in a vase, and it was the best painting in class, as usual. Mr. Hampstead even held it up in front of everybody and talked about how good it was. But what

I noticed and he didn't, and I don't think anybody else in class saw either, was the way you had all the stems in the vase curving and twisting around each other so they spelled out the words 'SCREW YOU,' all in capital letters."

I laughed. "Yeah, I wondered if anyone would spot that."

"I did. And I thought, *He's angry, just like I am.*" He stopped talking and cut me a look, like maybe he was worried I wouldn't like him comparing the two of us that way. "But mostly your lips—that was what really did it for me."

A little heat wafted across my cheeks again.

"I mean," he said, "it's true you were never all that nice to me, but when was the last time *anybody* fell for someone for being nice?"

My brain jumped straight to Tor, and I blinked and fidgeted with my scarf and hurried to change the subject. "How come I never noticed any of your work in art class? You're really good."

He laughed. "I half-assed all the assignments. For the one about joy, I covered the canvas in rotting food waste from the cafeteria Dumpster."

Franklin turned past the picture I'd made for Pete, past the aimless lines I'd drawn tonight, past the blank pages after that, all the way to the end of the book, where I'd done one more drawing on the very last page. I'd made a bunch of images dedicated to my brother, but this one was my favorite, which was why I'd redrawn it here. The second I saw it now, the ache the music was still pulling out of me strengthened. The piano playing had become stronger now, still beautiful, but more insistent.

The drawing showed Ethan having his head blown open. Except in my rendition, the moment was beautiful. This picture was different from the others in the Tattoo Atlas. Less bloody and violent, ironically enough. And in a weird way, happier. I'd drawn my brother's face wearing that big, open smile of his, like he felt no pain, and out of the blown-open top of his head streamed a flock of birds.

"That's Ethan," I said.

"I know. He *was* nice to me. When I was little, whenever he saw me out on Boreal Street, he'd say, 'Hey, Frankie,' and throw me a piece of Dubble Bubble. I felt sad when he died. I really did, even though you probably don't believe me after the stuff I said about him a couple days ago."

I touched the paper, stiff and crinkly from the watercolors. "I met the man who saw him get killed today."

"Today?" Franklin's voice sloped up a little in surprise.

"Just a few hours ago. One of the other soldiers in Ethan's unit. He said the guy who shot Ethan wasn't a guy at all. He was a kid. Ten or eleven years old. Probably scared out of his head. I'd never known that until tonight. And after I just told you at the lab I wished Ethan had pulled the trigger first or I'd done it myself. Instant karma, I guess."

"Don't feel bad," Franklin said. "You didn't actually kill anybody."

But would I have? I wanted to ask him. *If I'd been in that room in Afghanistan with my finger on the trigger, would I have been someone like you, Franklin Kettle—at least after you got the nanodrones stuck in your head—or someone like my brother?* I didn't even know for sure which answer to that question I would've preferred.

Franklin traced one of the ribbons streaming out of Ethan's head along with the birds. "What's that?" I'd written strings of words on each of the ribbons in tiny block letters. He turned the book sideways so he could read them.

"My brother's favorite poem. Emily Dickinson. 'The Brain Is Wider Than the Sky.' I think he liked it because he was into brains, just like our mom. He wanted to get a degree in psychology after he finished his tour of duty. Be a counselor. Help people."

Franklin squinted through his glasses. "It's too dark. I can't . . ."

"'The brain is wider than the sky,'" I recited from memory, "'For, put them side by side, The one the other will include, With ease, and you beside.'"

When I looked up, small flakes of snow had started wandering down to earth. As I'd recited, the ache in my chest had grown so strong it almost felt like real physical pain. The music playing into my ear and the lines of poetry I'd spoken aloud both seemed to express the exact same thing, a feeling I couldn't quite identify, except that it contained an undercurrent of incredible sadness. They all seemed to join together, the music, and the mournful wind chimes I could still hear in my other ear, and the image of my brother's face, and the poem he'd loved, and even the nighttime snow, they all reached through my rib cage, not like threads, but like thorny tendrils.

The song finally ended. The piano sounded the same note six times, like an alarm, and went silent. Franklin didn't say anything. He was watching the snow. I couldn't read his expression. He seemed to have fallen into a trance. According to my watch, it had just passed midnight.

I wondered if I should tell him what I'd learned tonight about the nanodrones. How killing Pete probably hadn't been his fault. I realized I hadn't even fully registered that fact myself yet. I'd spent so much time hating Ethan's murderer and hating Pete's, and now, in the space of just a few hours, I'd found out I had to completely change my conception of both of them.

But even so, I shouldn't tell Franklin. Not yet. If he found out the true story, he'd most likely want to make it public and clear his name. Not most likely—of course he would, and rightfully so. If the truth got out, it would ruin Mom, and however I might be feeling about her right now, I couldn't let that happen. For better or for worse, she was the only family I had left.

At some point, though, Franklin had to find out the truth.

I lifted the Tattoo Atlas out of his hands and cleared my throat.

"You need to go back, Franklin. Someone's going to find out you're gone."

"I'll be fine, Rem."

"You *are* going back, aren't you? You have all that circuitry in your head now. What if there are complications? You might even die."

He shrugged. Maybe that didn't make much difference to

him. After all, he'd planned on killing himself only a year ago.

"Please go back. I don't want something bad to happen to you."

He didn't speak, just nodded slowly, like he was weighing what I'd said, trying to decide if I meant it. He seemed different now, more closed off. His lips had pressed into a thin, flat line. The life had faded from his eyes. Maybe it was my mention of returning to the lab.

"I have an idea," I said. "How about I drive you back and drop you off nearby so you can sneak in again? And then I won't tell anyone what happened. It'll be our secret."

I watched him while he considered my proposition.

"Okay."

I let out a silent breath. "Okay. Good. I'll take you back then. I just need to run inside to get my car keys. It'll be safer if I don't take you into the house. Don't go anywhere, all right?"

He nodded. The lenses of his glasses reflected the lazy movement of the snow. I jumped up and trotted down the path to the house. Without a sound, I opened the back door. I started to grab my keys from the junk bowl on the kitchen counter, but then I stopped when I caught a glimpse of myself in the mirror hanging above. Had I really just offered to give a ride to a murderer who'd moments earlier confessed he'd had some kind of weird obsession with me for years?

Yes, I had. And not only that, I didn't even feel afraid. I'd doubted before as much as anyone, but now I could see it: Mom's technology *had* changed Franklin. It had made him a killer, and then it had made him . . . someone else. "I'm trying to be a good person," he'd said. I'd told him I believed him. And I really did.

My fingers closed around the keys. I slipped back outside and ran through the falling snow to the gazebo.

The blanket lay neatly folded on the bench. My Tattoo Atlas rested on top. Glancing around the yard, I saw Franklin had even smoothed over his footprints, so I couldn't tell which way he'd gone. I might've thought I'd imagined his whole visit, except for four large words traced in the dusting of snow on the floor of the gazebo: *DON'T WORRY GOING BACK.*

36

I lay on my bed staring at the shadowy ceiling for a long time after that, my stomach twisting and contorting while I wondered if Franklin would really return to the Mother Ship. And what if he didn't? What if someone found him wandering the streets of Duluth? If the news got out that Franklin had escaped just like everybody had feared he would, people would make assumptions. They'd think the capsule hadn't worked. They'd think he'd intended to do something horrible. Mom's project would get shut down. Maybe she deserved that, considering she'd built the project on lies. But she'd probably also have to take the capsule out of Franklin's skull. He'd go back to the way he'd been before all this started—not a murderer, perhaps, but also not whoever he was now.

Franklin had said he'd return to the lab, though. He probably hadn't stuck around in the backyard because he'd feared I'd get Mom or call the cops the second I stepped inside, which was understandable. If I hadn't learned what I had about him earlier tonight, I probably would've done just that.

After a couple hours of agonizing, I grabbed my phone and called Callie.

"This better be fucking important, Rem," she said, her voice thick with sleep.

I couldn't get myself to say anything, though. I always told Callie everything, but this felt too huge even to share with her.

"Spit it out," she said. "If this is about how I blew your stupid little secret and now Tor knows I know how the two of you liked to get steamy in the steam tunnels, I already said, I'm sorry but I'm not sorry. It's about time he—"

She broke off.

"What is it, Callie?"

"Nothing. I thought I heard a noise. Look, can we talk about this tomorrow? I mean it, Rem, enough with the middle-of-the-night phone calls. I want to be supportive and there for you and all that shit, but I also need my fucking sleep."

I rolled over in bed, the phone tight to my ear. She was right. I should just let her sleep. If I spilled the truth about Franklin's escape, how would she react? Would she understand if I tried to explain why I hadn't turned him in? Would she insist I go to the police now and tell them what had happened? Would she turn around and do it herself? And how much of the truth should I tell her anyway? Should I mention the part I'd learned Mom had played in Pete's murder? I couldn't explain the rest of it—how my feelings about Franklin could've changed so fast in such a short period of time—without divulging that too, could I?

"Right," I said. "Sorry. Go back to sleep, Callie. We can talk tomorrow."

A couple more hours passed before I finally sank into sleep myself. Right away, a dream pounced on me and swallowed me up. Except this dream felt different from my usual ones. I found myself back in the gazebo sitting next to Franklin. He had the iPod in his hand, and we each had an earbud in one ear, and that beautiful, heartbreaking thread of piano music was winding its way into my chest.

Then, as we listened, the lights went up, and we weren't in the gazebo anymore. We were sitting at the back of Ms. Utter's classroom from last year. I glanced at Franklin. He'd put on his Son of War mask. In one hand he still held the iPod, and in the other he gripped the black Beretta. Now the dream started to feel more like the ones I usually had.

Except with a few differences. Normally in these dreams, I was a bystander watching the action just like everybody else, but this time, when Franklin stood, I stood too, because I didn't want to dislodge my earbud, which for some reason seemed important. Also, all the desks in front of us faced backward instead of forward, so the moment I got up, the eyes of the whole class fastened on me. Tor, still enraged that I'd told Callie about the steam tunnels, watched me with the same dangerous look in his eyes I'd glimpsed that morning. Tears covered Lydia's freckly cheeks: in my dream she'd found out the truth about me and Tor. Callie sat back in her chair with her arms folded across her chest and her long bare legs crossed, regarding me with her trademark disapproving glower.

The whole class looked more like a grumpy audience at one of the drama department's horrible plays than a bunch of witnesses at a school shooting.

Apart from that, the dream continued the same way it usually did, pretty much just like the Big Bang had really happened. Franklin raising his gun and commanding Pete to say, "I didn't know Napoleon was that small." Pete's sweet face going slack. That sad dripping sound as he peed himself.

Then Pete changed into Ethan. That had happened before too. In my dreams those two deaths got mixed up all the time. Ethan wore dusty fatigues and held a rifle I knew he wouldn't fire. Franklin's finger massaged the Beretta's trigger, preparing to pull.

But then Ethan changed again, this time into a ten-year-old Afghan boy. Thick black hair. Eyes wide with fright. The rifle still in his hands.

Franklin turned to me and held out the gun. The mirrored goggles of his mask reflected my face back to me. I closed my hand around the handle and turned to the front of the classroom. The rest of the class scowled at me in silence. In my ear, the beautiful piano music unspooled.

As usual, the gun went *BANG* just as I woke up.

37

I didn't fall back to sleep until around five, which probably explains why I slept through my alarm that morning. When my eyes finally opened, my bedside clock said 8:47—twenty-two minutes after the start of first period. I'd had my phone's ringer turned off, but I'd gotten about a dozen calls from Lydia. Hopefully she and Callie and Tor had given up on me and taken their own cars in time to make class. I slapped on some deodorant, wrestled a paint-covered but otherwise clean sweatshirt over my head, and bolted to the garage.

I called Mom on the way to school. I still didn't feel much like talking to her after last night, but I needed to know for sure if Franklin had made it back to the lab, and if she'd found out what he'd done.

She picked up right away.

"Rem."

She sounded tense. My insides lurched.

"I'm glad you called. I didn't like the way we left things."

It took a second for my heart to find its rhythm again. Our

fight. *That* had her tense. Not Franklin's escape. I pulled the car over to the side of the road so I could concentrate.

"Sometimes," Mom said, "life presents us with situations where there are no good options and no right choices. Your brother's death was one of those. Pete's death was another."

"We don't live in a perfect world," I muttered.

"That's right. Believe me when I tell you it eats me up inside to think Pete might've died at least in part because of us. But just imagine how much more violence our technology might *prevent*. And whatever we did to Franklin before, I really think we're helping him now. It's still too early to tell for sure, but I really do."

A few snowflakes drifted past the windshield. They reminded me of the gentle snow that had fallen last night while Franklin and I sat in the gazebo. "I think you're helping him too," I said.

Maybe she was right. What she'd done to Franklin a year ago had been a mistake. And if she hadn't kept it a secret, that weird, dreamlike moment I'd shared with Franklin in the backyard—and that first kiss I still had no idea how to feel about—would never have happened. For some reason the thought of that made me sad.

"Have you seen him yet today?" I asked. "How does he seem?"

"Tired, which is understandable, considering what a strain these last few days must've put on him."

I exhaled. So he'd made it back. And it didn't sound like she suspected a thing.

"Are we okay, Rem?" Mom said.

I leaned the side of my head against the cold window. "I don't know. How are we supposed to just be okay after all those lies you told? And Mom, Franklin needs to hear the real story. That the shooting most likely wasn't his fault. That all this guilt he's feeling right now probably isn't his to feel."

"When the time is right," Mom said, "I'll tell him. I promise."

I almost asked her when that would be, but I stopped myself. Maybe because I knew she had no way of knowing, or maybe because I feared she'd just lie again.

"Rem, aren't you supposed to be in class?"

"I overslept. Don't worry, I'm on my way now. I'll talk to you later, all right?"

I hung up and took a few more breaths while I eased the Saab back onto the road. I kept telling myself everything had turned out okay. He'd gone back, just like he'd said he would. And hopefully he had as much computer and prison-escaping prowess as he'd claimed, and no one would ever find out what he'd done. My heart had just about slowed to normal speed by the time I rounded a bend in the road and Duluth Central appeared.

I almost ran into the car in front of me. It had come to a dead stop. Up ahead a crowd of vehicles clogged the roadway. Blocking their path, parked diagonally across the street, sat a police cruiser with flashing lights. More cop cars, many more, had pulled up behind it.

38

My heart went back to its dead sprint while I tried to make sense of the scene. A police officer in a big navy coat and furry hat stood in front of the cruiser, waving traffic away from the school. Closer to the building a couple ambulances stood among the idling police cars, and hordes of students milled around on the school's front yard. My hands clutched the steering wheel so tight the bones popped. What really chilled me was how *familiar* the scene looked. It felt like I'd just jumped back in time one year.

A honk from behind shoved me awake again. The cars in front of me had turned onto a side street, redirected by the cop. He waved me forward. I stopped next to him and cranked down the Saab's window. "What happened?"

"There's been an incident at the school," the officer said. "Class is canceled today, buddy."

"What kind of incident? Was anybody hurt?"

"We're still investigating. Right now, I just need you to turn here and proceed home."

The tightness of his mouth underneath his frosty mustache

told me he knew more than he was saying and it had him rattled. I cranked the window back up and followed the other cars down the side street. As soon as I noticed a parking space, I swerved into it, jumped out, and pelted back toward Duluth Central. Did all this have something to do with Franklin? The question played on a loop in my head.

The police still hadn't managed to clear the mob of students and teachers lingering in front of the school. I dodged past the cop redirecting traffic and plunged into the crowd. As I swam through the throng, I grabbed a few kids and asked what was happening, but no one seemed to know a thing. I knocked into a few others and had to shout apologies over my shoulder.

I'd almost made it to the school's main entrance when Lydia and Tor appeared in front of me, his arm around her shoulders. I seized Lydia with both hands. She looked up from her phone, and I got another jolt when I saw the tears streaking her cheeks.

"What is it?" I panted. "What the hell's going on?"

Her face crumpled as she clutched me back. "It's Callie," she choked. "Rem, she's dead."

My breath stopped. I twisted out of her grip and stumbled back a few steps, jostling someone behind me but not caring. The hot press of bodies around me had become unimportant, insubstantial, less solid than the words Lydia had just spoken. I threw Tor a questioning glance. *That can't be true, can it?*

He looked down at the trampled snow and nodded.

"How?"

Tor motioned for us to step farther away from the other

students. In a low voice he answered, "Somebody shot her." Now his face contorted too. "Last night, in the cafeteria."

The world around me seemed less real every second. Sort of pale, like an overexposed photo. The noise of the crowd had become tinny and distant. "What?"

"The police aren't telling people yet." Lydia swiped at her cheeks with the back of her hand. "I only know because I texted Billy."

Lydia had dated Billy Wakahisa for a couple months during sophomore year. He'd since graduated from high school and joined the police.

"He must be wrong," I whispered.

She shook her head. "I don't think so." Her face buckling some more, she added, "Where have you been, Rem? You weren't at your car this morning, you weren't answering your phone. I was scared something happened to you, too."

I turned toward the wall and pressed my palms against the rough, solid brick of the school, half-expecting my hands to go right through, half-expecting the whole building to come crashing down, half-expecting all this to reveal itself as nothing more than another of my nightmares. Because Callie couldn't be dead.

Lydia touched my shoulder. "Rem?"

"You said the cafeteria?" I asked Tor.

"Yes, but—"

I took off running before he could finish.

39

I dashed along the front of the school, my breath tearing from my mouth in ragged shreds that vanished as soon as they appeared. I hoped the police wouldn't see me as I hooked around the corner. From there I sprinted to the back of the building, my boots mushing through slushy snow, and clattered down the steps that led to the basement. I'd never tried opening the padlock myself, but I yanked on it the same way I'd seen Tor do. It took me five tries before the lock gave.

I pounded down the second stairwell. The heat of the steam tunnels swallowed me up. I threaded my way through them, jerking lightbulb cords as I went.

Once, a short while after Tor and I had first started coming down here, I'd suggested we explore a little. We'd never done anything like that since—Tor always wanted to get out of the tunnels as soon as possible once we'd done our business—but that day we'd crept up a random staircase and poked our heads through a door, only to find ourselves in an out-of-the-way corner of the school kitchen. I felt pretty certain I could find that same staircase now.

I rounded a corner, and the rickety wood stairs I remembered were standing in front of me. They squeaked and complained as I ascended to the basement level. After climbing a second flight of steps from there, I fumbled with a lock in the darkness and pressed a door open. Just as I'd hoped, the shadowy kitchen appeared empty. The police had evacuated the cafeteria staff along with everyone else.

That same question continued to repeat itself over and over in my mind: did all this have something to do with Franklin? But now other questions had joined it. Callie couldn't really be dead, could she? Had Franklin done it? Had I been all wrong about him? Jesus Christ, had I allowed something horrible to happen when I'd let him run off last night?

The sound of cops milling around and talking came from the cafeteria. A porthole window in one of the big swinging kitchen doors offered a place to look out without being seen. I drew close and peered through the dusty glass.

My eyes landed on Billy Wakahisa first. He stood only a few feet away. I flinched, afraid he might notice me, but he didn't. His face had gone white, sweat beaded his forehead, and his eyes stayed stuck on something in the center of the room. My own eyes started to burn and blur as I followed his gaze.

Callie was staring back at me. On the same spot where she'd shouted, "Kettlebot shot me!" in the middle of the Halloween dance junior year, a round lunch table lay on its side with her body slumped against it, two holes punched through her chest, her long legs splayed out in front of her. She had on the T-shirt and sweatpants she always wore to bed and, incongruously, her cork-heeled wedges. Her precarious mass of hair had collapsed. Black tendrils snaked down over her shoulders.

My body sagged toward the door, and I rolled to the side to keep from tumbling into the cafeteria. My back landed against the wall. I slid down to the floor, my knees up by my chest, my head tipped forward, my fingers clawing through my hair. My stomach writhed. I thought I might throw up any second. When I closed my eyes, I could still see Callie staring at me.

If I'd trusted Callie last night when I called her, if I'd kept her on the line just a little bit longer, maybe this wouldn't have happened. Maybe she would've stayed awake and her killer wouldn't have surprised her. Or maybe I would've glanced across the street at her house and seen something. She'd said she'd heard a noise. It must've been him, right there in her house at the very same time I was talking to her.

The person who killed her.

Franklin Kettle.

Because of course Franklin had done it. What other explanation made sense? The capsule hadn't worked. He'd faked his transformation. Maybe the nanodrones had left his brain's empathy centers permanently impaired. And last night he'd come to my house—Franklin, a mentally imbalanced killer, a subject of an experimental brain procedure—and I'd done nothing. What a fucking fool I'd been. I couldn't keep his escape secret any longer.

Except I still couldn't go to the police. Once people found

out Franklin had flown the coop and no one at Mom's lab had realized, it would finish her career. And her other secret, the one about the nanodrones, that might have to come out too. People would argue, probably rightly, that her negligence had resulted in *two deaths*. It might even mean she'd have to do time in prison. Maybe I didn't trust her right now, but she was still my mother, and I couldn't do that to her. I needed to tell her about last night. She'd figure out how to handle things from there. And at least I'd still know the truth and could make sure it came out eventually. When the time was right, like she'd said. That was what I told myself.

In the meantime, I couldn't risk telling Mom by phone. I had to do it in person. I had to go to the lab. Now.

40

My phone buzzed in my coat. Lydia had texted. *Where did you run off to? Are you okay? We're worried about you!*

I shoved my phone back into my pocket. I'd talk to her and Tor later.

In the cafeteria, the sounds of police activity had grown louder. I slid myself up the wall and lurched back to the narrow door in the corner that led down to the basement and the steam tunnels. After locking the door behind me and descending the two long flights of stairs, I stumbled through the tunnels in a daze and climbed back into the cold morning.

Again my phone vibrated, this time with a call from Mom. She'd probably heard about Callie's death and wanted to check on me. Again I ignored it. I'd see her soon enough.

By the time I reached my car, the urge to puke had grown stronger than ever, and I had to sit behind the steering wheel and do my stupid breathing exercises for a while just to fight it back. I kept thinking of how Franklin had gone moody and quiet last night before I'd left him.

And then I'd just let him go.

As I drove north along the shore, the frozen lake appeared and disappeared behind the bare trees. Callie had talked in her speech about how much her friendship with Pete and the rest of us had meant to her, and about how the five of us had always taken care of each other. "I just wish it had been enough to stop Pete from getting killed," she'd said.

It hadn't been enough to save *her*, either.

Over and over, Callie's death ricocheted through me. I'd wondered when the next calamity would arrive, and now it had. Another death. More fuel for my nightmares.

My best friend, gone.

I swerved into the lab parking lot, skidded into a space, and threw open the door just in time to spew vomit all over the pavement. It sprawled across the icy blacktop like an abstract painting. When I finished, I tipped my head against the doorframe and wiped the slobber off my mouth with my sleeve. I'd make it up to Callie, at least as much as I could. Somehow, I'd bring her killer to justice.

In my coat my phone buzzed one more time. I yanked it out and froze. The screen displayed a number I recognized. I'd seen it yesterday, and the day before that, when I'd received those digital paintings of my face.

I pulled my car door shut and put my phone to my ear.

"Rem?" Franklin said. "It's me."

41

"I know you did it," I snarled. "Callie was my best friend, and you killed her. You probably went straight from my house to hers, you fucking psycho. And then you put a gun on her and you got her to school somehow and you shot her."

"No, I didn't, Rem," Franklin said, his voice low but vehement. "I can see what it looks like, but I swear I didn't do it."

"Who did then?"

"I don't know, but it wasn't me."

"That's bullshit."

"Listen to me," he said. "After I left your house I ran straight back to the lab."

"Why didn't you wait for me to drive you?"

"I wanted to, but I didn't know if I could trust you. I thought you might try to turn me in. But you didn't. I know that now. Thank you, Rem."

I leaned my forehead against the cold metal steering wheel and squeezed my eyes shut. After all that puking, my stomach felt like a tight fist. The nausea still hadn't left me. "I called my mom this morning after she got to the lab, and she didn't sound like she suspected anything happened during the night, but that was before she heard about the shooting. She must know now. Does *she* think you did it?"

"I'm not sure. She's the one who told me about it, just a few minutes ago. She asked if anything unusual happened last night. So maybe she had a suspicion. As soon as I heard, I knew what you were probably thinking. I didn't want Callie to die, though, Rem. You have to believe me."

I rocked my head from side to side on the wheel and commanded my voice to stay firm. "You're in your room right now?"

"Yes."

"How are you speaking to me? You're using the iPod and the Wi-Fi network?"

"That's right. I have to be careful so they don't see me talking on the camera. I don't want to make them suspicious."

I lifted my head and peered at the huge glass structure rising out of the snow, towering above the trees. I imagined Franklin somewhere deep inside, curled up on his bed in a room without windows.

Through the phone came a tapping sound. "What's that noise?"

"One of my mice is crawling on my shoulder. Your mom's been letting me keep them in the room with me."

For a while I stared at the steering wheel and listened to the sound of Franklin's mouse nosing around him. "I have to tell, Franklin. You understand that, right?"

"Please don't. I know you don't really think I'm a psycho anymore. *Something's* been keeping you from letting your mom know I escaped up until now."

"I just—"

"Last night when I came to see you, did I *seem* like somebody about to commit murder?"

"How should I know, Franklin?"

"If I'd been planning to kill Callie," he persisted, "why would I go to your house first anyway? I could've just snuck out, killed her, and snuck back, and nobody would've known I'd ever left. But instead I went to see you, the son of the scientist in charge of the lab where I was supposed to be locked up. How does that make any sense?"

"A lot of what you do doesn't make sense, Franklin. You told me you broke out of there so you could play me a song on your iPod. *That* doesn't make sense."

But he had a point. And I knew one thing he didn't: the nanodrones had made Franklin kill Pete, or at least it seemed like they had, and Mom had taken them out of his head. Another argument in his favor. Plus, I'd spoken to Callie two hours after Franklin had left, which meant he couldn't have gone straight from my house to hers, like I'd just accused him of doing. Why would he wait all that time, when every minute he stayed away from the lab increased the likelihood he'd be discovered? Hope went through me like a tiny pinprick of light. Maybe he was telling the truth. Maybe I hadn't let something horrible happen after all.

"I didn't kill Callie," he repeated.

"Even if that's true, I should tell. If you didn't do it, you've got nothing to worry about. The police will get to the bottom of it."

"That's not how it works. You know that. If they find out I escaped from the lab last night, their investigation will stop right there."

I pressed my forehead against the wheel again. "Look, I understand why you're scared, but you're putting me in an impossible position."

"How about this then: just wait a few days. Give the police some time to find out who really did it, or at least turn up some clues. Can you do that?"

"I don't know, Franklin."

He breathed into the iPod's microphone for a while. His mouse continued to scratch and frisk in the background. "If you tell," he said, "people will think I did it. If people think I did it, they'll assume the capsule isn't working and have it taken out. And I don't want that to happen, Rem. I want the capsule to stay in my head. It's working. I know it is. I feel different."

"Different how?"

He let out a brief gasp of laughter. "Horrible, mostly. I felt horrible before the operation too, though. Back then I felt horrible and angry. I'd spend all my time thinking about all the things other people had done to me and how unfair life was. Now I feel horrible thinking about the things *I've* done. But I also have these moments when I feel really happy. I never used to feel like that, not even when I played Son of War. Last night in your backyard, when you listened to that song and showed me those pictures you drew, that made me feel happier than I've ever felt probably. Thinking about it now makes me feel happy too. And it doesn't even matter that you don't feel the same way about me that I do about you. I know you don't, I'm not stupid, but it doesn't even matter."

Outside, thick clouds blanketed the sky, with the sun lighting them up from behind.

"I also like being around the mice," he said, "especially now that they're not so afraid of me." I imagined him pressing his zigzag nose into his mouse's soft fur. "But not as much as you. I like being around you more. You're a much better kisser."

I closed my eyes and tried to think of something to say, but the tightness in my stomach seemed to have traveled all the way up to my throat.

"So yeah," Franklin said. "If I have to feel horrible, I'd rather feel horrible like this."

I gripped my cramping belly. My eyes still shut, I said, "Okay. I'm not going to tell."

"Thank you. Christ, thank you, Rem. You won't—"

"For now," I said. "But that doesn't mean I'm not going to tell ever. If you do anything to test my trust in you, I'm saying something. Do you understand me?"

"Yes."

"And Franklin." I opened my eyes and grabbed the metal steering wheel with my free hand. "Just so you know, if you try something *really* bad, like if you escape from the lab and come to my house again, but this time to do something to me so I won't talk—"

"Rem, I'd never—"

"—I'm leaving a letter in a place my mom will find telling her everything. So don't—" I squeezed the steering wheel tighter and peered again at the lab, the sky a uniform blinding white behind it. "So don't kill me, okay?"

42

About two seconds after I hung up with Franklin, my phone buzzed with another call from Mom. I almost ignored it again, but then I figured that would only make her worry.

"Honey." She didn't say anything else for a while, probably because she'd had enough experience with death to know whatever she might come out with would only sound inadequate. The two of us, we were death pros now.

I got through the conversation as fast as I could, mostly just telling her school was canceled and I was heading home. At least if my voice sounded strange, she'd figure it was because of my grief. Casting one more look at the Mother Ship, feeling suddenly paranoid she might glance out a window and spot my Saab, I started up the car and sped back toward the highway.

I went over and over what I'd just done the whole way home. My hands shook on the wheel. My nausea built and built until I thought I might puke again. I knew very well the longer I went without telling, the harder it would be when the time finally came, but the arguments Franklin had made felt so true. The

Franklin I'd talked to last night hadn't been someone planning to commit murder.

When I got home, I found Tor and Lydia waiting for me on the front steps. I parked in the driveway and got out of the wagon. "What are you guys doing here?"

"We wanted to make sure you were okay," Lydia said. "You weren't answering my texts."

Fresh tear tracks still marked her cheeks. Tor looked shell-shocked, the charming glint that usually inhabited his eyes snuffed out. Lydia peeled herself away from him enough to wrap her arm around me. She pulled me close, and I found myself nose to nose with Tor. We looked away from each other, embarrassed by our closeness even in the middle of our heartbreak.

A moment later, though, I forgot about the awkwardness with Tor. I forgot about Franklin and whether I should turn him in. I just thought about Callie. I softened into their arms, and together the three of us sobbed. That was another thing the grief counselor had told us: "It's good to cry. It's good to let out your grief. But as much as you can, do it with your friends. Help each other through this."

She'd been right about that, too.

"You just took off," Lydia choked, drawing back so she could look at me. "Where did you go?"

"I couldn't believe it was true. I wanted to find out if I could get close enough to see for myself."

"And did you?"

I felt Tor's eyes on me now. He knew I'd have made for the

steam tunnels. "No," I answered. "I couldn't find a way in." Loosening my grip on the two of them, I wiped my cheeks dry and glanced over my shoulder. Across the street, a police car stood in front of Callie's house. I'd noticed it as I'd driven up. "Did Billy tell you anything else?" I asked Lydia. "Do they know who did it?"

"I don't think so."

"I talked to Callie late last night, maybe two a.m. or so. She mentioned hearing a noise in the house while we were on the phone."

Lydia put a hand to her mouth. "So you were talking to her while her murderer was right there?" She hesitated over the word "murderer" like it was one of the swearwords she wouldn't allow herself to say. "All I can think is it must've been someone copycatting Franklin, going after his targets."

The nape of my neck prickled. "I thought nobody ever found out who Franklin's other targets were."

"I don't know, maybe nobody did, but it's not much of a stretch to think Franklin would've had his sights on Callie." She nudged a chunk of snow off the porch step. "Plus, last night I found something on the Internet. I was going to tell you guys about it this morning. A game. Son of War High."

Now the cold, prickly feeling washed from my nape all the way down my back. "What is it?"

"A player-built mod. Not an official Son of War release."

Tor squinted at her. "How do you know so much about Son of War all of a sudden, Strawberry?"

She slid a glance up at him, her cheeks reddening. "Yeah,

sorry, your girlfriend's a closet Son of War freak."

He started to say something else, but I cut him off. "So what's so special about it?"

"Last night I was reading a Son of War subreddit. I don't do that a lot, but I figured people would be talking about Franklin—you know, because your mom just did her procedure on him, and everybody knows he's way into Son of War—and I wondered what they'd be saying. One guy mentioned this obscure low-res mod someone made. Even though the game didn't use any actual names, a few details made the guy think it was based on the Big Bang. I was curious, so I did some digging and found the game, and he was right: it's basically the Big Bang, except packaged like Son of War. Same look, same rules. You have a mission."

"Which is?"

She sank onto the front step, her knees knocking together, and reached back to pull her ponytail over her shoulder. She twisted it between her hands while she spoke. "You're supposed to eliminate five targets in five specific places. Target One you're supposed to kill in the history classroom. Like I said, the game doesn't mention any names, but that target has a buzz cut and a letterman's jacket just like Pete's. Then Target Two has a bunch of black hair piled on top of her head. You're supposed to kill her in the cafeteria."

"And who are the other three targets?" Tor asked.

She flicked a gaze up at us, her forehead knitted. "Who do you think? The three of us."

Tor and I glanced at each other. Maybe a shiver had passed

down his back too, because he shoved his hands into his pockets like for once he felt cold in his thin long-sleeve T-shirt.

"You don't know who built the game?" I said.

"I don't think anybody does, but it must've been someone who knows a lot about Franklin and our school."

"What about Franklin himself?" Tor suggested. "Maybe he built the game before the Big Bang. Maybe it was how he prepped."

"It couldn't have been him," Lydia said. "Some of the details in the game come from the actual day of the shooting. Like, the dress I'm wearing in the game is the exact same color as the one I was wearing that day. The game had to have been created later, and Franklin was in custody by then, so he couldn't have done it."

Unless he could've, I thought. What if he'd hacked himself a connection to the Internet at the detention center the same way he had at the lab? But then again, could even Franklin manage to get himself online and design a whole video game from inside prison without anyone discovering?

"If it wasn't him," Tor said, "then it must've been someone else who was in the classroom with us that day. Someone who saw what dress you were wearing. Someone we know."

"Nil Bergstrom." The name just dropped out of my mouth.

"I figured it must be Nell too," Lydia said. "She loves Son of War just as much as Franklin does." Lydia refused to call her Nil. She thought the name was cruel, even though, as we'd reminded her many times, Nil used it herself.

"Do you think she based the game on inside knowledge of Franklin's plan?" I asked. "She and Franklin were pretty close.

Maybe he told her what he was plotting beforehand." My stomach was a mess of knots. Another wave of queasiness had started to build.

Lydia shook her head. "The police questioned Nell after the Big Bang, remember? They determined she'd had no prior knowledge of the attack. I mean, I guess they could've been wrong about that, but she might've just as easily come up with the idea on her own. Like I said, considering Pete was the first target, and the four of us were Pete's best friends, and Franklin lived on the same street as all of us, it's not exactly a huge leap to think we were all probably on his list."

Then how could Nil have known Franklin had named his mission Son of War High? I wanted to say. *Unless he told her, how could she have known that?*

"Admit it," Lydia said. "We've all sort of assumed the same thing, haven't we? That if it hadn't been for Ms. Utter, all five of us would've died that day?"

We passed around silent looks for a second, but nobody said anything. It did seem crazy that we'd never spoken about it out loud. Not even Callie, who'd usually said everything that went through her head, with a generous dollop of profanity mixed in.

"Anyway," Lydia continued, slinging her ponytail back over her shoulder, "whether we actually were Franklin's targets or it's just part of that game, what's really scary is that someone's following the game's playbook in real life. Or at least that's how it seems."

"So you're saying you think there'll be more murders?" Tor said.

Lydia stood and hugged herself. "I wish I knew." She grabbed Tor's shirt and twisted it in her fist. "I hope not."

I gripped the railing on the side of the front steps. The nausea still hadn't passed. "If Nil made the game, does that mean she killed Callie too?"

"Either Nell or someone else who knows both the game and us," Lydia said. "That's what it seems like to me."

My phone buzzed in my pocket. Mom had sent a text.

Would you send me a message when you've made it home, Rem? And lock the front door behind you? It's looking like whoever murdered Callie abducted her from her house.

"It's my mom. I should get inside and text her back. Lydia, do the cops know about the game? And about Nil?"

"I'm not sure. The game's sort of buried on the Internet. I'll tell Billy, just in case. You should let the police know about your phone call with Callie too."

I nodded. "I'll call them." The idea of talking to the police freaked the hell out of me, though, since it almost certainly meant I'd have to lie to protect Mom and Franklin. "And can you send me a link to the game?" I asked her.

Her eyebrows lifted. "Why? It's horrible. Trust me, Rem."

"I just want to see if I can spot any clues."

Lydia studied my face. I wondered if she could see I hadn't told everything I knew. But then she said, "Okay, I'll send it." She shook her head and pulled me and Tor close again. "I still can't believe it. How can this be happening?" Her fingers dug into my back. "Now we're down to three."

43

I locked the front door behind me and tapped Mom a quick message. I also checked the doors to the garage and backyard to make sure they were locked too. It wasn't even noon yet, but outside the clouds had turned so dark it looked like twilight.

I knew I should call the police, but the thought of it still made my stomach roil, so instead I sat down at my desk, tore a blank page from one of my sketchbooks, and wrote out a full confession for Mom, just like I'd told Franklin I would. My hands shook so hard I could barely write.

What Lydia had said about the Son of War High video game had sent my mind spinning in whole new directions. On the one hand, maybe it backed up Franklin's story by giving someone else a motive—a totally insane motive, but a motive—for killing Callie in just that way. But now I had a bunch of new questions snaking through my head. Who *had* built the game? Why? What did it mean? And the question that had been sticking in the back of my brain for almost a year cried out for an answer louder than ever: *had* I been one of Franklin's targets?

I slid the letter under my mattress. I figured if anything happened to me, somebody would find it there eventually. Opening my laptop, I found Lydia had already sent instructions for downloading the game from some obscure site. I settled onto my bed with a mug of Mom's coffee from that morning, now cold, and went to work.

When I finally got the game up on my screen, it looked a lot like the regular version, with SON OF WAR splashed across a black background in red letters. Then HIGH appeared below that. From there, instead of segueing into a dramatic, beautifully-rendered, explosion-filled opener explaining the backstory, the game cut straight to a view of Duluth Central High School. The level of detail didn't come close to that of the original—this looked more like a game from twenty years ago—but I still recognized the school's red-brick-and-limestone facade, the flagpole out front, even pixelated snowdrifts banked on the lawn on either side of the walkway leading up to the front steps. Digital high school students milled around in front of the building, putting off going inside in spite of the cold weather, the same way we always did in real life.

At the bottom of the screen, just like in the real game, hovered the score, time, and other game-related data, and next to those, in the right-hand corner, a button labeled MISSION DOSSIER. I clicked it and sucked in a breath. The screen now displayed pictures of the mission's five targets for elimination. The fourth one down wore a blue scarf around his neck.

I'd known I'd find something like this, but seeing a face

clearly meant to represent mine messed with my head anyway. My guts writhed like I'd swallowed a bunch of snakes. On the right side of the screen, across from the list of targets, the mission brief had appeared.

YOUR MISSION: KILL THESE ASSHOLES, IN THE ORDER IN WHICH THEY APPEAR ON THE LIST, IN THE LOCATION WHERE EACH ASSHOLE HUMILIATED YOU. THEN KILL YOURSELF.

I clicked on the first target. The one with the buzz cut. Pete. The mission brief vanished, replaced by a floor plan that resembled Duluth Central's, with a big red *X* near the location of Ms. Utter's former classroom. I moved down to the next target, who had a towering black hairdo and a smirking expression. Callie. The *X* moved to the cafeteria. The third target had reddish hair and freckles. Lydia. When I clicked on her, the *X* shifted to the school's main hall, right next to the cafeteria entrance.

I paused, my fingers hovering above my laptop's touchpad, before selecting the next target. The one with the blue scarf.

The *X* settled on the boys' locker room, marking the spot where I'd become, at least for a while, an asshole myself.

I leaned back against the headboard and tried to breathe deep. My lungs felt too small, though, or too weak. The red *X* on the map pulsed at me. I shook my head, hunched over my laptop again, and navigated back to the game's main screen. Under my direction, my avatar—Franklin, obviously—moved up the stairs, into the school, and down the hall. The details, though low-res, rang true. The ugly institutional green of the lockers. The twists and turns of the corridors.

Without having to think about it, I guided Franklin to Ms. Utter's classroom. By the time he got there, everybody else seemed to have arrived. I made him pause at the door near the front of the room so I could scan the other students. My cheeks and fingers went cold when I spotted a digital Jeremy Braithwaite seated in the middle of the room wearing a digital blue scarf. I imagined if I got close enough I might see digital paint smears on his shirt and hands.

Callie, Lydia, Tor, and Pete occupied their usual spots too, all of them with telltale details that made their identities unmistakable. Tiny Ms. Utter sat at the front of the room behind her enormous desk.

I steered Franklin to his regular place in the back. Class started. Ms. Utter began to speak, but in a muffled, indistinct voice, sort of like the grown-ups in old Charlie Brown cartoons. She motioned for Pete to come to the front of the room to make his presentation.

Pete started his speech, his voice similarly indistinct. I'd gotten so used to watching this scene unfold in my imagination and my nightmares, it felt bizarre to see a computer-generated version play out on my screen. Little by little, as Pete spoke, my muscles coiled tighter and tighter. I could feel the moment approaching, even though I couldn't understand the words Pete was saying. I selected EQUIPMENT at the bottom of the screen, which brought up the contents of Franklin's overstuffed backpack: the Beretta, some spare ammunition, a bowie knife, various other pieces of military gear, and the Son of War mask.

I selected that. The edges of the screen went dark, just like in the actual Son of War game, to indicate I was now looking through the mask's goggles.

Next I made Franklin pull out the Beretta.

My mouth had gone dry. My heart had started to drum. It felt like someone had taken control of my movements in the same way I controlled Franklin's. I used the touchpad to make Franklin aim the gun at Pete, who went silent. It reminded me of last night's nightmare, in which I'd held the Beretta in my own hand for the very first time.

I jumped at the *BANG* the gun made as if I hadn't caused it myself. The splash of blood on the whiteboard behind Pete's head looked just like I always pictured it. Pete's body disappeared behind the desks. All the other students stared at Franklin with approximations of shock and terror on their—*our*—faces.

Then I remembered Ms. Utter. I made Franklin turn and saw her sprinting along the side of the room. She'd already made it halfway to the back. The Beretta flew up. Three shots went off. She flew backward and landed against the wall with three bloody holes in her belly.

And just like that, I'd changed history. When Franklin turned back toward the class, most of the students were still in their places, stunned, but Callie, Lydia, Tor, and Rem—the Rem on the screen—had all made a beeline for the door, like they knew they were the next targets. Now I was probably supposed to make Franklin chase after them one by one, drag them to the appropriate spots, and execute them, all before the police arrived and took him down.

I didn't, though. Killing one of my best friends and a teacher I liked hadn't left me with the same euphoric feeling as killing anonymous soldiers had. I just felt tired, even though my heart continued to pound, and grubby, like crumbling smudges of paint covered my whole body instead of just my hands.

On the left side of the room Ms. Utter sat slumped against the wall like a discarded marionette. Lydia had been right: whoever had created this game had to have done it *after* the Big Bang. No one could've predicted Ms. Utter would do what she'd done. My eyes wandered over the class one more time, until they stopped on green-haired Nil Bergstrom. I imagined a smirk on her pixelated face.

44

The next instant, a digital security guard burst into the room with his sidearm drawn. "Drop the gun!" he yelled.

For a few seconds I tried to figure out how to make Franklin throw down the Beretta, but relinquishing a weapon was one thing I'd never had occasion to do while playing Son of War. The guard opened fire. The image on the screen danced as bullets drummed into Franklin's body. A film of blood cascaded down the screen.

"GAME OVER."

I shoved my laptop away from me and slumped against the headboard again, biting my thumb.

I needed more answers. Talking to Franklin again today was the last thing I wanted to do, but I couldn't think of any other options. Before I could change my mind, I grabbed my phone, found the number Franklin had used to call me earlier, and dialed.

He answered right away. "Rem."

"Can you talk?"

"Yes. It's okay. I'm alone."

"I just played Son of War High."

The line went silent.

"What the hell, Franklin? Did you make it yourself?"

"No," he answered. "How could I? The detention center didn't even have Wi-Fi. You can check yourself if you don't believe me."

"But you know about it. You know somebody made a sick, disgusting game out of that plan of yours."

"Yes. Nil told me."

"Because she built it herself?"

"No. It wasn't her. I don't know who built the game, and neither did she when she told me about it."

"You're sure you're not just saying that to protect her? If it wasn't you, she's the next obvious suspect. Whoever did it had to have been in the room the day of the Big Bang. The details are too spot-on."

"You're thinking whoever built that game must've killed Callie."

"It would make sense. I mean, as much as any of this makes sense."

Across from me a red background still spanned my laptop screen, with the words "GAME OVER" superimposed.

"She didn't build the game, Rem."

"Who else could've done it?"

"I'm telling you I don't know!" he snapped, forgetting the camera watching him.

"In the game," I said, "I was one of the five targets."

Again he didn't speak.

"Was I in real life, too?" I pressed. "Was whoever made the game right about that?"

"No way."

"Then how would this person have known about the locker room?"

"Everyone at school knew about that."

"So you didn't want to kill me?"

"No, Rem. I had feelings for you, remember?"

"But you said your feelings were more complicated then."

"I swear I didn't."

"Well, who *did* you want to kill? Because you said yourself yesterday you had *targets*, plural. Who were they?"

His breaths sounded shallow and uneven. "I don't want to talk about that."

"I think you have to. I'm the only friend you've got right now."

"I said I don't want to talk about it!" His voice had tilted toward hysteria. He caught himself again and inhaled and exhaled a few times. I wondered if he'd had a counselor with a kindergarten teacher voice teaching him breathing exercises at the detention center. More softly he said, "Why can't we go back to the way it was last night in the gazebo, Rem?"

"Because someone died, Franklin. My best friend."

"I know. It's all I'm thinking about. She didn't deserve what happened to her."

My laptop continued to pulse red. I smacked it shut. "I just don't want anyone else to die. Not you. Not me. Not any more of my friends." I shoved the laptop away from me and dropped my head back against the headboard. "You should probably hang up now, Franklin. Someone's going to see you all upset and talking to yourself on the security camera."

He let out a bitter laugh. "What's the difference? They already think I'm a psycho."

"Good point."

"You're right, though. I should go. You still won't tell?"

I rubbed my knuckles against my forehead. My head throbbed like *I* was the one who'd just had a bunch of scientists drilling into my skull. Playing the game had shaken me, but the reasons I'd had for believing Franklin hadn't killed Callie remained the same as before. And maybe I was getting closer to finding out who *had* done it. Maybe I owed it to Franklin to see this through, after what Mom had done to him, and after what I'd done to him too.

"I won't tell," I said.

"Okay. Good. Thank you. Because I'm pretty sure I can handle anything as long as you still believe in me."

After I got off the phone with him, I called the police and told them about my two a.m. call to Callie. The cop I spoke to asked if I'd noticed anything else unusual last night.

"Not a thing," I said.

45

When Mom got home that night, I could see the day had taken its toll on her too. The circles under her eyes had darkened even more, and her usually sleek gray hair looked frayed, with stray strands standing up from her head like a dull halo. She greeted me with a long hug, apologized for not getting away from work earlier, told me again how sorry she was about Callie. Out of habit, I put on my strong face—the one I'd started practicing after Ethan's death and perfected after Pete's—and told her I'd be okay. She lowered herself into a chair at the kitchen table and made an effort to smooth down her hair. I tapped my fingertips against the counter. More than anything, I wanted to go back to my room, bury myself underneath my covers, and sink into a hopefully dreamless sleep.

But Mom might've learned something important at the lab.

I got her bottle of red wine from the fridge and poured her half a glass. When I moved to put the bottle back, she patted the table. "Leave it here."

I set down the wine and sat across from her. "Do you know if the police have found out anything more?"

She shook her head. "I don't think so, but they aren't telling me much. They spent the whole afternoon grilling Franklin and combing the lab for clues, trying to figure out if there was any possible way he could've committed the murder himself."

I stiffened. "And?"

"I didn't get the impression they found anything conclusive. Dr. Hult did some investigating too. He studied the security footage. He talked to the guard who was stationed outside Franklin's room all night. He didn't turn up a thing."

I nodded. Franklin's boasts about his prison-breaking skills must've been accurate. I wondered how he'd stood up under the cops' interrogation. Hopefully Son of War had taught him some techniques for that too. "What about you, Mom?" I said. "What do you think?"

"I don't believe Franklin had any involvement in Callie's murder. I just don't see how it would be possible." She reached for the wine bottle. "Of course, there are other theories flying around the lab."

"Like what?"

Mom tipped some more wine into her glass. She'd emptied it without my noticing. "Gertie came to my office this afternoon asking if I thought someone might've killed Callie hoping to implicate Franklin and get our project shut down."

"Do you think it's possible? Would someone do a thing like that just to stop your work?"

"I think it's unlikely." She took a sip. "Then again, there are a lot of crazy people out there."

My mind went to Nil Bergstrom and all that stuff she'd said in Ms. Utter's class. She definitely disagreed with what Mom was doing. If she *had* killed Callie, could *that* have been her motive? It would also mean she'd plotted to frame her best friend for murder. Would she do something like that? I didn't know her very well. Maybe she was capable of it.

"You said in your text the police think Callie was abducted from her house?"

Mom nodded.

"And then what?"

"The killer seems to have driven her to Duluth Central in her car. The police found it parked on a street near the school. I also overheard the cops talking about some footage a security camera caught of the car driving by. The person in the driver's seat wasn't recognizable. He was wearing a bulky black coat with a hood." Her eyes rose from her glass of wine to meet mine. "Apparently he turned his head for a second. Underneath the hood he had on a Son of War mask."

46

I spent all of Saturday and most of Sunday in my bedroom. Mom brought me plates of food and a couple times tried to get me to come out, but mostly she just let me be. Every now and again I got up to look out the window. A lone cop in a cruiser appeared to be permanently stationed at the end of our block. Through Callie's bedroom window, I kept seeing Mrs. Minwalla drifting around the room like a ghost, touching the chaotic multimedia collages that hung from Callie's walls. If she'd never needed a reason to spiral into a depression before, she certainly had one now. I knew I should pay her and Mr. Minwalla a visit and tell them how sorry I was, but so far I'd been clinging to the lame excuse that I should give them space to grieve. I also knew I needed to keep digging into Callie's death so I could find out once and for all if I was right to trust Franklin. For now, though, I couldn't even bring myself to take a shower. The one time I tried to pick up my Tattoo Atlas and draw something for Callie, my pencil just sat there on the page like a stalled car.

On Sunday evening a text showed up on my phone from Tor, addressed to me and Lydia.

Ladies and gentlemen, I have an idea.

That right there made me sad, because we weren't ladies and gentlemen anymore. Just Lydia and Rem—one lady, one gentleman.

A second text followed. *Since last year's attempt at rebuilding the ice palace was unsuccessful, how about if we pop a few Fat Tires at my house tonight in honor of Callie?*

He was referring to the day a few weeks after the Big Bang when the three of us and Callie had tried to re-create the crystalline structure in my backyard, this time to memorialize Pete. It hadn't worked. Two of the walls we'd built had collapsed, and we hadn't been able to keep any of the candles lit with the wind blowing through. We'd huddled in the cold, dutifully sipping our beer, for about fifteen minutes before we'd called it a night and hurried back to our houses.

This time we weren't even going to try. Not that I minded. The fact that we had traditions for when our loved ones got murdered only depressed me anyway. Drinking beer at Tor's house sounded like a better alternative.

I still had reservations, though. Up until now, the one benefit—if you could call it that—of mourning Callie was that it had kept me from obsessing about the Tor and Lydia situation. There was nothing like the death of your best friend to put stuff like that in perspective. Spending time with the two of them now—and without a fourth person to act as a buffer—might just bring all that confusion and jealousy back to the surface. But shutting myself away wasn't doing me much good either. The four of us had hung out a lot after Pete's death last year, and it had helped. Maybe I needed to follow that grief counselor's advice and reach out to my support network.

Plus, Lydia might have heard more about Callie's death from Billy. I needed to find out what she knew.

I texted Tor back to tell him I was in.

We met up at Tor's place after dinner. His parents were still out of town. Lydia was dry-eyed this time, but the sorrow had settled into her face the same way it had after Pete's death, hollowing out her eyes and cheeks and turning her skin porcelain white behind her freckles. She balled herself up in a corner of the Agnarsons' gigantic leather couch with her knees hugged to her chest. Tor looked like a zombie too. He didn't even peel off his T-shirt for no reason five minutes after we were all together. We sat there in the cavernous, pristine Agnarson living room, picking at a plate of old-school tater tots Tor had warmed up in the oven (another Boreal Five tradition), Tor and I washing down the mouthfuls of deep-fried potato with gulps from bottles of Fat Tire he'd lifted from the fridge in the garage. Lydia stuck with water this time, but I caught her once or twice casting a longing glance at her purse. She must not have confessed to Tor about her secret smoking habit yet.

"Did you guys hear about the security camera footage?" I asked after we'd made it to our third round.

Lydia grimaced. "Billy told me. The killer was wearing a Son of War mask. Just when I thought this couldn't get any more horrible."

"But the cops don't know who it was?"

"I don't think so. Billy said they found a few other clues, though. They checked the Minwallas' house, and it looked like somebody had forced the kitchen door. The killer must've snuck all the way up to Callie's room and then walked her back out at gunpoint without waking anybody else."

"I still can't fucking believe it," Tor muttered. "That something like this could happen on Boreal Street." He moved closer to Lydia on the couch and folded her into his chest. I watched from the oversized armchair opposite.

"Why *not* Boreal Street?" I said.

He frowned at me. "What's that supposed to mean?"

"You just said it like we're special somehow, because we live way up here on our nice street in our nice houses and look down on everybody else." With my beer I motioned toward the view of the city and the lake outside the big picture window. "What should really be shocking is that it happens anywhere."

"Come on, Nice Guy, I was just—"

"Stop picking a fight, Rem," Lydia murmured.

She was right. I was picking a fight. Maybe it was the beer. I wasn't usually much of a drinker, and my head had started feeling warm and floaty.

I glanced out the window again. In the darkness, the drifts of snow in the front yard had turned a luminous blue. Class politics aside, I knew what Tor meant. We'd all grown up on

Boreal Street. It had always felt like the safest place in the world. But danger seemed to be marching closer and closer. First my brother had died, but in a faraway country. Then Pete, at our school. Now someone had stolen Callie from right out of her bed. Even home wasn't safe anymore. "Do the police know how the killer got into the cafeteria?" I asked.

She shook her head. "I don't think they have that part figured out yet."

"Did they find anything in Callie's car, maybe? Fingerprints, hair, that kind of thing?"

"Not as far as I know."

"What about the video game? Did you tell Billy about that?"

"He said they'd look into it."

"Because if the killer *is* copycatting Son of War High, you're next on the list."

"Yes, I'm aware of that, Rem. But Billy said the cops are keeping our block under surveillance around the clock."

"And our suspicions about Nil Bergstrom? You mentioned those too? I told the cop I talked to about her, but he just said something vague about how they'd 'thoroughly investigate all leads.'"

"Jesus, Rem, relax," Tor said. "You don't have to grill her. It's been two days. The police will figure it out. If it was Nil, they'll nail her."

"It's okay, Tor," Lydia said. "Yes, Rem, I told Billy about Nell." She settled her cheek against Tor's chest. In a small, private voice, she said, "Tor, I don't think you should stay here alone tonight. It might not be safe. Come stay at my house."

"Where? In the guest room?"

"Of course in the guest room."

He grinned, his eyes recovering a hint of their mischievous gleam. "Because I think me staying at your place might be *more* dangerous, not less."

I swallowed the last of my beer. My head felt even floatier now. I grabbed another tater tot and scribbled it around in the puddle of ketchup on the plate.

"Come on, Tor," Lydia said, pulling away from him. "You shouldn't joke like that. Not now."

"Sorry, Strawberry. You're right." Tor cupped her cheek in his hand. In that kind voice he used only sparingly, he said, "It's just that when we lose people we care about, we have to hold even tighter to the ones who are still with us."

Before he could draw her in for a kiss, I stood up and said in an unnecessarily loud voice, "Hey, is there any more beer in the garage?"

They both glanced at me, startled. "There should be," Tor answered.

"Great. Wonderful. Thanks." I barreled through the kitchen and out the garage door. My face burned. So did my chest. My belly seethed like a washing machine. I leaned my elbows on the Agnarsons' Range Rover, hoping I wouldn't puke for the second time in three days. Although as much as I hated barfing, the thought of doing it all over the Agnarsons' unspoiled pearl-white hood did have a certain appeal.

Then I noticed I'd defaced the hood without realizing it:

my fingers, smeared in ketchup the same way they usually got smeared in paint, had left messy smudges on the opalescent paint. Like I had in the cafeteria a few days ago, I nudged the ketchup around on the white surface, mopping it into the shape of a blood spatter.

The door opened and closed behind me. "Are you okay?" Tor said. "Are you sick?"

"How could I not be after watching that?" I turned around to face him. "Tell me, Tor, does it not even enter your head how seeing the two of you together might make me feel? Or does it actively turn you on? Because I'm not into this new game you're playing."

He glanced over his shoulder, worried Lydia might hear. "I'm not playing any games."

"Bullshit. You love that I'm jealous, and you love that I can't say a thing about it because, unlike you, I actually care about Lydia's feelings."

"I care about Lydia too, Rem. I'm not perfect, but I do." He stepped closer and gave my chest a few hard taps. "And just in case you don't remember, *I'm* the one who should be pissed here, after the way you've been running your mouth about the tunnels. But since Callie died, I've been trying to honor her memory by forgetting about that."

"Maybe you should honor her memory by not being such a dick."

Tor's face started to twist. For a second I glimpsed that rage I'd seen for the first time a few days ago, but he managed to recover himself. "I'm going to ignore that because I think you've had a little too much to drink."

"I've had just enough." I shoved my chest up close to his, not even caring the guy was twice as big as me. That burning feeling in my rib cage had roared into an inferno. "You know the thing about Callie? She totally had you pegged. She knew you were a pathetic closet case all along. And idiot me, I was always making excuses for you. 'Maybe he's really bisexual.' 'Maybe he's just scared and confused.' I was determined to put the most positive spin on everything you did. And that was my fault. I was just so smitten with you I couldn't bring myself to think a bad thing about you. But you know what I'm starting to realize?" I reached past him and banged my fist against the button for the garage door. "Callie was right all along. You're just a fucking pig."

I started to turn away, but then I reached for him one more time.

"Hey!" he said, flinching away from me. Actually *flinching.* Away from *me.*

But I just swiped my palm along his cheek, leaving a satisfying streak of bright red ketchup glistening there like a bloody gash. Then I walked out into the cold night. "No more Mr. Nice Guy," I muttered over my shoulder.

47

I needed to tell Lydia about me and Tor, just like Callie had said I should. I could see that now. And if that meant Tor never talked to me again, so be it. My fear of him rejecting me was the real reason I'd stayed quiet all along, even though I'd never admitted it to Callie, or even to myself, and that fear had made me a coward. Callie had been right: I needed to man up.

But first I had to deal with the Franklin Kettle situation.

At school the next day it felt as if the place, and everyone in it, had jumped backward one year. The halls had gone quiet, just like in the days following the Big Bang. Students and teachers walked around with stunned expressions on their faces. When they talked, they did it in low, careful voices, like they didn't want to wake someone sleeping nearby. I passed by the cafeteria, but the entrance was locked, with brown paper taped inside the small windows in the doors. Yesterday we'd received an e-mail from Principal Chen saying we'd have to bring our own lunches and eat in the gym until further notice.

The e-mail had also mentioned we'd have to attend a special

assembly first thing Monday morning instead of going to our regular first-period classes. We'd had an assembly after Pete's death too. Our first day back at school—that time we'd had two days of class canceled, not just one—we'd all herded into the gym, where Mrs. Chen had droned on and on about the importance of processing our feelings. The speech had gone on for so long that by the end we'd all managed to fully process our grief into boredom.

Today, once again, all seventeen hundred of us tromped onto the shuddering bleachers. Lydia and Tor sat down by the front, but I chose a spot near the top. Ever since I'd let Tor have it the night before, my chest had continued to burn hot. It was like a voice in my head—a voice similar to Franklin's when he described the emotions of characters in old episodes of *Friends*—had said, *You are mad. You are mad as hell at Tor.* And I'd finally realized it was true. I'd always assumed I loved Tor with the pure white of true love, but more and more since Tor had taken up with Lydia, I'd started to see all the other colors swirled in. Blue for misery. Green for jealousy. Red for rage.

I couldn't help but wonder if Franklin had been describing something similar when he'd said his feelings for me before the Big Bang had been "complicated."

Until I told Lydia the whole truth, though, I figured I should keep my distance from both her and Tor as much as I could without raising her suspicions.

When Mrs. Chen walked out and got us quieted down, she didn't launch into a speech like she had last year. Instead she said, "Ms. Utter has asked to say a few words."

The room got another notch quieter. Ms. Utter appeared, a tiny figure on the floor of the gym with a step stool under her arm, and crossed to the podium. I winced inwardly as I pictured a pixelated version of her slumped against the classroom wall with three bullet holes in her belly. Giving my head a little shake, I stuffed the memory away. She stepped onto the stool and cleared her throat.

"In two days," she said, "it'll be the one-year anniversary of the shooting that ended Pete Lund's life. Callie Minwalla was going to give a speech for the memorial assembly. She was one of Pete's best friends. And now she's gone too.

"We still don't know the details of what happened, so I don't want to say too much about that, but one thing we do know for sure is that Callie's death, like Pete's, was shocking and horrible and senseless. All of us here are wondering how this could've happened. Again."

Ms. Utter stared at the podium for a long time. When she started talking again, her voice had thickened.

"Callie was known around school for having a foul mouth and a sardonic sense of humor. But she had a big secret: at heart she was an optimist. She gave me her speech to read last week and asked me what I thought of it. I told her it was beautiful and hopeful. And I told her she had to get rid of all the swearwords."

A soft murmur of laughter went through the gym.

"I'm not the optimist Callie was." The edges of Ms. Utter's words had blurred. Had she started crying? I couldn't tell from that distance. "What I'm about to say isn't hopeful or beautiful.

Callie was going to speak about how much her friendship with Pete meant to her, and about how she hoped it would become possible to help Franklin Kettle and people like him, and about how she really believed our world was becoming a better place, even though awful things still happened.

"As a historian, I can tell you she was right. Right now we're living in the least violent age in human history. But I have to say, knowing that doesn't bring me much comfort on days like today."

She stopped again. Swayed a little. For a second it almost looked like she might fall off her step stool. I tensed. Had she been drinking more than usual?

"Because there's still too much violence," she said. "As a historian, I can *also* tell you the kind of atrocity that happened here on Friday will continue to happen for just as long as we as a country keep up this bullshit love affair of ours with guns and violence and killing people."

Principal Chen, standing off to the side of the basketball court, snapped to attention. Her footfalls echoed through the room as she speed-walked toward the podium.

"We spend our days watching movies and playing video games chock-full of killing," Ms. Utter said, her voice growing stronger, but also more slurred. "We still administer the death penalty, even though the rest of the world rejects it as barbaric. Our police can't seem to stop shooting innocent and unarmed people. And God forbid we ever pass a meaningful gun control law. We insist on keeping guns in our houses for hunting, for recreation, for self-defense. So how are we supposed to expect our criminals and psychopaths not to kill if we keep doing it ourselves? When are we going to pull our heads out of our goddamn asses and *wake up*?"

Mrs. Chen had reached the podium. She grabbed Ms. Utter by the arm, flashed a tight smile at the rest of us, and drew her down from the step stool. A ripple of murmurs flowed across the bleachers. My face burned just watching. I had to look away.

When I did, I noticed something I hadn't earlier: Nil Bergstrom had sat down right in front of me. Somehow I'd missed her shock of radioactive-green hair. Her huge backpack slouched on the bench next to her, taking up the space of a whole person. The top of it had come unzipped a little, and inside, I could just make out the corner of a black notebook, the same kind I'd always seen Franklin scribbling in during class. My hot cheeks turned cold, and I forgot all about Ms. Utter. I glanced at Nil. Like everyone else, she had her eyes on the gym floor, where the assistant principal was escorting Ms. Utter away from the podium. Principal Chen had pushed the step stool to the side and started talking into the mike. I caught the words "processing our feelings" while, with a slow, careful hand, I reached for the zipper on Nil's backpack.

"Because if we ignore our feelings," Mrs. Chen said, "and keep them trapped inside, they'll just fester."

My fingers wrapped around the zipper pull. Bit by bit, I dragged the zipper to the side, every nerve in my body buzzing.

Mrs. Chen's drone continued. "It's okay to feel sad. To feel scared. To feel angry even." This with an awkward gesture toward the door through which Ms. Utter and the assistant principal had just disappeared.

I bent closer, searching for the Son of War sticker or Franklin Kettle's name written in red ink down the side, but I couldn't see either yet. I reached for the zipper again.

Nil turned to her backpack.

I flinched away, praying she hadn't noticed me. It didn't seem like she had. She pulled her phone out of one of the smaller pockets and started playing a game.

"We need to talk about those feelings. Set them free. And always remember what our grief counselor taught us last year: breathe. Iiiiinhale. Eeeeexhale."

I waited a few moments and focused on my breathing. *Iiiiinhale. Eeeeexhale.* Then my fingers crept toward the backpack one more time. Sweat beaded my forehead as I drew the zipper a little further, my movements steady and controlled. I still couldn't see the Son of War mask, but maybe this was the back cover and the sticker was on the other side.

The next thing I knew, the gym had erupted with noise and movement. Everyone standing up, grabbing their things, talking. The assembly had ended. Mrs. Chen had dismissed us to our second-period classes. Nil swung her backpack onto her shoulder—without seeming to notice what I'd done, thank God—and headed toward the stairs, her head down and her shoulders hunched.

I edged along my row and fell in behind her. As the mob of

students tromped down the bleacher stairs and funneled out of the gym, I made sure to keep her wild green tangle of hair in my sights. I trailed her through the noisy halls, weaving past other students, staying close but not too close. The Son of War patch on her backpack glowered at me.

We'd almost reached Ms. Utter's old classroom at the far end of the school. The throng had thinned. Nil veered toward her locker and started fiddling with the combination. I tried to stop a discreet distance behind her, but with all the people jostling by, I had to stay pretty close to see anything.

Nil's backpack landed on the wood floor with a thunk. She squatted down to unzip it. I bent forward, peering over her shoulder, straining to see.

She pulled out the notebook and tossed it into her locker. It landed on top of her other books, and this time I got a clear look at the thing. Black cover. Frayed corners. Son of War sticker. *FRANKLIN KETTLE* written down the side in red pen. A crackle of electricity went through me.

Nil shot to her feet and glared at me through narrowed eyes. Without looking away, she reached behind her to slam her locker shut. "May I help you?"

I shook my head, took a step back, and let the rush of students carry me down the hall.

48

I spent the rest of the day obsessed with that notebook. Why Nil had it in her possession wasn't clear to me, but the fact that she was carrying it around made me more suspicious of her than ever. Plus, I wanted to get my hands on it. It had to be important. Otherwise why would Nil have kept it from the police, when they clearly would've wanted a piece of evidence like that? Why would she be walking around school with it a full year after the Big Bang? Maybe if I read it, it would help me understand Franklin and reveal all those things he wouldn't talk about. Maybe it would somehow clear him of Callie's murder.

But how to get it? Nil wouldn't just hand it over if I asked her, would she? And she'd seen me see it. Would she even carry it around in her backpack anymore after today?

By the time I said good night to Mom and went to my room, I hadn't come any closer to an idea. I also felt exhausted. A week of more troubled sleep than usual had caught up with me, so even though I had enough on my mind to fill ten Tattoo

Atlases, I was out about five seconds after my head hit my pillow.

Then, hours later, I snapped awake again. I'd heard a clattering outside the window by my desk. I rolled over, adrenaline pounding through my body. A silhouette appeared, caught in the moonlight filtering through the roller blind. I grabbed my phone and held it to my chest.

But I didn't dial. I didn't yell for Mom either.

The window slid open. A cold wind blew the blind inward. As it batted back and forth, clacking against the window frame, I caught a glimpse of an orange hoodie.

I slipped out of bed, crept toward the window, and gave the cord one hard pull. Franklin appeared, his glasses glinting, a screwdriver in his hand.

He waved. "Oh, hi."

I seized a handful of his hoodie in my fist. "What the hell are you doing here, Franklin? *Again?* No, wait, don't tell me. This time you have some really interesting whale song you want to play for me."

He tilted his head and squinted at me like *I* was the crazy one. His teeth clacked. His shoulders juddered up and down.

"For Christ's sake."

I helped him inside.

"Thanks," he said, flopping on my desk chair and rubbing his arms. "It's colder tonight."

"So how come you didn't steal a goddamn winter coat for yourself if you're such a master thief?"

From out in the hall came Mom's voice. "Rem? What's going on? Are you okay in there?"

My heart's frantic pace doubled now. I wrenched the window back down. "Fine, Mom," I called. "I just couldn't sleep. I opened the window for a second to get some fresh air."

"Do you need anything?"

"Nope. I'm just fine." I clutched the corner of my desk, my heart still tripping and stumbling, and waited for the sound of Mom's bedroom door closing at the other end of the house. To Franklin I whispered, "What were you thinking? My mom's just down the hall! And there's a cop car on the street!" I gave a sharp tug on the cord to pull the blind down. "You beg me not to say anything because you're terrified people will think you killed Callie, and then you do something like this."

"I wanted to see you, Rem."

I stood gripping the cord and sighed. His shivering had subsided. I glanced at the window. "How did you get it open anyway?"

"It wasn't locked. You can tell from the outside." He got up and pushed the blind to the side to point at the window lock. "See? Every house has at least one unlocked window. It's like a rule."

I pulled him back. "For Christ's sake, Franklin, get away from there. The cop's going to spot you."

"Don't worry, he fell asleep. I already checked."

I pointed at the screwdriver in his hand. "What's that for?"

"I used it to push back the screen, and then I wedged it under the window frame until I could fit my fingers and pull the window the rest of the way up."

"Why didn't you just knock?"

"I wanted to surprise you."

I dropped my head in my hands. "Jesus."

"Plus I wasn't sure you'd let me in."

"Well, I did, didn't I?"

He grinned. One of his eyebrows edged up above the chunky black frames of his glasses. "That's true. You did."

His eyes had landed on my bare chest. I'd completely forgotten I only had on a pair of boxer briefs. I grabbed a T-shirt from the floor and yanked it over my head. "I thought I told you if you did anything to test my trust in you, I'd tell."

He stopped grinning. "Come on, Rem, what did I do?"

"You broke out of the lab again!" It took every bit of my self-control to keep my voice down. "Have you broken out any other times?"

"No."

"Good, because—"

"Except last night."

"What? Why?"

"Why do you think? To see you. But you weren't here. I saw you leaving Tor's house through his garage. It sounded like you two were having a fight. I figured you probably wouldn't be in the mood to see me after that, so I went back to the lab. What did you mean, 'No more Mr. Nice Guy'?"

I sat down on my bed. "None of your business."

He dropped into my desk chair again and wheeled around to study the ink and paint streaking my desk. "Seriously, I didn't mean to stress you out, Rem. But at least there's a bright side."

"Oh yeah?" I snapped. "What's that?"

"I snuck out last night and nobody died."

"You want me to throw you a party?"

Franklin touched the desk's surface, tracing his fingertips over the smears of paint. "You seemed pretty pissed at Tor when I saw you. It made me wonder if he was the reason you were sad the other day, before Callie died."

He sat with his elbows on the desk, his fingers slowly moving, while he waited for me to say something. He'd pulled off his hood, so I could see the back of his skull, the pale skin visible through the dark stubble. On the spot where he'd had his surgery, the gauze and medical tape had now been replaced by a single large square Band-Aid.

"He was," I said.

Franklin nodded, like he didn't need me to tell him any more, but I went on anyway.

"I have a thing for him, I guess. We used to mess around down in the steam tunnels underneath Duluth Central. He's not out, so it was a big secret. But lately he's been dating Lydia. He's been lying to her, acting like a jerk to me. Then he got incredibly mad when he found out I'd told Callie what we'd done. He slammed me against a door, said some ugly things, threatened me. So I suppose I've been feeling mad. And hurt. And jealous. And confused about what I should do."

The muscles of Franklin's jaw flexed.

"Are you okay? Are you mad at me?"

He shrugged. "I figured it was something like that. Mostly I'm just mad at Tor for treating you that way. He must be an idiot not to realize how amazing you are."

I probably blushed. I wasn't used to hearing that kind of talk pointed in my direction. "Tor can be a bully sometimes. I guess you know that. Probably better than anyone."

His fingers stopped. "Probably."

"Sometimes I wonder if he even thinks other people really exist."

Another shrug. "Well, sure, but do any of us?"

"What do you mean?"

"Don't *you* ever secretly ask yourself if maybe you're the only one that's actually real and everyone else is just, like, a character in a video game? A bunch of pixels on a screen? It makes sense, if you think about it." He knocked his skull. "We're trapped in here. We can never experience the world from inside someone else's head. So isn't it only logical to doubt whether anybody else is real?"

I raked my fingers through my hair. "I guess. But we can *imagine*, and isn't that almost as good? I think that's what Emily Dickinson was getting at in that poem I read to you. The one Ethan liked so much."

"'The brain is wider than the sky,'" Franklin murmured.

"Yeah. Like, the brain can *encompass* the sky through imagination. In the poem Dickinson talks about how we can imagine the sea, and we can imagine God, and we can imagine our way into other people's heads, too."

He turned toward me halfway, so I could see the profile of his crooked nose. "You're talking about empathy."

"I guess I am. Maybe that's one of the things that makes the human brain so amazing. You're right that we're trapped in our heads. Believing other people exist is sort of a leap of faith, like believing God exists. Maybe that's why we evolved to have empathy. It helps us make the leap."

"Because otherwise life is just . . ."

"Son of War," I finished.

I thought of the notebook I'd glimpsed today in Nil Bergstrom's backpack and, for a split second, considered asking him about it. But no. Better to keep that to myself for now. Instead I leaned forward and rested my elbows on my knees.

"I want to talk to you about something, Franklin. I've been a bully too. I want to apologize."

Franklin rotated the chair to face me but kept his eyes on the floor. "Okay."

"These last few days, ever since I started talking to you, getting to know you—or at least this new you—I've thought a lot about that day in the locker room. Then seeing my name on the list of targets when I played Son of War High made me think about it even more. Franklin, what I did was unforgivable."

It had happened toward the end of sophomore year. Phys ed had just finished, and we'd all tromped into the locker room to shower and change. I hated this part of the school day, because I didn't want anyone to see my mostly naked body, and because I didn't want to get caught peeking at anyone else's mostly naked body either. True, I'd already come out of the closet the year before, and people hadn't seemed to have a problem with it, but I still didn't want them to think I was the gross kind of homo who scoped out other guys in the locker room.

Luckily, the Duluth Central boys' shower had individual stalls, so at least I didn't have to deal with *all* my business and everyone else's flying around in the open. As soon as I'd finish showering, I'd retreat to my locker in the corner, pull up my boxer briefs underneath my towel, and throw on the rest of my clothes while keeping my eyes on the banged-up green lockers.

On this particular day I'd just yanked up my undies and slung my towel over my locker door when my eyes slipped out of their safety zone and landed on Franklin Kettle. He'd taken a locker a few down from mine. He still just had on a towel.

My glance turned into a look. I'd never noticed Franklin's body before. I'd always been too busy in the locker room keeping my eyes to myself. He had a slim build, but his whole torso was sectioned off into perfect units of muscle. I'd never in a million years have suspected such a thing existed under his clothes.

Maybe I let myself stare more than I would've otherwise because I didn't quite think of Franklin as a full-fledged person. He was just Kettlebot. He was pixels on a screen. So it surprised me when my gaze skipped up to his face and I found him looking back at me. Not with surprise or anger, and not straight into my eyes, of course. He was looking at my body the same way I'd been looking at his.

The next second I shouted, "What the fuck are you staring at me for?" The words seemed to fly out of my mouth all by themselves.

All the other boys in that part of the locker room jerked their heads around, Tor and Pete included.

"Keep your eyes to yourself, pervert," I snarled, my face searing.

The locker room exploded with yells and barks and laughter. Fingers pointed at Franklin, who just stood there in his towel with his eyes—partially obscured, as usual, by his hair and his glasses—still on me, but darkening now, his nostrils flaring, his lips puckering, his face tilting downward as it filled with anger.

The noise just grew louder. A few guys, Pete among them, whipped out their phones to capture the moment. Others insisted Franklin had a boner. Then a random kid named Eric must've decided he wanted to find out for sure because he yanked off Franklin's towel. That jerked him out of his trance. He covered himself, turned back to his locker, and rushed to put on his clothes. The mockery went on, though. I let myself melt into the audience, laughing and yelling along with the others, but maybe a little less loudly.

I guess that incident should've tipped me off that Franklin was gay long before he told me himself. Maybe in the same way I'd never quite thought of him as a person, I'd never quite thought of him as having a sexuality, either. A day or two after the locker room episode, down in the steam tunnels, Tor said to me, sort of teasing but sort of not, "Hey, I saw the way you were checking out Franklin in the locker room before you started yelling at him. Should I be jealous?" I probably blushed, but I laughed it off and said, "Are you kidding? Hell no." Because the thought really did seem ridiculous. Not even worth talking about seriously.

"I'm sorry," I told Franklin now. "I was an asshole. I only did it because I was still insecure about being gay myself. It had nothing to do with you, really."

"Yeah, I get it."

I glanced at my hands. I'd managed to wash them since art class earlier that day, but some green paint still showed in the creases of my palms. "Something's been running through my mind lately," I said. "I guess I have a reputation around school for being nice, and considering we live in a state known for its niceness, that must mean people think I'm *extra* nice or something. But a couple days before she died, Callie told me being a *nice* person isn't the same as being a *good* person, and I think she was right. My brother was good. Not me." My eyes rose to the picture of him on the shelf above my desk. His big grin. His warm eyes. "I remember once when I was nine and Ethan was turning thirteen, I painted a T-shirt for him for his birthday. At the time I was so proud of that thing, but I can tell you now it was hideous. Big purple and green and pink swirls all over it. Not the kind of thing a cool kid should ever wear outside the house if he wants to stay cool. But Ethan wore it anyway, all the time. And the really ironic part is, pretty soon other kids in the neighborhood decided it was the height of fashion and asked me to make shirts for them, too. Even Tor and Pete."

"I remember those," Franklin said. "They *were* hideous."

"And thanks to Ethan, for a few weeks, they were everywhere. Ever since he died, I think me being nice is just my lame attempt at being good like him."

"I bet lots of people feel that way. But what you're doing right now, covering for me even though most people would turn me in, that isn't just nice." He'd swiveled the chair around to look at Ethan's photo too. He turned back to me now, and for the first time I really noticed in his face and body what the last few days, and all the remorse he must've been feeling, had done to him. The way his shoulders hunched, and the haunted look in his once empty eyes, reminded me of Sam Durham, that soldier from Ethan's unit. "You're right that you were an asshole that day sophomore year," he said. "I hope it wasn't unforgivable, though. If it was unforgivable, what would that make what I did?"

I stared down at my hands again. "Of course. I'm sorry."

The house, the whole neighborhood, was quiet. I couldn't even hear Mrs. Kettle's wind chimes. The moonlight filtered through the blinds, giving them a pearly glow.

"It's strange," I said. "When I think back on what I did that day in the locker room, I feel like it was me, but at the same time it was a completely different person. Sort of like those nightmares you told me about, where it's you about to kill Pete, but it's also not you."

He nodded.

"You know, before Mom did her operation on you, I didn't think it would work. I never admitted it to her, but I couldn't imagine how you could just flip a switch in a brain and turn one kind of person into another."

"You mean like this?" He grabbed my old paperback copy of *Dr. Jekyll and Mr. Hyde* from the shelf above my desk.

"Exactly. I thought that kind of thing only happened in books."

He studied the novel's garish, melodramatic cover. "I didn't think it would work either, but your mom told me external influences change the way the human brain functions all the time. Like psychotropic drugs. Depressants. Antidepressants. Antipsychotics. Those all change your personality. Even alcohol."

"I guess."

"Or when you masturbate. That would be another example."

My face must've turned tomato red. "Excuse me?"

He smirked. "You know, when you take your hand and—"

"Yes, I know what masturbation is, but how is that relevant?"

"Haven't you noticed how when you masturbate your brain fills up with all these dirty thoughts, and then the second after you, you know, finish, it's like all those thoughts suddenly seem disgusting and you can't believe you were just thinking them? I've always found that really weird."

"Yeah," I said, hoping to plow right past the whole masturbation thing, "my mom talked with me once about how drugs and stuff can change your personality. It never quite convinced me, though. Those things don't change *who you are*. They just sort of . . . tweak it a little."

"Did she ever tell you about Phineas Gage?"

"Phineas who?"

He pulled up his feet so he could sit cross-legged on the chair. "He was a railroad worker back in the nineteenth century. Everyone thought of him as this great guy, a hardworking, upstanding citizen. Then one day there was an explosion that drove a big iron rod straight into his eyeball, through his brain, and out the other side of his head. No one expected him to survive, but he did . . . and all of a sudden he was nothing like before. He was lazy. Mean. Crude. A completely different person. The rod had damaged his brain in just the right way."

I inclined my head from side to side. "Okay, but what about something like what happened to you? Somebody changing for the better? Has *that* ever happened?"

He nodded. "Your mom also told me about another guy. He had an accident sort of like Phineas Gage's. He was suicidal, and for some reason he decided it would be a really good idea to kill himself with a crossbow. The arrow went all the way through his brain but didn't kill him, and just like Phineas Gage, he became completely different. Before the accident, he was violent, antisocial, and depressed. After, he was calm, peaceful, and happy. Like, *really* happy. The arrow must've hit the perfect spot, because he lived the rest of his life in pretty much a constant state of bliss. Can you imagine that?" He stared at the moon glowing through the blinds. The pearly light painted his face a pale blue.

"Yeah, it sounds pretty cool." I glanced at the book Franklin had set on my desk and the half-shadowed face on the cover. I wondered again if I should tell him the truth about the nano-drones. I wanted to. But not now. I still couldn't be sure how he'd react. I needed to prove his innocence first, get him safe and in the clear. I needed to give Mom a chance to prepare. Then, hopefully, the truth could come out. For now I said, "I just want you to know, Franklin, even though I didn't believe in my mom's procedure before, I do now. I can see you're different. People do change. I suppose they're changing all the time. Like, I was a different person that day in the locker room. I was still getting used to being out of the closet. I was self-conscious. I was scared. Not that I'm not all of those things now. Just less."

"And what you did didn't really have anything to do with me anyway, like you said before."

I peeked at his face and found myself wondering again what he'd look like without his glasses.

"Except maybe—"

I stopped myself. Now I'd started thinking about what he'd look like without his orange hoodie. I'd started imagining the body hidden underneath his clothes.

"Except maybe it did," I finished.

"Did what?"

"Have something to do with you."

I got up, my face searing hot. Franklin did too. We stood face-to-face in the narrow space between the desk and the bed, our bodies leaning in toward each other a little. With both hands,

I lifted off his glasses and set them on the mattress behind me. The sight of his face, bare and beautiful, drained half the oxygen from my lungs. For a second I wondered if it was rude that I'd just pulled off his glasses like that, without even asking. If I'd taken the liberty with him because I still didn't believe he was a real person. I hoped I hadn't. I didn't *think* I had. Right now Franklin felt to me like the most real person in the world.

And he didn't look like he minded what I'd done. His eyes—a gray that usually appeared so much duller behind the lenses of his glasses—had settled on my mouth. His lips—full and purple-red, like he'd just eaten a handful of blackberries—parted a little.

I caught his chin with my fingers and lifted it. Little by little, his eyes slid upward until they met mine. This time, unlike those other fleeting moments when we'd made eye contact over the last few days, he held my gaze. I realized if you got close enough and really looked, you could see so many colors flecking the gray of his irises. So much space inside the black of his pupils. And I could feel him really looking into my eyes too. As if I'd become as real to him as he had to me.

Slowly, slowly, we brought our mouths together.

Until a scream sliced through the night, slicing us apart. Franklin and I stumbled back from each other, breathing hard. We bolted to the window and I wrenched the blind aside.

The scream had come from Lydia's house. Up the street, the police officer stationed at the end of our block had already jumped out of his cruiser, gun drawn.

"Get away from the window!" I said, pushing Franklin back toward the bed.

Another scream. It was Lydia, I was sure of it. The cop had reached the Hickses' front walk. Lights had started snapping on behind their upstairs windows one by one.

"What's happening?" Franklin grabbed his glasses and jammed them on.

"I don't know. I'm going to find out. Listen, don't go anywhere. Hide under my bed." I grabbed him by the shoulders and hustled him down to the floor. "You can't let anyone see you, especially if something just happened. I'll be back soon."

"Maybe you shouldn't—"

But I'd already pulled on a pair of sweatpants and flung open my bedroom door.

Mom stood in the hall in her robe. "Did you hear that, Rem? It sounded like somebody screaming."

I made sure to yank my door shut behind me. "I know. I'm going to check it out."

"Honey, it could be dangerous. Why don't you—"

"I'll be careful." I jumped into my sneakers but didn't bother with my coat or scarf. The next second I was outside, sprinting down our walkway and across the icy street toward the Hickses' house. Now, though, I didn't hear any screaming coming from within. Only silence.

49

I bounded up the Hickses' front steps and skidded to a stop just outside the open door. Inside, a huddle of people had gathered at the base of the staircase. I picked out the cop's big winter coat, Mr. Hicks's bald head, Mrs. Hicks's blue robe, a too-large T-shirt with the words DULUTH CENTRAL CARIBOU hanging on the skinny frame of Lydia's younger brother. But what about Lydia? Where was she?

Then I spotted them through the crowd of bodies: two pale legs stretched out on the lowest steps in just the same way Callie's had been when I'd seen her dead on the cafeteria floor.

"Rem?" Mrs. Hicks had noticed me.

"Lydia." The word sounded more like a gasp. I barely had enough breath to speak. "What happened? Is she—"

The crowd parted. Lydia appeared, sitting at the bottom of the staircase.

Alive.

I almost passed out right there on the doorstep. "I heard you scream," I panted. "Are you okay?"

She covered her face with her hands. "I'm so embarrassed." Peeking through her fingers, she said, "I'm sorry I scared you, Rem. I thought I heard something outside my window. It was probably just a nightmare."

"No nightmare would make you scream like that." Her dad crossed his arms and cast a grim glance up the stairs. "I heard it too. There was someone outside."

"But whoever it was didn't get in?" I said.

She fidgeted with the hem of her pajama shorts and shook her head.

I gripped the frame of the Hickses' front door. My heart had slowed a little. At least I knew Franklin had been in my room, attached to my mouth, when all this had happened. Already my mind had started working. Could this be the proof I'd hoped to find that Franklin hadn't killed Callie? If so, could it prove his innocence in other people's eyes too?

The police officer's walkie-talkie blared static. A voice said, "We're almost there. Over."

"That's my backup," the cop said. "We'll have to check the house just in case." He turned to me. "Son, I appreciate your concern, but I need you to go back home."

"Sure," I said. "Talk to you later, Lydia?"

She gave a weary nod. I closed the front door and raced across the street, my body still buzzing. Now all I could think about was telling Franklin what I'd learned: that I might have what we needed to clear his name once and for all. Mom stood in the doorway waiting for me, her winter coat over her shoulders, her hair in disarray. "What happened?"

"Lydia heard something outside her window," I said, hurrying past her into the house. "She thinks it was probably nothing. Look, I should get some sleep." I rushed to my room, hoping she wouldn't find my brisk behavior strange. The second I'd pressed my door shut, I whispered, "Franklin? I have some news. Good, I think." I dropped to my knees to look under the bed.

Of course. Gone again.

But he'd left behind the screwdriver he'd used to pry open my window. It lay balanced on the angled surface of my paint-smeared desk, next to my old copy of *Jekyll and Hyde*.

50

When Lydia called about an hour later, I saw her name on my phone's screen and answered halfway through the first ring.

"What's going on?" I said. "How come the cops are still there? Did they find something?"

I'd been watching her house through the window. Less than a minute after I'd left, two more police cruisers had joined the one already parked at the end of the block. They hadn't gone yet.

"Oh, Rem," she whispered. "I think I really messed up."

A little over an hour ago, Lydia had been awoken by noises right outside her window, just like I had earlier that night. She'd sat up screaming, but instead of finding a Son of War mask staring in at her, she'd glimpsed a face she knew: Tor's. He'd come to surprise her, the same way he had a few nights ago.

The next instant, he'd disappeared. Her scream had startled him, making him lose his balance and fall. That had prompted Lydia's second scream.

"Is he okay?" I asked.

"He's fine. I talked to him on the phone a few minutes ago. But when the police searched the house, they found his footprints in the yard and signs he'd climbed up the trellis."

"Did they track him all the way back to his place?"

"No. They don't know it was him. If my dad had any idea Tor was trying to get into my room, he'd never let me set eyes on him again. But now everybody thinks it was the killer who was trying to get into the house. My dad's flipping out. Rem, he's sending me away with my mom to stay with my grandma in Saint Peter."

"When?"

"First thing tomorrow morning. My mom's already packing."

"For how long?"

"I don't even know. Until all this blows over, I guess."

I got up from my bed and went to the window again. All the lights in the Hickses' house had stayed on. The three police cruisers still stood in a line along the far side of the street. I'd already noticed Franklin had managed to smooth out the snow outside my window, apparently without anyone spotting him. Our front yard looked as pristine as a blank canvas. That reassured me at least. If the cops searched the rest of the block for signs of a skulking murderer, I didn't think they'd find any here. But now that I knew Lydia's prowler wasn't the killer after all, that also meant I no longer had an alibi for Franklin.

"Don't you think maybe you should tell the police the truth, Lydia?" I asked. "It might throw off their investigation if they go on thinking it was the murderer who tried to break in tonight.

And then maybe your dad wouldn't make you leave town."

She heaved a breath. "I hate lying, but I just can't do that to Tor. Plus my dad terrifies *me,* too. He'd probably send me to my grandma's anyway, just to teach me a lesson."

I couldn't argue with that. I knew all about keeping secrets I probably shouldn't.

51

The next morning, at the same time we all usually met up to drive to school together, Lydia ran across Boreal Street to hug me and Tor good-bye. Her mom already had their car running; her dad watched us with his arms crossed and a frown on his face. She held Tor a long time, her cheek crushed against his thin long-sleeve T-shirt, but she couldn't kiss him with her dad there.

Her eyes glistening, she straightened his earmuffs and ran back across the street to her parents. A minute later Tor and I were rumbling to school in the Saab.

"And then there were two," he said.

I didn't reply.

"Are you still mad at me?"

"Why wouldn't I be?" I snapped. "By the way, I'm only giving you a ride today because I didn't want Lydia to suspect there was something weird going on between us. After school you're on your own."

"I still don't see what you're so worked up about."

"You treat me like shit, Tor. It's like you don't care about other people at all. I swear, sometimes I wish my mom could put a fucking capsule in your head too."

He threw up his hands. "What the hell are you talking about?"

"You rub your relationship with Lydia in my face. You act like what we do together's dirty and disgusting. Aren't those the exact words you used in the cafeteria the other day?"

"What a load of bullshit. I already explained how it is with me. I never lied to you about that. If you'll recall, I even tried to end our thing last week because I was worried about how it was affecting *you*."

"Then two days later you were hitting on me again."

He shook his head, disgusted. "For Christ's sake, grow up. Take some responsibility. I never forced you to do a single fucking thing. Come on, Nice Guy. I'm still waiting for you to tell me what I've done that's so goddamn horrendous."

"You—"

I stopped myself. *You might've gotten my brother killed,* I'd almost said. Jesus, where had *that* come from? I bit my lip and stared at the road.

Tor shifted in his seat to look at me. He had a Band-Aid on his forehead where he'd bumped himself falling off the trellis. In a gentler voice—the voice that up until a few days ago had never failed to puree my insides—he said, "Look, I know Lydia told you what really happened last night. When I climbed up to her window—"

"Can you just not talk for a while? I'm really not interested."

He pressed his lips together, faced forward, and slammed his fist against the Saab's hard dash. But he stopped talking. I'd never bossed Tor around like that before, and I had to admit it felt good. Sitting next to him now, I didn't even feel an urge to bury my face in his neck and breathe in his chlorine scent.

As we coasted through the snowy streets, my thoughts drifted to Franklin. Was *he* the reason Tor didn't have the same hold on me he'd once had? That second kiss we'd shared last night, what the hell did it mean? Had I really gone from having feelings for a mere asshole to having feelings for a sociopathic killer?

But Franklin *wasn't* a sociopath. The capsule had changed him. Over the last few days he'd done more to show how much he cared about me than Tor ever had. He'd spent probably hours drawing detailed portraits of my face. He'd escaped from custody multiple times just so he could spend time with me.

He'd actually wanted to kiss me on the mouth.

What did it *mean* that he'd changed, though? If the gadget in his head had made Franklin the person he was now, was I having feelings for a real person at all? Just thinking about it was enough to scramble my brain. I supposed it was like we'd been saying last night: people changed all the time, for all sorts of reasons. But if people changed all the time, what was it we fell in love with when we fell in love with someone? An idea? An illusion? There had to be *something* there that didn't change, right?

Not that I was falling in love with Franklin.

We turned a corner, and Lake Superior came into view. The dark sky hung low above it. The weather app on my phone had warned of a blizzard hitting later today, and I could already feel it building. I glanced in the rearview mirror and saw the Hickses' Lexus had fallen in behind me, with Lydia's mom in the driver's seat and Lydia slumping unhappily next to her. Even if her dad did have a scary overprotective streak, I knew he'd done the right thing sending her away.

Which made me wonder if I should think about leaving town too. My name was next on the list.

52

A sub was standing in for Ms. Utter again today. He'd just called class to order when the door opened and Abigail Lansing slipped in.

"I hope you don't mind," she said to him, the earnest furrow already in place on her forehead. "I have an announcement about the assembly tomorrow."

He shrugged and waved her to the front of the room.

"I wanted to tell you all myself," Abigail began, "because I know many of you in here were close to Callie Minwalla." She gave me and Tor a significant nod each. Summoning a teary gleam to her eyes, she said, "Callie was deeply involved in putting together the memorial for Pete Lund that was scheduled for tomorrow. During that time, the two of us became very close, which has made her loss especially hard for me personally." She bit her lip as if to hold back a sob. "Principal Chen and I have decided to move ahead with the assembly as scheduled, but now we'll use the time to honor both Pete and Callie. Because she would've wanted it that way."

Bullshit, I wanted to yell. Callie had always hated assemblies like that. "That's Principal Chen's solution to every problem," Callie had quipped after she first heard about the Big Bang memorial. "Throw a fucking assembly at it." What would she have said if she'd known she'd be the subject of two assemblies in one week? I wasn't sure, but it would've involved a lot of swearwords.

I kept my mouth shut, though. Abigail wiped the dramatic track marks from her cheeks and left. After that, the sub spent most of the hour reading out of the history textbook in a dry-mouthed monotone. I didn't mind. I stacked some books on my desk, laid my cheek on top, and stared out the window at the snow, which had just started to fall.

And I worked on my plan.

53

Mom had said she'd have to work late that evening, and maybe even stay at the lab overnight depending on how bad the snowstorm got, which would make executing my plan easier. At around seven I drove to Nil Bergstrom's house, just a few blocks over from Boreal Street. I'd been there once before, when we'd been paired together for a science project freshman year—an excruciatingly uncomfortable experience.

I parked halfway down the block. My vintage Saab didn't exactly blend in, so I didn't want to bring it too close. At least the snow had picked up enough that a white blanket was already forming over the bright yellow hood and roof. I got out and crept closer.

By the light radiating from the little house's windows, I could see the snow had smoothed out the rutted front lawn, stacked itself on top of the low chain-link fence enclosing the yard, dusted itself across the gray aluminum siding. Nil's bedroom occupied a detached garage covered in the same gray siding and standing off to one side. I peered at the garage's small windows, straining to see if she was inside, but I could only make out an inconclusive low blue glow.

Stepping over the chain-link fence, I slipped under the shelter of some trees that separated the Bergstroms' yard from their neighbors'. The snow made a soft, dry crackling sound as it landed in the tangle of branches above me. I had to wade through deep drifts even here, but at least the trees would help keep me hidden. I made my way to the garage and crept along the wall farthest from the house until I reached a window. That bluish light continued to filter through the glass. Crouching low, I peered over the sill.

The room didn't look all that different from how I remembered it. A large folding table stood against one wall, with three monitors on top—the source of the blue glow. A couple keyboards and lots of papers, soda cans, candy bar wrappers, and other trash covered the rest of the table's surface. Two PC towers were tucked underneath. Across from the table stood a bed, unmade, with black sheets sagging onto the floor. Nil had painted the walls black too. Son of War posters hung here and there, the mask with its trapezoidal goggles staring out from multiple directions, and there were also a few for old bands like Marilyn Manson and Nine Inch Nails.

Then my eyes caught on something new: an arrangement of hunting knives decorating one wall, their shiny blades standing out against the matte black paint. Even from where I stood, even in the low light, I could tell how sharp the blades were. Or maybe I just imagined I could.

But at least I couldn't see anyone inside. The room appeared still, the bed empty, the computers dormant, their screens all on screen savers displaying contorting blue geometric shapes. I brought my face all the way up to the cold glass and scrutinized the interior. Just below one of the monitors, bathed in its bluish light, a book lay on the table, partially covered by a crumpled potato chip bag. I could still see its black cover, though, and the letters written along the side that spelled *FRANKLIN KETTLE*.

I pulled out the screwdriver Franklin had left in my room last night and studied the window. Nil had locked it. I could tell right away. But hadn't Franklin told me every house had at least one unlocked window? I just had to hope that rule counted for detached garages too. I edged along the wall to the next window, located above Nil's bed. I cupped my hands around my eyes and put my face to the glass, my heart banging.

This one she'd left unlocked.

And if she'd been careless enough to do that, maybe that also meant she hadn't tricked out her room with security cameras—something I wouldn't have put past someone as tech-savvy as her. But then again, I reminded myself, so what if she had? If she found out I'd broken into her room, what could she do? Report me for stealing the notebook she'd been concealing for the past year? I could always tell the police the truth, or part of it anyway: that I'd seen her carrying the journal around and wanted to find out if it was the one that had belonged to Franklin. Perhaps using poor judgment, I'd decided to investigate myself. Nil had a lot more to lose than I did.

I wedged the screwdriver between the window and the frame and wiggled it up and down. It took me a while, but I finally managed to force a gap just big enough for my gloved fingers. The window squeaked and groaned and finally flew upward. I stood there panting and sweating, not even believing what I'd just managed to do.

Headlights flashed across the outside of the garage. I dropped to a crouch and spun around, my heart going triple-time now. A car had pulled into the driveway next door, but the trees between the Bergstroms' property and the neighbors' screened it from view. The car's doors opened and closed. The neighbors murmured to each other as they hurried inside. I didn't think they'd seen me.

After taking another few seconds to let my heart calm down, I knocked my boots against the wall to get off as much snow as I could and swung my legs over the sill one by one. Scraps of snow still landed on the black sheets, but that couldn't be helped. I'd reposition the messy bedclothes to cover the water marks before I left and hope for the best.

I stepped from the bed onto the floor—old shag carpeting, the same shade of green as Nil's hair, mostly covered with dirty clothes and towels—and pulled the window down to keep out the snow. As I turned around, I noticed the hunting knives again, and my heart hiccupped. I squeezed my eyes shut, shook my head, and forced myself to focus. Whatever I'd gotten myself into, it was too late for second thoughts now. I waded through the mess, past Nil's giant backpack lying in the center of the floor, to her cobbled-together computer setup on the far side of the room.

Before I even got to Franklin's notebook, I noticed something else underneath the trash on the folding table: a blueprint of Duluth Central High School. Had she used it to create the floor plan for the school in Son of War High? Why else would she have something like that lying around?

I pulled the journal out from under the potato chip bag and ran my finger over the worn sticker on the cover and the red capital letters running down the edges of the pages. The answers might all lie in here. I started to shove the book into my coat pocket, knowing I should leave fast, but then I stopped, stared at it another second, and opened to the first page.

I found myself gazing at a portrait of my own face.

Franklin must've drawn the picture a couple years ago. My hair was sort of spiked up in front, the way I'd worn it when I was a freshman and sophomore. But this image was just as graceful and detailed as the ones Franklin had made at the lab and messaged to me.

I closed the book again. When Franklin had created this portrait, he hadn't had a capsule in his head that gave him a conscience, or a bunch of nanodrones that made him a murderer, either. He'd done it with the brain he'd been born with . . . which meant the original Franklin couldn't have been *that* different from the Franklin I'd kissed, right?

I raised the journal one more time, chose a random spot, and parted the pages, splitting the *FRANKLIN KETTLE* in red ink down the middle.

The notebook opened to a picture of a masked Jim Colby holding an enemy soldier from behind and slitting his belly. Blood jetted in all directions. The victim's intestines, rendered with obvious relish, spilled out over his pants. The depiction of his muscly bare chest and Colby's, and the way the two of them were locked tight together, gave the image a weird homoerotic element too. I flinched and looked away. Why was I doing this to myself? Hadn't I known I'd probably find something like this? As much as I might want to, I couldn't blame *all* Franklin's darkness on Mom's nanodrones.

But even though I knew I should just put the journal away and get the hell out of that place, I couldn't make myself stop. Not until I found what I was looking for.

I paged through the book. It contained all sorts of things. Abstract doodles. Notes on Son of War strategy. One full page consisted of the word "earwig" repeated over and over in that precise, blocky handwriting of his. More drawings. Many violent, some not. They all had a strangeness, though, that made me think of the images in my Tattoo Atlas.

I reached a page labeled *SON OF WAR HIGH* in big letters. Underneath, Franklin had drawn a detailed picture of the Beretta M9 he'd used to kill Pete. The next two-page spread contained a floor plan of the school, drawn with the help of a ruler. Red arrows plotted a route through the halls to various locations, marked with *X*s. Ms. Utter's classroom. The cafeteria. The main hall.

The locker room.

My chest cinched tight, making it hard to breathe. I turned another page.

> *YOUR MISSION: KILL THESE ASSHOLES, IN THE ORDER IN WHICH THEY APPEAR ON THE LIST, IN THE LOCATION WHERE EACH ASSHOLE HUMILIATED YOU. THEN KILL YOURSELF.*
>
> *PETE LUND*
> *CALLIE MINWALLA*
> *LYDIA HICKS*
> *REM BRAITHWAITE*
> *TOR AGNARSON*

My hands had started trembling so hard I could barely turn the pages. On the next one, Franklin had put *TARGET ONE: PETE LUND* at the top and stapled Pete's headshot, clipped from the yearbook, next to that. Below he'd written *TARGET ONE MISSION DETAILS: Isolate Pete in the history classroom. During his presentation maybe? Make him say, "I didn't know Napoleon was that small." Shoot him. Take the remaining four targets prisoner.*

On the facing page Franklin had written a long, dense passage that appeared to lay out his reasons for wanting Pete dead.

I didn't read it carefully, but it seemed to focus on the prank Pete had played on Franklin during his presentation. I noticed phrases like "stupid jock" and "Tor's underling" and "can't think for himself."

I turned the page. *TARGET TWO: CALLIE MINWALLA.* Under *MISSION DETAILS*, Franklin had put, *Escort the remaining targets to the cafeteria. Make Callie say, "Kettlebot shot me." Shoot her.* On the facing page was more ranting, this time about how Callie had thought she'd been so clever at the Halloween dance, pegging Franklin for the stereotypical school shooter, but she'd find out just how well he could play that role.

Next page. *TARGET THREE: LYDIA HICKS. Proceed to the main hall near the cafeteria entrance. Make Lydia say, "Nobody wants you here anyway." Shoot her.* Another rant followed. Lydia had probably been right that nobody had wanted Franklin at Duluth Central. So what? He hadn't wanted them, either.

I eased into the chair in front of the folding table, feeling dizzy now. Stars strobed in front of my eyes, and my lungs seemed to have stopped working altogether, but I forced myself to turn one more page.

My face stared back at me, the photo stapled next to my name. *Proceed to the boys' locker room. Make Rem say, "Keep your eyes to yourself, pervert." Shoot him.*

The words blurred on the page. I shook my head and squinted until they came back into focus enough for me to keep reading.

He's a phony, Franklin Kettle had written. *He likes to think he's such a nice guy, but really he only acts nice when he can get something out of it. People he doesn't think are important, like you, he barely even looks at.* Lower down: *Even if it's true that somewhere deep inside he's a freak like you, that doesn't mean he wants to be, and that doesn't mean he could ever care about you. Face it, he wouldn't lift a finger to save your life.* Then, all the way at the bottom of the page: *Just forget about him. Just get rid of him. Just shoot him.*

I let the book drop onto my lap and stared at the blue shapes folding and refolding themselves like origami on Nil Bergstrom's screens. From somewhere deep in my brain came that grief counselor's kindergarten voice. *Iiiiinhale. Eeeeexhale.* But it didn't do any good. My breath was coming in weak, jagged pants.

Then a noise broke the silence.

I flew out of the chair and whirled around, searching for the noise's source. It sounded like a buzzing, close by, right next to me. I could hear it, but I could feel it too.

It took me a full ten seconds to realize my phone had started vibrating. I yanked it out of my coat. The number Franklin had been using lit up the screen. Without even thinking, I touched the answer button and put the phone to my ear.

Franklin had already started talking, his voice low but full of excitement. "I probably shouldn't even be calling right now, they might come any second, but I wanted to say I'm sorry I ran off again, I just figured I should get out of there, but I read the news today and saw Lydia Hicks didn't get killed or anything, which is great, so two nights out and still no more deaths, and by the way, that was another amazing kiss, I think we're getting really good at th—"

"You lied to me, asshole."

The rush of words stopped dead. "What do you mean?"

His journal had fallen onto the carpet, open and facedown, when I'd jumped out of the chair. Its front and back covers splayed outward like the wings of a dead crow. "I found your notebook. You lied to me when you said I wasn't a target. You wanted to kill me."

His reply didn't come for a while. "I—I was different then, Rem," he stammered. "I didn't tell you because—"

"Don't even bother. I don't want to know." I snatched up the book.

"Where did you find it?" he asked.

"In Nil's room."

"But why were you—"

"*I'm* asking the questions. What's she doing with it?"

"I told her where I'd hidden it the first time she came to visit me at the detention center. I asked her to destroy it for me. She said she had."

"She didn't. I'm in her room right now, holding the notebook in my hands. And I also found a blueprint of the school. I'm guessing she must've used this stuff to create Son of War High. I bet there's even more proof on her computer. And I bet you knew about it too. Another lie."

His breath had started to speed up, just like mine had. "I did know she built the game, okay? She told me about it just before I got transferred to the lab. It made me mad, because Son of War High was supposed to be for me only, not for just anyone to play."

"Either way, it's sick. And then I suppose she decided to play it in real life, so she shot Callie."

"Rem, no," Franklin insisted. "That's exactly why I didn't tell you she built the game. I knew you'd assume she must've killed Callie, but I promise she didn't."

I glanced at the array of knives on Nil's wall. "I wouldn't be so sure. This girl's a psycho, Franklin."

"She's not." His voice was growing more unsteady, more desperate. "Please don't think she did it. She's my best friend."

"That doesn't make her innocent. The police need to know about this. I'm going to call them. Tell them what I found here."

"Please, Rem. Don't do it."

I yanked at my scarf to cool down my neck, which felt fiery hot. "Did you know Lydia left town this morning? That means my name's next on the list. Nil could be plotting to kill me right now. If you cared about me as much as you say you do, that would mean something to you."

"I do care about you. More than anything."

"Then how could you lie to me like you did? My mom might've rummaged around in your brain a little, but could she really change you? I started to think she had, but now I don't know."

While I talked, I smacked the journal down on the table and flipped through it until I found the snapshot of my face. At the bottom of the facing page, the words *Just get rid of him. Just shoot him.*

"I *have* changed, Rem. I know seeing that notebook probably freaked you out, but that's who I was, not who I am. Be mad at that person. Don't be mad at me."

"This isn't about that," I retorted, even though my eyes hadn't budged from those ugly words he'd written about me. "You lied to me. About Nil. About your plan. How am I supposed to trust you after that?"

"What about last night? When we—"

"I'm going to forget about last night," I fired back. "I suggest you do too."

He sucked in a breath like I'd punched him in the belly. "Don't say that. I'll visit you later. We can talk about this. Just please don't say that."

"I'm hanging up now. I'm calling the police. So I wouldn't sneak out tonight if I were you."

"Please—"

I hung up and started dialing 911.

I only got as far as 9. An arm grabbed me from behind and a cold blade pressed against my throat.

54

"Drop the phone."

I recognized Nil's surly snarl. The knife leaned into my Adam's apple, squeezing my windpipe. My phone thunked as it hit the carpet.

"What are you doing here?"

I tried to answer, but only a thin choking sound escaped my mouth.

She yanked away the knife, spun me around, and pushed me up against the folding table. A soda bottle and a few papers fell to the floor.

"Answer me," she growled, the knife still raised. Spikes of green hair fell down over her face, screening her eyes. "You're in my room. That's breaking and entering."

Even without the knife choking me, I still couldn't seem to make my voice work. I grabbed the table behind me for support, and a few more pieces of paper spilled onto the green shag.

She noticed the notebook lying open on the table. "Doing some snooping?"

"That's right." I managed to force out the words in a throaty rasp. "I know everything. That you created Son of War High. That you killed Callie. And now you want to kill me. But you can't do it here, right? You have to take me to school. Make me say the phrase in the book. That's the only way you can get your points or whatever in that disgusting game of yours, right?"

She took a step back and tossed her hair out of her eyes.

I pressed on, the adrenaline really kicking in now, making me brave. "Anyway, it's too late. I told other people I was coming here. Lydia. Tor. If anything happens to me, they'll know who did it."

Still she didn't say anything. She just stared. Had she bought my bluff?

Then a huge laugh exploded from her mouth. She backed up a few more steps, doubled over, and guffawed so hard tears ran down her cheeks. "*That's* what you think?" she panted. "You think *I'm* the killer?"

My cheeks burned. "The evidence is all here. The notebook. The blueprint of the school. You designed Son of War High, and now you're making it real. You're finishing what your friend started."

"I built Son of War High, sure," she said, wiping her eyes. "But how does that make me a murderer? Why would I kill Callie?"

Because you're sick, I wanted to say. *Just like Franklin was, and maybe still is.*

She folded her arms across her chest. "Think about it, genius.

Do you honestly believe you're the first person to have the brilliant idea that Franklin's best friend might be Callie's killer?" She pointed across the room. "For your information, that door was one of the first ones the cops came knocking on last Friday."

"So?" I kept my grip on the table. "What happened when they came in here and found all this stuff? How come they didn't take the notebook?"

She smirked. "They never made it inside. I have an alibi for the night of Callie's murder, you idiot. My mom was in the hospital dying of ovarian cancer. I was with her all night. The rest of my family was there too. Nurses, doctors, goddamn orderlies. They can all vouch for me. I never left until my mom kicked the bucket at seven fifteen a.m."

My face felt even hotter now. "I'm sorry. I didn't know."

"That you're an idiot or that my mom died?"

"About your mom."

Her eyes dropped away from mine. She twisted up her mouth, maybe to keep her chin from trembling, and tried to reestablish her toughness by giving a nonchalant shrug. "Understandable. Callie's death was more high profile. My mom's got lost in the shuffle."

"Why are you even in school this week?"

"My dad thought it would do me good to get away from all the talk of death around here." Her mouth twisted into a sardonic smile. "So instead I get treated to two death-related assemblies in one week at school."

"That sucks."

"No kidding." She toughened her face up some more: back to business. "Listen, I didn't kill Callie," she said. "If you want to, you can call the police and ask them yourself. Then you can also explain to them what the hell you're doing inside my room when I sure as hell didn't invite you in."

I studied the floor and didn't say anything. Around my boots, a wet mark had darkened the clumpy green carpeting. My phone lay a few inches away. I grabbed it and jammed it into my pocket.

"Who were you talking to when I came in?" Nil asked. "Sounded like you were mad."

I looked up. So she didn't know I'd been talking to Franklin? I hadn't been sure how much she'd heard. "Tor. He didn't think I should be breaking into your place."

"Maybe you should've listened to him."

A gust of wind shook the garage. The storm had picked up outside. We both glanced over at the windows and the snow swirling behind them.

"Why did you create Son of War High?" I asked.

"Because I felt like it, all right?" she snapped, turning back to me with eyes flashing. "Because it was something to do. Because I was bored. I didn't really kill anyone. Whatever Franklin has wrong with his brain, I don't have that. I'm just fucked up in the usual ways."

"I'm not convinced," I said. "I played your game myself, you know. Only someone really sick could've come up with something like that."

Nil grinned. "I'm guessing that means you didn't win."

My hands squeezed the table so hard my knuckles popped.

"So what do you want to do?" she asked. "Take me to your mom's lab so she can drill a hole in *my* head and stick in one of her capsules?"

"Maybe that's not such a bad idea."

"Make me meek as a house pet. No free will. No individuality."

"That's not what the capsule does. And even if it did, it would still be better than being a monster." Those images Franklin had drawn in his notebook flashed through my mind. That page with the word "earwig" written over and over. The list of targets with my name on it. "Franklin was a monster. He was obsessed with violence. And you don't seem any different." I nodded at the knife still clutched in her fist.

She raised the blade and admired it. "You got me. I'm obsessed with violence. So is every other human on this planet. It's just that most people don't admit it. Take your mother, for example."

"She's trying to *stop* violence. That's the whole reason she invented the capsule."

"Is that what you think?"

"That's what I *know*."

Her smug grin grew even wider. "Then you must not be reading what they're saying about your mom's little project on the Internet."

I narrowed my eyes at her. "What are you talking about?"

"You really think your mom got all that funding and that sleek, high-tech new lab just so she could be a do-gooder and get rid of violence? Do you have any idea where most of her money comes from? Go on, take a guess."

I just shook my head, my gaze shunting away from her face.

"DARPA. The Department of Defense's emerging technologies agency. Your mom's working for the military, sweetheart."

"Sure, according to some paranoid Internet conspiracy theorist." My voice didn't sound as steady as I wanted it to. "Why would the military want my mom's technology? So American soldiers can go into enemy territory and methodically implant each and every person living there with a capsule to make them nonviolent? That sounds like a great strategy. Much more efficient than, say, a bomb."

Nil chuckled. "Do yourself a favor, Rem." She opened her door. An icy blast of air swept into the room. "Go home. Do some googling. Find out what your mom's really up to."

I stood there a second, not quite believing she'd just let me go.

"Go on." She flicked her knife toward the door. "Get out of here."

"You're wrong about my mom."

"Sure I am." She turned to hang the knife on the wall among the others. "Keep telling yourself that."

While she had her back to me, I slipped Franklin's notebook into my coat. Then, without another word, I hurried past her into the storm.

55

I cleared the snow off the Saab's windows, dove in, and barreled home. Franklin's journal lay on the passenger seat next to me. I flipped it over to hide the Son of War sticker and pointed my eyes forward, at the snow scribbling across the windshield. My brain right now felt just like that snow: seething, chaotic, flying in a million different directions. Too many questions. Too many fears. Too many people I didn't know if I could trust. One person in particular I didn't even know if I *wanted* to trust anymore. Images from the notebook kept flashing in front of my eyes, split-second pictures sketched on the windshield by the snow. Fragments of sentences whispered in my ears as if carried by the wind. *He's a phony. Just get rid of him.*

I tried not to think. The lake had appeared on my right—or, at least, the big dark space where I knew the lake lay. I ordered myself to make my brain like that. Above the lake's surface, the storm raged, but down below lay only frozen water and, underneath that, some oblivious, slow-moving fish. The image reminded me of one of the lines from that Emily Dickinson poem: *The brain is deeper than the sea.* I whispered those words to myself like a mantra as I drove.

I'd just pulled into the garage when my phone buzzed with a text from Franklin. He'd sent a link to a Dropbox folder, without any explanation. The folder contained hundreds of files. I couldn't tell what kind, and I didn't feel like finding out.

I'd just started putting my phone away when I got another text, this time from Tor.

Feeling shitty. Thinking about Callie. All alone over here. I know you're pissed at me, but can you come keep me company? Just for a little while? Please?

Tor admitting he needed me. I didn't think he'd ever done that before. It was true he'd looked pretty wrecked ever since Callie's death. Maybe googling Mom's project and looking at the files Franklin had sent could wait a while.

Okay, I texted back. *But just for a few minutes.*

56

When Tor opened his kitchen door, he looked even worse than he had the last time I'd seen him. Disheveled, and not in his usual hot way. He had crumbs and food stains on his tank top and gym shorts, and his wispy blond hair was sticking straight up.

"Thanks for coming, Rem," he said. "It looks pretty bad out there."

He led me up to his room. On the floor lay an open pizza box with the rest of the pizza he was wearing all over his clothes. He plopped down on the edge of his bed and dragged his fingers through his hair.

"What the fuck's happening to us? Pete and Callie dead. Lydia gone."

"I don't know, Tor."

I'd been thinking the same thing. As angry as Tor made me, at that moment I wished he'd look up at me with that glint in his eye and say he had an idea. Some crazy, wonderful scheme that would make us forget all about what was happening. But he didn't. All the crazy, wonderful schemes seemed to have drained out of him.

The bedroom windows groaned as the wind pressed against them. I watched the snow outside flurry past. In spite of my best efforts, my brain still felt scrambled too. Images from the notebook kept forming and disintegrating in my head. An enemy soldier's guts spilling out. The floor plan of our school, with a route plotted through it joining five red *X*s.

Like a stray snowflake, a thought leaped out of the chaos into the front of my brain.

"Tor?" I said. "What did *you* do to him?"

He lay back on his bed and wiped his hands down his face. "Who?"

"Franklin Kettle."

He groaned. "Do we really have to talk about that again?"

"When I played Son of War High I never noticed where Franklin was supposed to kill you. The rest of us each did one specific thing to him in one specific place. But you . . . I remember you coming up with that nickname for him, egging on the rest of us sometimes, making little comments to him here and there, but apart from that, no one specific thing. What did *you* do?"

"That video game's probably based on nothing, remember? We don't even really know he wanted to kill me."

What about the notebook, though? I wanted to ask. I hadn't made it to Tor's page. I couldn't even picture where Franklin had placed Tor's *X* on the floor plan he'd drawn. He seemed to have sequenced his targets to create the most efficient route through the school, but I'd never bothered to notice where the route terminated.

Still, I did know one thing: Tor had most definitely been one of Franklin's targets. "You seriously think Franklin would've wanted to shoot Pete but not you?" I said.

"How should I know? The guy was insane."

"A sociopath," I murmured.

"Whatever. Moving on. Any new information about who killed Callie? I mean, it had to be Nil, right?"

I dropped into Tor's desk chair and rubbed the back of my neck. I felt so tired of having this conversation. With other people, and inside my own head. My eyes wandered over Tor's room and caught on a Son of War box sitting on his media stand next to his game console. These days it felt like everywhere I looked I found that mask staring back at me.

"But she's still been going to class," Tor continued. "The police haven't arrested her. Now that Lydia's gone, I was thinking about calling Billy myself, seeing if I could find out anything from—"

"Nil didn't do it," I said. "She didn't murder Callie. She has an alibi for that night."

He lifted his head off the bed to look at me. "How do you know?"

I shrugged. I didn't feel like getting into that whole story. It would just make me sound like a nut job.

"So who did kill Callie?"

Another shrug. That was exactly the question I was trying not to think about.

"Franklin? Do you think maybe he escaped from the lab after all?"

I stiffened, fighting back the urge to jump to his defense. What if he *had* done it? I had to admit that possibility, didn't I?

"If he didn't do it," Tor said, "and Nil didn't do it, who else could it be?"

"I have no idea, Tor."

He dropped his head on the mattress and stared at the ceiling. "I bet it was Abigail Lansing. She was probably desperate for somebody else to make posters and get tattoos and cry pretty tears for." He let out a hollow laugh. "I tried talking to one of the cops hanging around outside, but he wouldn't tell me a thing. 'The investigation is ongoing. Don't worry. We have Boreal Street under constant surveillance, and Duluth Central as well. Nothing will happen to you.' I told him that didn't exactly overwhelm me with confidence."

I nudged the pizza box with my toe. Feeling generous, I said, "Lydia was right, you shouldn't be here alone, Tor. If you want you can stay at my place tonight, in the guest room."

He shook his head. "It's okay. My parents are coming home tomorrow."

"It took them long enough."

"They had trouble getting tickets or something. Whatever. I'll be fine tonight. It's nice having company now, though." He sat up and pulled his tank top over his head. "Hey, can you do me a favor? My neck and shoulders are killing me. Can you give me a rub?"

As usual, the sight of his bare torso made me blink, like a

bright light had switched on right in front of my eyes. "I don't think that's a good idea, Tor."

He hiked up the corners of his mouth, a little of the Tor Agnarson glint returning to his eyes, while he pitched his tank top into a corner. "Come on, Nice Guy."

When I still didn't move, his eyes dropped to the bed, the glint extinguished. His huge shoulders hunched forward. The grin left his face. It was probably the first time ever I hadn't jumped right away when he'd said the word.

"Last night, when I went over to Lydia's house," he said in a quiet voice, "I was going to break up with her."

"Why?"

He picked at a dried splash of tomato sauce on his shorts. "I think with Callie's death and everything, I'm just having a hard time focusing on a relationship."

"Lydia seemed to believe you were having trouble focusing on the relationship before Callie died too."

"Well, there's also been the Big Bang memorial coming up. Plus I've been thinking Callie might've been right about my relationship with Lydia threatening the integrity of our group." He lifted his eyes to meet mine. "I know it was bothering you, Rem. I swear I didn't mean to hurt you. I'm sorry if I did."

It made me feel good to hear him say that, but I still didn't budge from the chair. "I don't believe those are the only reasons," I told him.

He scraped his fingers again through his wispy, chlorine-fried hair. "I guess I felt like I didn't deserve her."

"Why not?"

"It's complicated. That day in the bio lab when Lydia and I first got together, I had this weird freak-out. We were cutting into our stupid dead cat, and it made me think of Pete, and how that could've been me. *Should've* been me, probably, because you're right, Rem, I'm ten times the asshole Pete ever was. I broke into a cold sweat. I couldn't breathe."

"Lydia told me about it."

"Yeah. She was so sweet and patient with me. She talked to me in this soft voice. She made me feel better. I thought, *She's the kind of person I want to marry. Have kids with. Spend the rest of my life with. She's a good person.*"

"Yes, she is."

"And I figured maybe she could make me a good person too. But now I realize I was just kidding myself. I'm an asshole, and there's no changing that."

Outside, the storm continued. A sudden gust rattled the windows in their frames.

"Maybe all that's true," I said, "but it's not why you were going to break up with her. I want to hear you say it."

He looked away again. "I don't know what you're talking about, Rem."

"You're gay, Tor. Say it. You're gay."

"I already told you—"

"She deserves to know. You don't have to tell everyone. But you have to tell her."

He clamped his hands over his ears. "For Christ's sake, would you stop lecturing me? Get off your goddamn homosexual high horse and just"—he looked up, a tortured expression on his face, and banged the mattress next to him with his fist—"come over here."

Not the most tactful invitation I could've imagined. At least he'd apologized for hurting my feelings, though. That was something. And he really did look like he needed support. I'd never seen him like this before. So naked. Not physically—I'd seen *that* plenty—but emotionally. I got up and perched on the edge of the mattress. He bent forward, dropping his forehead on my shoulder. His back swelled as he took a breath. I breathed in too. The smell of chlorine and sweat filled my nose. He unbuttoned my shirt and put his lips on my chest just below my clavicle.

"But I want you to kiss me on the mouth," I said. "Can you do that?"

He didn't answer. His lips stayed where they were.

I didn't stop him, though. I let him keep going, even though I'd promised myself I wouldn't do this again, even though I'd thought I'd finally learned how to stand up to him, because what I'd said to Franklin last night was true. I wasn't good. I was just nice. And underneath the nice, I was an asshole, just like Tor. In spite of all the horrifying stuff I'd read in Franklin's notebook, in spite of the fact that he might've killed *two* of my best friends, in spite of everything, I felt a twist of guilt, like Franklin could see me betraying him with Tor at that very moment. I glanced over at the window, the one that looked out on my backyard, half-expecting to see him there gazing up at us.

I didn't. But I froze anyway. My whole body went cold, like I'd just taken a nosedive into a snowdrift. I lurched to my feet and stared outside.

At the gazebo.

Where Franklin and I had sat the night of Callie's murder.

"What's wrong?" Tor said.

Tor had seen us that night. Or at least he could have. Easily. Earlier that same day, he'd found out Callie knew about the steam tunnels, and it had made him crazy with rage. The way he'd looked at me, the way he'd slammed me against that door, I could've believed he'd do almost anything to protect his secret. And then . . . what if he'd seen Franklin visiting me in my backyard? What would he have done?

"Rem? Hello?"

My eyes went back to the Son of War box on his media stand. I'd never known he played the game before. If Tor played Son of War, maybe he'd discovered Son of War High on the Internet, just like Lydia had. Maybe he'd figured if something bad happened to Callie, people would find out about Franklin's escape eventually and blame it on him. Especially if Callie's murder in real life looked just like her murder in Son of War High.

"Hey, say something."

Hearing Tor come up behind me, I spun around, knocking over a couple swim trophies balanced on the sill. One of them crashed to the floor and the gold-colored plastic smashed.

"Jesus!"

I sidestepped away from him while he bent down to pick

up the pieces. He stood, both of his huge hands gripping jagged shards of plastic. His eyes, dark under his jutting brow, stayed locked on me. Just above that, a Band-Aid still covered his temple where he'd banged his head outside Lydia's house.

What if Tor hadn't gone to Lydia's to break up with her? What if he'd gone there to kill her too? Maybe he'd feared that she'd figured out his secret. But then he'd slipped off the trellis, and after that she'd left town, so he'd had to let that murder go.

Now I was next.

"What the hell's going on, Rem?"

Come on, say something. Make an excuse. Get the hell out of there. At first, though, I couldn't even remember how to form words, let alone think of something to say. He squinted at me again. Maybe trying to decide how much I knew. Whether I'd figured out the truth.

"I just don't think this is right, Tor." I buttoned my shirt with shaking fingers. "Lydia's one of my best friends, and one of yours too. I can't do this behind her back anymore." I grabbed my coat and blue scarf.

"She isn't even in town."

"I know, but that doesn't change how I feel. You need to talk to her first." I turned toward the door, walked straight into the chair, and tumbled to the floor.

"What the hell's with you?"

He tossed aside one of the trophy pieces and stretched out his hand to help me up. The other shard of the trophy—once a swimmer with outstretched arms, now splintered, knife-sharp, glinting gold—was still clasped in his opposite fist. I scooted backward, blundered to my feet without touching his hand, and wrenched open his bedroom door.

"Come on," he said, "don't go."

"My mom's home making dinner," I babbled. "She knows I'm here. I told her I'd only be gone a little while."

He padded after me down the steps to the front hall. "It didn't look like she was there a few minutes ago."

I shot a look back at him, my heart hammering. He still hadn't put down the trophy piece. "You were watching my house?"

"Not watching. I just glanced out the window and saw you pulling into your driveway. That's when I texted you."

Almost there. Almost safe. I grabbed the knob of the front door.

"Rem, why don't you—"

I swung the door open. A gust of wind howled into the room, scattering white flakes all over the hardwood floor.

"Christ, Rem!"

"I really have to go. I'll call you later, okay?"

I pulled the door shut behind me and sprinted across the front yard, throwing glances over my shoulder as I went. Tor was a shadow in the living room window, motionless, watching me run.

57

I didn't even pause to stomp the snow off my boots. I just ran in the front door and through the house, not caring about the slushy trail I left behind me, flicking on lights as I went, grabbing my car keys out of the bowl in the kitchen, hustling into the garage. The Saab's door released a sharp whine as I flung it open. I landed in the driver's seat and blundered the key into the ignition.

Then I stopped, breathing hard. The corner of Franklin's notebook peeked out from under the passenger seat, where I'd left it. I shot a glance around the garage, checking to make sure Tor hadn't somehow followed me in here, before snatching up the book. I opened it to the Son of War High section and flipped fast past the map of the school and the pages for Pete, Callie, and Lydia. I couldn't help it, I paused on the pages about me. My eyes skipped down the long diatribe Franklin had written. *He's a phony. Face it, he wouldn't lift a finger to save your life.*

I shook my head to stay focused and turned one more page.

Right away the right-hand side of the spread devoted to Tor drew my eye. Instead of scrawling a rant explaining why he'd wanted to eliminate his fifth target, Franklin had colored the entire page black. Neatly, systematically, with the same fine-point rollerball pen he'd used to write everything else. It must've taken a long time.

On the left-hand side, under *MISSION DETAILS*, Franklin had put, *Take Tor down to the steam tunnels.*

My breath snared in my throat.

Make Tor say, "When you die, no one will give a shit, and no one will remember you." Shoot him in the head.

I set the book on my lap, propped my forehead against the cold metal steering wheel, and stared at the page. What had Tor done with him down there? The same thing he'd done with me?

No. Something worse. Whatever had gone on, Franklin hadn't wanted it to happen. It had left him so full of rage he couldn't even put it into words.

A soft creak made me jump in my seat. I searched the garage through the windshield and side windows, my pulse picking up speed. The door to the house stood open, rocking a little on its hinges. But I'd closed it behind me when I'd come in, hadn't I?

I banged down the Saab's old-fashioned door lock. I needed to get out of here. Find someplace safe. Talk to Mom and talk to the police, finally. I reached up to click the garage door remote clipped to the visor.

A loud whine filled the garage. Then a few seconds of clanging.

Then silence. The door stayed shut. The opener had broken down again. Last time this had happened, we'd had to open and close the door manually until we'd found a repair person.

I sat in the Saab a second, my hands on the steering wheel, my back clammy with sweat. I cast my eyes around the garage one more time. Nothing. I pulled the lock back up and eased the door open a crack. Stopped. Listened.

In one rush, I shouldered the door the rest of the way open, swung out my legs, and sprinted toward the garage door. I'd almost made it when a voice said, "Why are you running, Rem?"

58

I let out a yell. My car keys clattered to the floor. I whipped my head around and caught a flash of traffic-cone orange in a corner.

A hoodie.

Inside the hood, a pair of glasses.

Franklin stepped forward. "Sorry. I keep scaring you. I promise I'm not doing it on purpose."

I grabbed his shoulders—because I was happy to see him, and because I thought I might keel over if I didn't—and panted, "You want to stop scaring me? Try ringing the goddamn doorbell once in a while. Jesus, I thought you were Tor."

"Why Tor?" His voice sounded funny. He'd stiffened when I'd taken his shoulders in my hands. It took me a second to remember he probably thought I'd already reported him and Nil to the police. After the way I'd reamed him over the phone, I couldn't blame him for being standoffish.

"Because he's the one who killed Callie," I said. "I'm sure of it. Just a few minutes ago I was up in his room, and I realized he had a clear view of the gazebo in my backyard, and the rest just clicked into place."

Everything else I'd figured out tumbled from my mouth in a breathless rush. Franklin listened without saying a word, just studying the drain in the middle of the garage's concrete floor, his nostrils expanding and contracting as he breathed.

"So right away I left his place and raced over here. I was afraid he might come after me. That's why I was acting like a maniac just now. He could probably see I'd figured things out. We're probably in danger. You don't have a gun, do you?"

His forehead scrunched. "Why would I have a gun?"

"I don't know. Look, I'm sorry for what I said to you before, Franklin. Tor's a monster. I see that now. He killed Callie. Tried to kill Lydia. Probably wants to kill me. And I know he did something horrible to you too. I read your notebook. I know he took you down to the steam tunnels."

Franklin flinched. His hands squeezed into fists.

"It's okay," I said, "you don't have to tell me about it. It just makes me so mad to think I didn't realize what he was before this." I noticed my own hands had balled themselves up too. I uncurled my fingers and shook them out. "The good news is we can go to the police now. We don't have to lie anymore."

"Do you have proof it was him?"

"Not yet, but I'm sure if we tell the police what we know, they'll find something."

"That won't be good enough."

A faint banging came from outside. Something blowing

in the storm probably, but the noise made me antsy anyway. I imagined Tor pounding on the front door, trying to get into the house. "Look, we can talk about it on the way. Right now we have to get out of here. I still think Tor might try something."

I started pulling Franklin toward the car, but he didn't budge. "What were you doing in Tor's room just now?"

I stopped. The wind outside screamed.

"The same thing you do with him down in the steam tunnels?" Franklin asked. "Because it sounded like when he takes *you* down there, you like it."

I took a step back and shoved my hands into my coat pockets. "He texted me when I got home. He was upset about Callie. At least that was what he said. He asked me to go over there and keep him company."

"And you didn't mess around?"

Hot blood pulsed behind my cheeks and forehead. "Not exactly."

Franklin gnawed his lower lip. "The way you kissed me last night, I thought . . ." He gave his head a sharp shake and lunged forward to grab my car keys from where I'd dropped them on the floor, swiping his arm angrily. He must've misjudged the distance, because instead of grabbing them he knocked them to the side. They skated across the floor. He chased after them. Stopped. Dropped to his hands and knees.

"What happened?" I said.

"They fell down the drain."

"But we need them. We need to get out of here."

He studied the drain a minute before sitting back on his heels and shaking his head. "They're gone."

My stomach twisted itself inside out. I could've sworn I'd just heard more banging outside. "Look, my mom has a spare key for when she needs to move my car, but I think it's in her office, and she keeps that door locked. Maybe you could pick the lock, though. I mean, you're good at that kind of stuff, right? Or else we could just bash the door down. With everything that's happening, I bet she'd under—"

"Can you just tell me something, Rem?" He hadn't risen from his spot on the floor next to the drain. "How do you feel about me?"

I fiddled with the partly unraveled end of my long blue scarf. "That's a complicated question, Franklin. Way too complicated to answer right now, when someone's probably trying to kill us."

"No, it's not. It's really simple. Do you care about me?"

"Of course I do, Franklin."

"What about if I'd never had the procedure? Would you still care about me then?"

"Now that's definitely too complicated—"

"Tell me."

I took a careful breath. "I guess I probably wouldn't. At least not the way I do now."

He nodded.

"I'm sorry if that's not what you wanted to hear, but I don't want to lie to you. I don't want to just be Mr. Nice Guy. I want to be honest, especially with you."

He ran his palm over his shaved head. His fingers probed the Band-Aid at the back of his skull.

"Look," I said, "I'm sorry I went to Tor's tonight. And I'm sorry for what I said on the phone too. I was confused. This is a confusing situation. The important thing is I've figured out who killed Callie. I know how to clear you. Can't we forget all the other stuff and move on?"

His fingers dropped away from the hole in his head. He nodded. "You're right." He stood and turned to face me. His eyes looked as dull as they had during our first session at the Mother Ship. "Show me where your mom's office is, and get me a flash-light and a nail file. I can get the door open for you."

59

Franklin crouched next to Mom's office door, a penlight between his teeth, and went to work. A few minutes later, the door swung open.

"I'll look for the keys," I told him. "Can you check the house? Make sure all the doors are locked? And the windows, too. We shouldn't forget about those. You taught me that."

He didn't say anything, just gave a silent nod and moved off. I bit my lip as I watched him head toward the front door. He hadn't spoken a word since the garage. It was like his face had slammed shut again.

I went into Mom's office and switched on her lamp, figuring I'd start by searching through her desk drawers. I didn't make it that far, though. My eye had already caught on a row of empty wine bottles lined up against the wall on her desk. In front of them lay a hand-addressed envelope. According to the return address, it had come from Sam Durham, the soldier who'd visited the house the other day. I thought again of what Nil had said about a connection between Mom's work and the US military.

Did this have something to do with that? But this letter didn't have the appearance of official correspondence. It looked personal. And Sam had said he was a civilian now, hadn't he? Judging from the postmark, he'd sent the letter the day after his visit.

I slid the single folded sheet of paper from the envelope, dropped into Mom's office chair, and read.

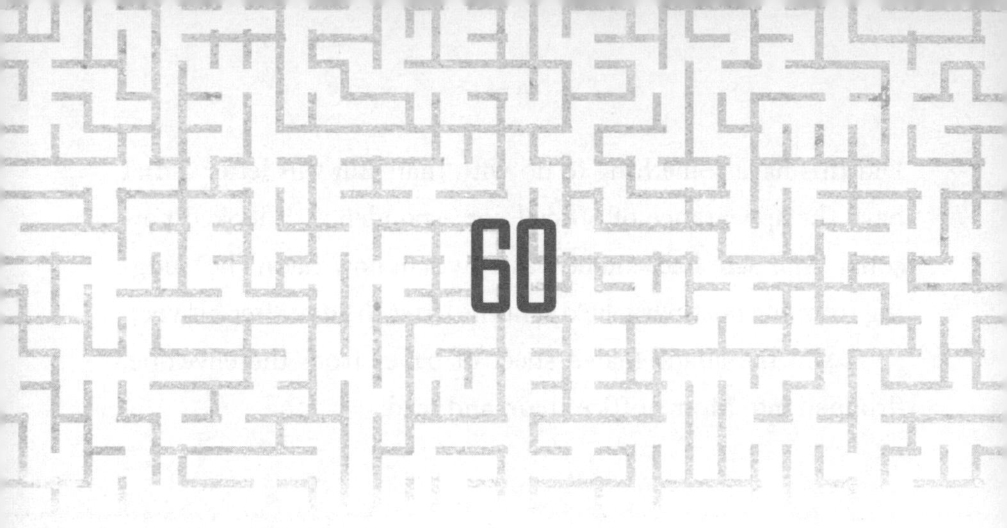

60

Dear Dr. Braithwaite,

I hope you don't mind me writing you this letter. I figured an e-mail sent to your work address, which is the only one I have, might too easily be seen by the wrong person, and I mean this message for you alone.

I realize I already stated my case to you in person a few days ago, but that was before the death of that poor girl, Franklin Kettle's classmate. I honestly don't know if Franklin had anything to do with that. Her killer could just be a copycat, but as I write this, the police are saying they aren't ruling out any possibilities.

Was it him, Dr. Braithwaite? Was that girl's death somehow related to your project? I'd like to think it wasn't, but I'm afraid that might not be the case.

You're a good person. I could tell when I met you at Ethan's funeral, and I had the same feeling about you after talking with you yesterday. But I still disagree with what you're doing. I believe good people are capable of doing bad things. If I've learned nothing else from my time in Afghanistan, I've learned that.

I think I understand your reasons, though. You imagine this procedure might prevent deaths like your son's. You imagine if you could've switched your son's conscience off the way you switched Franklin's on, maybe he would've fired his weapon and he'd still be alive. But let me tell you, I did fire my weapon, I did kill that child, and whatever I am now, I'm not sure you'd call it alive.

The child was crying. Did I mention that? Maybe that was what stopped Ethan. No one in that room wanted to be a killer, but only Ethan chose not to fire his weapon. And your project seeks to suppress the part of the brain that kept your son from shooting a weeping child? I'm sorry, but I can't believe that's right.

When I saw you, I promised I wouldn't say anything publicly about the true nature of your work. I'd still like to honor that promise, but I'm finding it harder and harder to do so. I beg you, Dr. Braithwaite, stop what you're doing. Don't make Franklin your guinea pig. Stop turning his conscience on and off like a light switch. It's wrong. It's cruel. It's dangerous.

Yours truly,
Sam Durham

61

I grabbed my phone and dialed Mom, my heart thudding. "Answer," I chanted under my breath. "Answer. Answer. Answer." I shook off my winter coat while I waited. Sweat drenched my armpits and slid down my back. I listened for sounds of Franklin moving around but couldn't hear any. Just the roaring of the storm. No banging, either. Whatever had caused that noise earlier had gone silent just before we'd entered the house.

Mom finally picked up. "This isn't a good time, Rem, I'm right in the middle of—"

"You lied to me *again*." The rage in my voice as I growled the words startled even me. "I just read Sam Durham's letter. What the hell does he mean when he says you're turning Franklin's conscience on and off like a light switch?"

"Calm down, Rem. Listen to me. There are parts of the project that are classified. Sam Durham isn't supposed to know about them either." She'd shifted into press conference mode again and was speaking in smooth, precise sentences. "He has an indiscreet friend at DARPA, one of his buddies from the unit.

I'm sorry, I know this is hard to hear, but I can't discuss the confidential aspects of our work, even with—"

"Bullshit, Mom. Tell me. Is it true you're exploring military applications for your capsule? Figuring out how to make sociopathic supersoldiers or something?"

She didn't answer right away. I imagined her in her office jabbing her thumb with her fingernail. "Those aren't the words I'd use. We're working on technology that can ease soldiers' moral inhibitions in certain combat situations."

"And how's Franklin involved?" I demanded.

"Rem, let's talk about this when I get—"

"No, Mom. It has to be now."

The banging noise outside had started up again, like an echo of the banging inside my own chest.

"I think you're blowing this out of proportion," Mom said. "The capsule we installed in Franklin's brain emits pulses of energy that stimulate his empathy centers, like I explained to you the other day. But we can also modulate the pulses so they inhibit his ability to feel empathy instead, the same way the nanodrones did."

"And make him like he was when he killed Pete." My fingers tightened around the letter, crumpling it. I wanted to yell and scream at the top of my lungs. I wanted to reach through the phone and shake Mom and demand to know how she could keep lying to me, her own son, this way. But right now I needed to concentrate. I took a breath to help steady my voice. "So have you tried inhibiting his empathy yet?"

"We're just starting that phase of testing."

"What about on the night of Callie's murder? Did you turn him back into a sociopath then?"

"No, Rem. That couldn't have been him. Dr. Hult verified he was inside the lab all night."

I swallowed through a dry throat. The banging continued. I tried to listen for Franklin again, but wherever he'd gone, he still wasn't making any noise. I hunched over Mom's desk and dropped my voice. "No, he wasn't. He figured out how to hack the lab's security and escape."

"That can't be—"

"I saw him, Mom. He came to our house."

She released a slow exhale. "Dear God. And you didn't say anything?"

"No, I didn't."

"But why—"

"Are you sure the capsule's setting couldn't have gotten switched that night?"

"I don't know." I could hear her struggling to keep her voice under control, the same way I was. The press conference smoothness had fallen away. "The lab's computer system monitors and controls the capsule when it's within range of the Wi-Fi network. Dr. Hult used the system to search for irregularities the morning after Callie's death. He didn't find anything. But if Franklin figured out how to hack our system . . ."

"You think he might've changed the setting himself?"

"It's possible. Oh God, could he have?"

I crushed the letter some more. Why would he do that? He'd *wanted* to feel empathy. He'd said so himself. Unless that had been a lie. I'd seen how much suffering his newly acquired remorse had caused him. Had it finally become too much for him to take? That still didn't make sense, though. The argument he'd made himself still held: why would he have come to visit me just before the murder? The Franklin I'd seen in the gazebo, the one who'd played me that music and argued with me about tattoos and given me that unexpectedly mind-blowing kiss—he hadn't been someone planning to kill.

"And that's the only way to control the capsule?" I said. "Just the computer system?"

"No. There's one other way. Dr. Hult also installed a fail-safe inside the capsule itself in case our computer system ever went down. The capsule contains a microphone and voice recognition software. It's programmed to switch between modes when it hears one of two phrases."

"And what are they?"

"For God's sake, Rem," she said, losing it now, "why didn't you tell me Franklin got out of the lab?"

"Mom, the phrases!"

I shot a glance over my shoulder, hoping Franklin hadn't heard.

When Mom spoke again, my pounding heart came to a full stop. "You remember that Emily Dickinson poem? Ethan's favorite?"

62

At that moment Mom was standing at the floor-to-ceiling window in her office and staring at the snow barraging the glass as she held her phone to her ear. Just as I'd imagined, the nail of her left index finger jabbed the numb pad of her thumb, searching for some sensation.

"The first verse makes the capsule inhibit Franklin's empathy centers," she said. "The last one stimulates them."

"And how do you have the capsule set now? You said you'd just started the next phase of testing. What does that mean?"

"We changed the setting on the capsule to inhibit his empathy for the first time a few hours ago. We thought we'd give his brain a chance to adjust while he sleeps. We plan to start testing tomorrow." She shook her head at the window like I was standing on the other side, out in the storm. "I know what you're probably thinking of me, Rem. But I want you to know I did this for Ethan. You can understand that, can't you?" She turned away from the glass. "Now tell me, has Franklin escaped any other times?"

I didn't answer. She looked at the phone screen to check the connection.

"Rem? Are you there?"

Mom's eyes went wide. She lunged for the door and flung it open.

"Gertie?"

The lab tech looked up and yanked out an earbud blaring something dissonant and experimental sounding. The rest of the main lab stood empty. Everyone else had gone home.

"When was the last time you checked on Franklin?" Mom said.

"A few minutes ago. Why?"

"Check now."

"Something wrong?"

"Goddamnit, Gertie, just do it."

Gertie tapped on her keyboard and pulled up an image of Franklin's room on her screen. Mom stood behind her with her arms crossed over her chest. "Fast asleep," Gertie said.

On the screen Franklin lay on his side, his face visible, his eyes closed.

Mom pressed her lips tight together while she studied the image. "Let's go have a look."

She took the elevator down one floor, charged out through the whooshing doors, and banged down the corridor in her high heels. Gertie hurried after, her asymmetrically cut hair bouncing as she went. Mom didn't offer any explanations on the way. She was too busy trying to call me back on her phone.

"Is he in there?" She fired the question at the guard outside Franklin's room.

He looked confused. "Of course he is."

"Have you taken any breaks? Even for a minute?"

"Just once, to visit the restroom."

Mom elbowed him away from the door and peered through the little window. A shape lay on the bed beneath a mound of white covers. Gertie squinted over her shoulder. "There he is, just like on the—"

"No. On the monitor he was facing this way. He didn't have the covers over his head."

She pulled down her badge and touched it to the reader.

"Are you sure you want to wake him?"

She yanked open the door and flicked the light switch. Bright light poured down, turning the room white. The shape under the covers didn't move. Gertie and the guard crowded into the room after Mom and stood near the wall, mute, as she tore back the sheets. A few pillows lay underneath. No Franklin.

"What the—?" Gertie whispered. But she wasn't looking at the bed. Mom followed her gaze to the Plexiglas cage on the nightstand.

That was empty too.

Mom smoothed her helmet of hair and took a careful breath. Without another word, she left the room and walked all the way to the end of the corridor, where another floor-to-ceiling window looked out on the blizzard. The snow hurled itself at the pane so hard you'd almost believe the tiny collisions might eventually shatter the glass. Mom pressed both her palms against the window, tilted back her head, and let out a scream. It was every bit as loud as the one she'd released when she'd found out Ethan had gotten shot. Then she sagged against the glass, like the cry had drained her of all her strength.

"Not him too," she whispered. "Please, don't take him too."

63

I'd heard Mom tell me she'd changed the setting on Franklin's capsule, but nothing after that. The phone had disappeared from my ear. I spun around in Mom's chair to find a figure in a long black coat and a Son of War mask looming in front of me.

Inside my body everything seemed to stop working. My lungs collapsed. My heart gave up its pumping. My muscles turned to mush. Somehow I managed to push myself back until my chair had jammed itself against the desk. The masked figure tossed my phone to the floor. Part of me still wondered—*was* this Franklin? Or Tor? Or someone else even? But then he opened his coat, and I caught a glimpse of bright orange. From an inside pocket he pulled out his notebook.

"What are you doing?"

"Nil told me she has the high score in Son of War High." Franklin's voice, muffled by the mask, sounded just as hollow and dead as it had on the day of the Big Bang. "But even so, she's only ever managed to kill three of you. It's *my* game. I want to do better. I should have the high score."

"Franklin, that's—"

"Let's see how I'm doing so far, shall we?"

He spun my chair around and banged the book on the desk in front of me. He flipped through it until he found the pages devoted to Pete. Leaving the notebook open on the desk, he pulled two more items from his coat: a mouse and a Beretta M9. The mouse writhed as he pinned it over the little picture of Pete's face. He brought the barrel of the Beretta right up to the mouse's head.

"Bang!"

I jumped. He'd rammed the gun into the little skull, splattering blood and brains all over Pete's smiling face. He tossed the mouse away, turned the page, and took out another mouse. He pinned it over Callie's photo.

"Bang!"

I wanted to look away, but I couldn't. He turned to Lydia's spread. Held a third mouse up to her headshot. Positioned the barrel.

This time, he opened his fingers, and the mouse scurried away, jumping off the desk and disappearing behind a filing cabinet.

Franklin turned me around again. He took out his last two mice and held them up in his fist. They squirmed and squeaked and blinked their black beadlike eyes. "I need you two for the high score." He stuffed the mice away again and patted the pocket. "Anyway, everything I wrote in that notebook is still true. Especially the stuff about you. Tonight proves it. You don't give a shit about me."

"That's not true," I said, the words more breath than voice. "Please, Franklin, just put away the gun. The capsule's making you act this way. It's not really you."

"You're wrong, Rem. When I was whining and feeling remorseful and wanting you to like me, *that* was because of the capsule." He slammed the notebook shut, mouse guts and all, and stuffed it away in another of his bulky coat's pockets. "I know they've been messing with it. Turning it on and off. You think I don't know that?"

"Not just turning it on and off. They've been switching it between two different settings. Franklin, listen to me. A year ago, when you first went to the lab—"

"Quiet!"

He shook the Beretta in my face. I jerked away from him and slipped from the chair onto the floor. My head banged against the desk.

"I'm tired of you twisting things around with all your talk," Franklin said. "It doesn't matter. When this is all over, everyone's going to find out what your mom and the rest of them have been doing to me, and I'll have my revenge on them too."

I clutched the back of my head where I'd banged it and tried to pull my brain into focus. The poem. I needed to recite the poem. The first verse I knew. It was the one I'd included in my Tattoo Atlas picture, the one I'd recited for Franklin the other night. But what about the last? The one that would turn him back into the Franklin who could feel empathy?

"'The brain is just the weight of God,'" I said. "'For, lift them, pound for pound,' . . ." I licked my lips. "'For, lift them, pound for pound,' . . ."

Franklin's mask cocked to the side, like he thought I'd lost it. From another pocket he pulled a roll of duct tape. He made a circular movement with the barrel of his gun. "Roll over on your belly."

I stared at the tape, my breath fast and uneven. He wanted to tie me up. So he didn't plan to kill me right away. He wanted to take me to school, like he had Callie. *That means you still have time.* I tried to concentrate on that. *Just do what he says. You still have time.*

He motioned with the barrel again. "Hurry up."

I obeyed.

"'The brain is just the weight of GAAAH—'"

Franklin drove his knee into my back, stopping my words short and driving the breath out of my chest. He yanked my hands behind me and wound the tape around my wrists.

"'The brain is just the weight of God, For, lift them, pound for pound,' . . ."

Now he rolled me onto my back. He crouched above me, another piece of tape ready in his hands. He must've stowed the gun in his pocket, but with my wrists bound, I couldn't do a thing except thrash around on the floor. Sweat slid down my forehead and stung my eyes. The scraping noise of my breath filled my ears. The mask's mirrored goggles flashed above me, impassive.

The last part of the poem came back to me in a torrent.

"'And they will differ, if they do, As syll—'"

He smacked the tape hard over my mouth.

64

Franklin grabbed me by my shirt, hauled me to my feet, and marched me out to the main living area. With one hand he kept a grip on my taped-together wrists. With the other he drove the barrel of the Beretta into my back.

"Sit down on the floor with your back against the wall," he said, probably following the military protocol he'd learned from Son of War. He wrenched open the sliding glass door leading to the backyard. Cold wind gusted into the room. Outside, the snow didn't swirl anymore. Now it drove past in horizontal sheets. On the back porch, up against the railing, a seated figure cloaked in snow hunched and trembled.

Franklin delivered a kick to the figure's midsection. It snapped to life, tossing and twisting and wrestling against itself, banging against the porch. That was the noise I'd heard earlier. The snow blanketing the figure went flying, revealing hulking shoulders, a broad bare chest, wispy hair now crusted with ice and sticking out in all directions. Tor had his hands tied behind his back, like me, and bound to one of the porch posts. Duct tape covered his mouth. He still only wore that grubby pair of gym shorts. Not even anything on his feet. His usual exhibitionistic, weather-blind dressing habits taken to a nightmarish extreme.

"Settle down or I'll blow your head off," Franklin muttered.

Tor's body stopped its flailing but continued to shake. Franklin kept the gun on him with one hand while with the other he took out a knife and cut the duct tape fastening his wrists to the post.

"Get up. Go inside. Stand next to Rem." To me he said, "Stand up."

Tor staggered across the carpet, tracking snow. His bare feet had turned rigid and bluish-white, the toes frozen in contorted positions.

Franklin slid the door shut and leveled the gun at us both. "I bet you can guess where we're going." He waved the Beretta, motioning us toward the garage. We filed through the door he opened for us. He flicked on the light and from another of his coat pockets produced the keys to the Saab. He must've palmed them earlier when he'd claimed they'd fallen down the drain. Unlocking the rear, he said, "Get in."

It took some struggling for both of us to cram ourselves into the way back with our hands tied behind us. The small backward-facing bench seat was narrow because of the wheel wells on either side, so Tor and I ended up crushed against each other. Tor's shivering had diminished but hadn't stopped. Or maybe he was just shaking from fear.

Franklin used more duct tape to fasten our ankles to metal loops attached to the floor. He didn't hurry. Instead he moved with precision, still acting out the part of the highly trained Son of War soldier. Maybe that explained why he had the mask on too. Maybe his game required it.

He grabbed a gray wool blanket from a shelf and tossed it over us. Its stale smell filled my nostrils. Dim light filtered through the weave of the wool.

"Behave yourselves."

The rear hatch slammed shut.

Some time passed while Franklin hauled up the garage door. Under the blanket, Tor's fast, noisy breathing and my own turned the air between us humid. I caught the tang of his chlorine-and-sweat smell over the stale stink of the blanket. Our eyes met for a second. What a lunatic I'd been, over the last week and especially the last twenty-four hours, bouncing from theory to theory, making accusations left and right, when the truth was the killer had always been the most obvious suspect of all. And Nil and Tor were innocent.

Although I still wondered what had gone on between Tor and Franklin down in the steam tunnels. Something Franklin had said during our first session together came back to me: *Maybe there* is *no innocent, really.*

Maybe that went for all of us.

The Saab roared underneath us. It eased backward. I could feel the storm swallowing us up little by little. The wind rocked us from side to side. The snow hit the windows like millions of tiny BBs. The car dipped as it rolled from the driveway onto Boreal Street and paused as Franklin changed gears.

I remembered the police cruiser parked on the side of the road. How much time had passed since I'd talked to Mom on the phone? Five minutes? More? By now Mom must've gone to check Franklin's room and found him missing. She'd call the police, knowing I'd be in danger. They'd send a bunch of cruisers and get in touch with the cop guarding our street. He'd see my car pulling out of the garage in the middle of a violent storm and know something was up. He'd stop Franklin, maybe a shootout would follow, in which hopefully no one would die. And it would all be over.

Only that didn't happen.

The Saab pulled forward. Outside I couldn't hear any sirens. Only the howling of the blizzard. Next to me Tor writhed back and forth until the blanket slipped off his head and mine, just in time for us to see the police cruiser parked at the side of the street, with the cop in the driver's seat fast asleep.

65

I thought Franklin might stop the car to pull the blanket over our heads again, but he didn't bother. No one else had ventured out in the storm. We had the roadway to ourselves. I watched the pavement roll away behind us and get swallowed up by the darkness and the driving snow. Sitting here in the rear of the wagon made me think of the picture I'd drawn in my Tattoo Atlas of Pete in the way back with the bullet hole in his head. *Don't forget I'm back here.*

Up front, Franklin hunched over the wheel, the black coat adding bulk to his shoulders, its hood pulled low over his face to conceal the mask. He didn't say a word during the trip.

We pulled into a spot in one of Duluth Central's faculty parking lots. The police must've had a car here too, but Franklin had probably done reconnaissance and knew where to go to stay clear of the cops. Anyway, in this storm, we probably could've passed within ten feet of a police cruiser without the cop inside seeing a thing.

Franklin appeared at the back of the Saab, his long coat

whipping in the wind. The hatch groaned open. He pulled his gun out of one pocket and the knife out of the other and cut our ankles free. Then he stepped back while we struggled out through the hatch. The cold bit into my skin in a thousand different places. I didn't have my coat on, just a button-down and jeans, but at least I had more protection than Tor, who'd already started convulsing again.

Tor and I swam through the wind toward the back of the school, with Franklin behind us holding his gun and barking commands over the roar of the storm. He guided us to the stairway that led down to the steam tunnels. Snow had flooded the stairwell, but Franklin jabbed us in the back with the Beretta and waved us forward. We waded down the steps. By the time we reached the bottom, the snow came up to our waists. An especially strong gust of wind swept more snow over us, and chunks of it landed on my head and shoulders. It made me think of someone shoveling dirt into a grave.

Franklin leaned past us and, with a single practiced movement, wrenched the padlock open. We spilled inside and shuttled down the second flight of stairs, a single swaying bulb lighting the way. With my hands tied behind my back and snow making my sneakers slick and terror making my body weak and loose, I had to concentrate hard to avoid slipping.

We reached the hot, dark tunnels. Franklin continued marching us in front of him and barking directions at each intersection. I could tell he knew his way around down here better than either of us. After three turns, I was lost. We made slow progress, Tor and I never getting too far ahead. We couldn't: only Franklin had his hands free to reach up and turn on lightbulbs, so he had us walking into blackness.

"I should thank you for showing me these tunnels, Tor," he said. "Best hiding place ever. I had an extra mask and guns and ammunition and this coat squirreled away down here, just in case I needed them. I never expected I'd be coming back for them a year later. It pays to be prepared, I guess."

Here and there we passed narrow wood staircases leading up into the school. Franklin stopped us at one of them and waved us up with his Beretta. Once we all reached the basement, he had us wait there while he climbed a second flight and unlocked the door at the top. He came back down.

"Go up."

I recognized the odor before I even reached the top of the stairs. Sweat and chlorine. A stronger, more sour version of Tor's smell. All of a sudden my forehead felt hot and cold at the same time. With my mouth taped up, I couldn't seem to pull enough air in through my nostrils anymore. The duct tape sucked against my mouth as I struggled to breathe.

We stumbled into the boys' locker room. The only light filtered in through small rippled-glass windows near the top of one wall. A few used towels draped over benches and hung from open locker doors.

My breathing sped up even more. Again I forced myself to focus. In a second, Franklin would march me over to that spot in the corner, rip off the duct tape, and tell me to say the words

I'd said two years ago, the words he'd written down in the book. *Keep your eyes to yourself, pervert.*

But when the moment came, I wouldn't say that sentence from the journal. I'd recite the last verse of the poem instead. I just had to get out the words before he pulled the trigger. I remembered them now. The lines seemed to glow inside my head.

Would the change in his brain happen fast enough to save me, though? Would the magic words transform him just like that? I had no idea, but at least there was hope.

Franklin directed Tor to wait off to the side. To me he said, "Go stand over there." He prodded me with the gun, but my legs barely had the strength to carry me forward. I felt like I was still wading through snow. Once I reached the far corner, Franklin turned me around and grabbed a corner of the duct tape covering my mouth. The goggles of his mask reflected back to me my heaving shoulders and pale face and wide eyes. The final stanza of the poem was there, on my taped-up lips, ready to spill out.

But he didn't pull.

"No." He shook his head. "You don't get to talk. I don't care if I lose a few points. I don't want to hear your voice anymore."

He backed up a few steps and raised the Beretta. My vision blurred. It took me a second to realize I'd started crying. He hadn't pulled off the tape, but I tried to say something anyway, maybe the poem or maybe something else, I didn't even know, but it came out a formless moan. His finger tightened on the trigger. Next to me a locker lolled open like an empty coffin. *This is it*, I kept thinking. *This is it. This is it.* Me dying here, in this room, at Franklin's hand. It didn't feel real, but at the same time, it felt absolutely inevitable. I closed my eyes, pressing out tears.

I didn't hear a gunshot. I heard a crash. When my eyes snapped open again, the mask and gun had disappeared. Tor had barreled into Franklin, and the two had rammed into the lockers. The gun skated across the concrete. They slid to the floor and wrestled there, their bodies a writhing mass.

Tor was a lot bigger than Franklin, but he still had his hands tied behind his back, just like I did. Franklin punched him with his fists, jabbed him with his elbows, even knocked his head, metal mask and all, against Tor's. The blow stunned Tor, but only for a second. He kicked Franklin hard in the belly. A strangled grunt came from inside the mask. Franklin clambered away from Tor, who struggled to his feet and lunged after him like he wanted to keep on kicking. Rolling onto his back, Franklin reached into his coat for something.

A second Beretta.

The room exploded with noise and light. In the darkness that followed, I could just make out black spots of blood dotting the green lockers behind Tor.

He staggered backward and banged against the lockers, his big shoulders slumped. I couldn't tell where the bullet had hit him. Franklin, on his back ten feet away, couldn't seem to tell either. He hesitated, the gun sagging a little, like he wanted to see what Tor would do.

Tor did this: he released an animal roar through the duct tape covering his mouth and lunged forward again. His eyes bugged with rage. He vaulted over one of the benches bolted to the floor. Another gunshot slammed through the room. Tor spun around a full turn but stayed standing.

By then, though, I'd had time to remember I was a human being with legs and a brain and the ability to do something. Before Franklin had a chance to pull the trigger a third time, before Tor had a chance to make a third suicide charge, I rushed forward, shoving into Tor, pushing him behind a freestanding bank of lockers, out of range of Franklin and his guns. Once we were in the clear, I kept right on sprinting for the exit, hoping Tor had the strength to follow me. It sounded like he did. We raced toward the door that led to the playing fields and freedom.

And stopped.

If we'd had our hands free, getting out would've been a simple matter of turning the lock and twisting the knob. But we could do neither of those things. And behind us, Franklin had just staggered around the bank of lockers with a gun in each hand.

Not far away, the door that led to the basement stood open, the bulb over the landing still lighting the way down. Tor and I scrambled toward it. Franklin let off one more gunshot. The two of us sailed through the narrow doorway, Tor's foot hooked on something, and together we tumbled down the stairs.

66

As much as it would've hurt to fall down those stairs under normal circumstances, it hurt ten times more doing it with our hands tied behind our backs. No hands to slow down our fall. No hands to protect our heads. The concrete steps kept rearing up to punch us over and over, and there was nothing we could do about it. By the time we reached the basement, we'd built up so much momentum we catapulted directly onto the narrower wood staircase leading to the steam tunnels and kept on falling.

We landed in a heap at the foot of the steps. Every inch of my body hurt. My shoulder screamed like I'd broken it, or maybe popped my arm bone out of its socket. A sharp shard of tooth floated inside my mouth, but with my lips taped shut I couldn't spit it out. The still-lit electric bulb above our heads swayed, making the shadows slant this way and that. Some scuffling sounds came from two flights above us.

Below me, Tor didn't move.

At first I thought maybe the fall or the gunshots or both

had finished him, but then his chest expanded, and from his taped-up mouth came a weak moan.

The noises above grew louder. I glimpsed a shadow moving around all the way at the top of the second flight of stairs. I made a sound, sort of an urgent groan, hoping it would rouse Tor, but he didn't respond.

I rolled off him. Ignoring the pain, I pressed my back against the concrete wall and, shoving my feet into the floor, slid myself to a standing position. Tor still hadn't budged. In the locker room doorway, Franklin appeared, the Berettas in his hands. He looked weak from Tor's kick, though, and propped his shoulder against the doorframe as if unable to stand on his own.

I gave Tor a push with my sneaker and made another noise.

He rolled onto his back, but his eyes stayed closed. Blood smeared his bare chest and engulfed the pizza stains on his shorts. It looked like one of the bullets had torn through his thigh and the other had grazed his rib cage just below the armpit. So he might live, but only if he could get up in the next few seconds, before Franklin could pump a third bullet into him.

Franklin staggered down a couple steps. He raised the gun. I jerked back, behind the wall at the base of the staircase, out of his line of fire. From my protected position, I kicked Tor one more time. If he didn't get up, I'd have to leave him.

Tor's eyes shot open, wide and crazy like they'd been up in the locker room. He rolled away from the foot of the staircase just as Franklin let off another gunshot. The bullet plowed into the concrete floor. Tor put his back against the wall like I had and started to lever himself to his feet.

Franklin's shoes smacked against the stairs as he made his way down. His footfalls sounded unsteady. Even so, the second I saw Tor was upright, I turned and pelted back the way we'd come, following the path of illuminated lightbulbs. Tor fell in behind me. But when another *BANG* filled the tunnel, I realized keeping to the lit corridors only made us easy targets. I dodged to the side, down a pitch-black passageway. With one shoulder pressed against the wall for guidance, I barreled into the darkness.

Tor stayed close behind me. I could feel his hot breath on my neck. My pulse pounded in my temples so hard I thought the pressure might crack my skull. A few times my body glanced against a searing pipe, but the pain only made me go faster. The adrenaline coursing through my body almost made me feel like I was playing Son of War again.

But no, that wasn't it at all. Franklin was the one playing the game. I was just a target now. Pixels on a screen.

I kept going, making turns at random. The darkness was absolute, like someone had painted everything velvet black. I tripped on the uneven concrete and staggered whenever we reached a corner. Tor's sluggish footfalls sounded behind me. I strained to hear Franklin, but aside from my own grunts and footsteps and Tor's, I couldn't make out a thing.

After a while, the pain started to overpower the adrenaline. My shoulder throbbed. My legs felt heavy. I had no idea how long we'd been running or how far we'd gone. I'd hoped I'd stumble across a staircase that might lead us out of this maze, but so far I hadn't. And even if I did, how would we unlock the door at the top with our wrists tied? Tor's breathing behind me had grown more ragged. I wondered how much farther either of us could go on.

Not very far at all, it turned out. I smacked face-first into solid concrete a second later, and when I turned and traced my shoulder along that wall, I ran into another. After a few seconds of feeling around, I figured out we'd blundered into a dead end. I started leading Tor back the way we'd come.

Then I lurched to a halt.

I finally heard footsteps, headed this way.

I stumbled backward, elbowing Tor to move back too. We hit the dead end again. I slid down to sit on the floor, and as I did, my forearm scraped against a bolt sticking out of the wall. I sucked in my breath and then prayed Franklin hadn't heard.

His footsteps sounded closer now. Steadier too. He'd recovered from Tor's kick.

I leaned forward, lifted my hands behind me as much as I could, and dragged the duct tape binding my wrists across the protruding bolt's sharp, jagged end. Moving my arms hurt, but with all the pain pulsing through the rest of my body, I barely noticed. I kept at it. The sawing seemed to work. I could feel the duct tape give way little by little. I was making some noise, but with luck, the mask covering Franklin's ears would muffle the sound.

The footsteps continued, slow but rhythmic.

Now I had to stop. I hadn't freed myself yet, but I feared Franklin had come close enough to hear my movements, even through the mask. I got very still and hoped Tor would keep quiet too. Maybe if we pressed ourselves close to the wall, Franklin would feel the dead end but miss us and go back down the corridor.

The footsteps had almost reached us. I focused on keeping my body absolutely motionless even though every part of it screamed. On drawing in slow, quiet breaths even though my lungs were starving for air. I squeezed the sharp fragment of tooth between my tongue and the roof of my mouth. Next to me, Tor made no sound. With every step Franklin took I could hear the rubber soles of his sneakers make gritty contact with the rough concrete.

Then the sound stopped. Had he touched the wall above us? Did he realize he'd reached a dead end? I waited for the squeak of his sneakers heading back in the other direction, but that didn't come either. It was like he'd vanished entirely, though I knew he hadn't. My eyes strained to dig through the darkness, searching for the flash of his mask's goggles in the velvet black.

Nothing. And still no sound, either.

Until Franklin spoke, his mouth inches away from my ear. "Did you forget? My mask has infrared goggles, just like the one in Son of War does." Something cold pressed against my left temple. "I can see you, Rem. I could see you all along."

67

The sensation of the gun barrel against my skin disappeared. Franklin took a few steps back, his sneakers crunching against the floor. I squeezed the tooth in my mouth so tight it cut my tongue. I should've realized before. Of course he could see in the dark. Why else would he have followed us without bothering to turn on the lights?

With a pop, light flooded the corridor. I squinted against it. As I eased my eyes open again, Franklin appeared above me, a dark figure next to the swinging lightbulb, the mask still covering his face, the two guns still in his hands, one aimed at Tor, one aimed at me.

Next to me Tor made a weak grunt but didn't move. A puddle of blood had formed underneath his wounded thigh.

"I have to do this right," Franklin said. "Both of you get up and come back to the locker room with me, and I'll make sure it doesn't hurt."

At that moment something came over me. I exploded to my feet like the floor was electrified. Wrenched my wrists

apart, tearing away the partially sawed-through duct tape like tissue paper. Tackled Franklin, sending us both crashing to the floor. Wrestled one of the guns from his hand. It was like I'd just turned into Jim Colby, with one of the world's top-ranked players at the controls. My body thrummed. My eyes bugged the same way Tor's had up in the locker room. I could see them mirrored in the mask's trapezoid-shaped goggles.

I didn't fire the gun, though. Instead I tore away the tape covering my mouth and pinned Franklin's shoulders to the concrete floor.

"'The brain is just the weight of God, For, lift them, pound for pound, And they will differ, if they do, As syllable from sound.'"

I waited, breathing hard, staring into the mirrored lenses, searching for some sign of what was happening behind them. I couldn't find one. There was only the heaving of Franklin's chest and the muffled, raspy sound of his panting.

Then from inside Franklin's mask came a roar. He twisted to the side and bucked me off him. My head and shoulders slammed against the wall behind me. I still managed to keep my grip on the gun, though. Scrambling to my feet, I wheeled the barrel around to point it at Franklin.

But Franklin had pushed himself up too. The two of us stood there, each with a Beretta aimed at the other. Here it was, finally: my chance to do what my brother couldn't. *Like this, Ethan. Like this. Like this.*

Except how could I know which Franklin I'd be killing? That was what stopped me. Would it be the Franklin who'd killed

two of my best friends? The one I'd spent the last year hating? The one who haunted my nightmares? Or the one I'd kissed? He hadn't put down his gun, but he hadn't fired, either. The mask continued to give away nothing.

I should pull the trigger. I knew that. If I fired right now, no one would blame me.

"Franklin?"

He didn't answer. He held his gun with a steady grip.

I tried to swallow, but my throat felt like sandpaper. "Franklin, we don't have to do this." I put up my hands, pointing the Beretta at the ceiling. "I'm not going to do this."

I eased the gun down and set it on the floor.

The Beretta in his hand still didn't budge.

"You should know something," I said. "A year ago my mom injected experimental nanodrones into your brain. She thought they'd just monitor your brain activity, but they actually disrupted it. *They* made you shoot Pete, Franklin. It wasn't really you. And now the capsule's been messing with your brain again. Inhibiting your empathy, the same way the nanodrones did. But I just switched it back. At least I hope I did. See, that poem I recited, it's a fail-safe. There's a mike built into the capsule. If someone speaks the first stanza of the poem, like I did by accident the other night when we were in the gazebo, the capsule switches over to interfering with the empathy centers in your brain. If someone speaks the last stanza, the one you just heard, the capsule goes back to stimulating your empathy centers."

I stopped talking and waited for him to say something. Tor

panted softly, waiting too. I shifted the piece of tooth to the inside of my cheek. The metallic taste of blood spread through my mouth from where I'd cut my tongue.

"So they've been playing me like a video game." Franklin pumped the gun handle a few times, tightening and relaxing his grip, but he didn't lower it.

"You told me a few days ago you could handle anything as long as I still believed in you. I still believe in you, Franklin. I still believe you have the ability to care about other people."

Even as I said it, though, I understood it didn't make any real difference how much I believed in Franklin. I knew there was good inside him. I'd seen it. I knew there was evil. I'd seen that too. But in the end, what mattered was which way his capsule happened to be switched. For better or worse, science had reduced the whole huge question of good and evil to a matter of electric impulses.

Or maybe it had always been like that, and science had just finally allowed us to see it.

I waited.

Little by little, the gun sagged in Franklin's hand. Then it clattered on the concrete.

The muscles in my body unclenched. I slumped backward against the wall and slid all the way down to the floor. A warm, dizzy feeling flowed through my head as my lungs started working again.

Franklin pulled off the Son of War mask. There it was, finally: his strange, beautiful face, with its sharp angles and twisty nose. His eyes, red and wet, met mine. With the mask gone, the illusion of the Son of War supersoldier had vanished. His shaved head and jutting cheekbones and skinny neck made him look more like a starved and tortured prisoner of war.

"How am I supposed to figure out who I am if people keep flipping switches in my brain?"

"I'm sorry, Franklin. It's not fair what they've done to you. But listen to me: one thing you're not is a killer."

"Yes, I am."

"The electronics in your head, *they* killed Callie and Pete, not you."

"I pulled the trigger, didn't I?"

"Yes, but—"

"So I'm a killer. I have to take responsibility for my actions."

"Not if someone else was controlling your brain. It wasn't your fault."

"There's no way to know if the nanodrones and the capsule made me kill. I was pretty screwed up before your mom went anywhere near my head. And what if I'd never even had any devices put in my brain? What if we knew for sure I was just born a sociopath? I guess you could say *that* wouldn't be my fault either. But I'd still have to take responsibility for killing, wouldn't I?"

Still lying there on the floor, I turned my head to the side to stare up at the concrete ceiling. "I don't know. The whole concept of responsibility . . . I'm not even sure I know what it means anymore."

"It has to mean something, doesn't it?"

"I suppose. Look, you're not a killer today, then."

Franklin shook his head. His eyes filled. He threw the mask to the side, fell to his knees, and hunched forward, his spine making the same curve Sam Durham's had. "I'm a killer today, too. I killed those mice at your house."

He slid his hand into an inside pocket of his black coat and pulled out the two mice he'd stowed there earlier. He peered into his cupped palms.

"Are they alive?" I asked.

He nodded. His thumb brushed their fur. He set them on the floor, and they skittered off.

"See?" I said. "You're not a killer *right now*."

The reassurance seemed insufficient. Idiotic even. Once the little creatures had rounded the corner and disappeared, I shifted my position on the floor, and pain stabbed through me. A gasp jumped out of my mouth. I'd felt no pain when I'd wrenched my wrists apart a few minutes ago, but now I could tell it had made my injured shoulder even worse.

"What's wrong?" Franklin spun around and crouched next to me.

"I'll be okay."

Little by little, the pain receded to a tolerable throb. He watched, his hands hovering near me like he wanted to help but didn't know how.

I shot a glance at Tor. He'd finally passed out, maybe from blood loss. The puddle under his leg had grown. We needed to get him out of here. "Your capsule's working the right way again, Franklin. I can tell. You told me you'd rather be like this, remember? You said it was hard, but it also made you happy."

He sat back on his heels, his spine settling into an even deeper slump. "Maybe I liked being this way because I *was* this way. When I was the other way—out for blood—I wanted to stay like that, too." He pulled his glasses from a pocket and slid them on. "That night in the gazebo, after you recited the poem, I could tell something had changed. My head started filling up with all these angry thoughts. I really was going to go back to the lab, like we talked about, but then the idea came into my head to stop by school and check if anyone had found the stuff I'd stashed in the tunnels. When I got down here, everything was still where I'd left it. I put the mask on and just kept feeling angrier and angrier. I decided now that I was free I needed to finish the game. So I went to Callie's house."

I flinched. Looked away. Almost put my hands over my ears.

"By the time it was over," he said, "it was getting late. So I went back to the lab and used the iPod to sneak into my room. Then I hacked into the program that monitors my capsule to see if I could figure out what had happened to it. Right away I could tell there was more to your mom's project than she and the other scientists were letting on. For some reason they'd given the capsule two settings, and it looked like some kind of auxiliary subroutine had gotten tripped and caused the capsule to switch to the other setting while I was out.

"I realized the only way I could keep the scientists from

finding out what I'd done, the only way I could keep the game going, was if I turned the capsule back the way it had been before and erased any record of the switch in the system. But I didn't want to do it because I liked being the way I was. No remorse. No fear. Just anger. The anger didn't feel *good* exactly, but it was so *easy*. So *familiar*.

"I had a feeling your mom would turn the empathy back off eventually, though. All I had to do was wait. So I changed the capsule's setting and became good Franklin again. And as soon as I did, this tidal wave of guilt crashed over me. I was so afraid you'd find out what I'd done. I hacked into the system one more time, disabled that auxiliary subroutine so the capsule wouldn't get accidentally switched again, and started telling you all those lies. I wanted you to keep believing in me. After our kiss last night, I wanted you to kiss me like that again. I wanted you to feel that way about me for as long as possible.

"But once I got off the phone with you tonight, I realized you were right: I shouldn't have been lying to you. And I shouldn't have been putting you and other people in danger by keeping what I'd done a secret. I was being greedy, and I couldn't do it anymore. That's why I sent you the Dropbox link. Did you get it?"

I nodded. "But I haven't looked at the files yet."

"I wrote out a confession. And I copied all the surveillance footage and other files related to the project from the lab computer system. I figured whatever your mom and her team were really up to, you should know about it, and maybe the files would help you figure it out. Then I sent you the text message with the link, and I thought it would all be over."

He dropped his head forward and touched the Band-Aid on the back of his skull.

"But then an hour later," he said, "I felt another shift in my head. I guess that was when your mom changed the setting on the capsule again. I started thinking about what you'd done to me sophomore year in the locker room, and what you do down here with Tor, and that stuff you said on the phone about wanting to forget our kiss. The anger came back." He dragged his fingers forward over his stubbly scalp. "The way I've been feeling about you these past few days, the way I've been feeling about everything, it reminds me of that optical illusion where you look at the picture one way and all you can see is a vase, and you look at it another way and all you can see is two profiles, but you can't see it both ways at the same time. That's how I've been seeing the whole world, and I don't know which way is real. The vase or the profiles."

Franklin glanced at the mask lying on the floor a few feet away, its mirrored goggles pointed toward him. With his sneaker he nudged it until it faced the wall. He tipped forward, burying his face in the space between my neck and shoulder, careful to choose the side I hadn't injured. I put my arm around him.

"I know how confusing this must be," I said. "My mom had no right to do what she did. But Franklin, we'll find a way out of this."

"That was your mom you were talking to on the phone before, right? She must know I escaped by now."

"Probably."

"If people know I could escape, they'll realize I killed Callie. They'll find out I tried to kill you."

"I'll make my mom tell people the truth. About the nanodrones. About the capsule. I'll go to the press and tell them myself if I have to."

"The end result will be the same. The project will get shut down. They'll take the capsule out of my head. I'll be like I was before all this happened. Back then, I guess it's possible I wasn't an actual killer, but I was close. Those nanodrones wouldn't have had to give me much of a nudge." He sat back so he could look at me. "I won't care about you anymore, Rem. Not in the way I do now."

I imagined Franklin's dead eyes and tiny, cruel smile returning. The thought chilled me. "Run away, then. Just go, before they can take it out."

He shook his head. His fingers went back to the hole in his head. "This was supposed to be a limited trial. The battery in the capsule only lasts ten days. They'd have to do another surgery to make the change permanent."

"But that means you only have—"

"Three days left."

I stood and paced back and forth down the narrow corridor. "So what if we lie? There has to be a way my mom and I can cover for you. She owes you that at least. She won't tell anyone you escaped. I won't say a word about what happened tonight."

"What about . . ." Franklin nodded at Tor. He lay there in a sprawl against the concrete wall, still unconscious, his body slick with sweat and blood.

"We could ask Tor to keep the secret too," I said.

"Why would he do that? I just *shot* him, Rem. Plus, even if he did go along with it, how would we explain his bullet wounds?" He let out a small, joyless laugh. "Too bad we can't just say he did it."

I stopped pacing. "Franklin, no."

"A little while ago you really thought he had. Remember how it all fit so perfectly? We could make that the truth. We could tell about the steam tunnels. How he came down here with you but wanted it kept a secret. We could say he found the stuff I hid. Used one of the guns to kill Callie, thinking he'd pin the murder on me. After that he tried to kill Lydia but failed. Lydia can back up that part herself. Then he came to your house when I'd snuck out to visit you, and he took us back here. His plan was to kill us both and make it look like I'd done it." His eyes inched toward one of the two matte black Berettas lying on the concrete. "But we managed to get the gun away from him. And kill him instead."

My throat squeezed as I tried to swallow again. I couldn't even tell if he was serious or not. "I've been angry at Tor too, Franklin. I think it almost made me happy to believe he was a killer. Like it justified all the rage I'd been feeling. He treated me like shit. He treated Lydia like shit. And what he did to you must've been much, much worse. But we can't kill him."

Franklin's eyes stayed on the Beretta another second. He licked his lips. The fingers of his right hand fidgeted, like they longed to pick up the weapon. Then he looked away. "I know." He shook his head. "What he did to me down here . . . it wasn't even that bad, Rem. I mean, it was bad, but not what you were probably imagining."

"So what did he do?"

Franklin's eyes darted toward me. "He kept me away from you." He shrugged out of his bulky coat, which puddled on the floor around him. He looked even skinnier in just his orange hoodie. "It happened sophomore year. About a month after everybody laughed at me in the locker room, I got to math class early one day, and so did Tor. We were the only ones there. I had my notebook out, and he started goofing around, saying, 'What do you write in that thing anyway?' He grabbed it before I could stop him and opened up to the first page. He saw a picture I'd drawn there. Of you."

I nodded. "I saw it."

"He turned some more pages and saw some more drawings I'd done of the two of us. Stupid corny things I'd written about you. I tried to grab it back, but he held it up over his head, and by then other people had started arriving for class. I was afraid he'd show them what he'd found, so I got quiet and went back to my desk.

"At the end of class Tor came up to me and said if I wanted to get the notebook back, I'd have to meet him outside the back entrance of the school at midnight that night. I didn't know what else to do, so I met him there, and he took me to the tunnels.

"When we got down there, he turned on a light, and I saw he'd covered all the walls in photocopies of my corny drawings of me and you. That made me lose it. I ran at him from behind, howling like a crazy person, but he just turned around and gave me one little pop, and my whole face exploded. That's how I got this." He flicked a finger at the mountain range twisting down the center of his face. "He said the walls upstairs would look just like the walls down here unless I promised to stay away from you. I guess he wanted you all to himself.

"'Don't talk to him,' he said. 'Don't look at him. Don't go near him. If you think anything could happen between the two of you, you're kidding yourself. He already thinks you're a freak. How could he possibly care about you? How could anyone? When you die, no one will give a shit, and no one will remember you.'"

Franklin's hands had squeezed into fists, just like they had back in my garage.

"I don't think I'd ever felt so angry before. And the funny thing was, I knew he wasn't *really* keeping you from me. You already thought I was a freak, just like he said. But it didn't matter. I hated him so much anyway. With every muscle in my body, I hated him. One of the main objectives of my mission was to prove him wrong about no one remembering me."

He noticed his clenched fingers and, with effort, unclenched them.

"But it wasn't like he deserved to die for something like that," he said. "And he still doesn't. I understand that, Rem."

"It's okay. We'll think of something else."

"I already have."

Franklin picked up one of the Berettas, touched the barrel to his temple, and put a second hole in his head.

68

The blood that splashed across the concrete wall looked different from the blood I'd seen splashed across the whiteboard in Ms. Utter's classroom. Instead of bringing brilliant color to the surface, it soaked into the gray concrete, turning it black.

Franklin pitched to the side. More blood pooled on the floor around his head like a black halo. His glasses, knocked off by the gun blast, lay next to him. I lunged forward, ignoring the flare of pain in my shoulder, dropping to my knees, searching for something to do, but I felt as useless as if I'd still had my hands tied behind me. I couldn't see the back of his head, couldn't tell how much of it he'd blown away, but I didn't want to.

"Franklin, can you hear me?" I sputtered like an idiot.

But he did hear me. His eyes blinked open. They were crossed at first, the two of them wandering around on their own like lost animals. Little by little, they straightened themselves out and focused on me.

"Why the hell did you have to do that?" I said. "Why—"

He lifted a finger as if to put it over my mouth, but he only managed to raise it a few inches. "Don't worry," he whispered. "It doesn't hurt." His eyes lost focus and looped around some more. "I feel amazing, actually. Remember that guy who tried to kill himself with a crossbow? I think I hit the same spot." He let out a weak laugh. "I always knew I was a good shot."

Something warm touched my fingers. The puddle of blood had reached my hands. It nudged outward rhythmically, lapping like gentle ocean waves—in time with his heartbeat, I realized.

"We could've figured something out," I said. "Maybe there's still time. I'm going to find a phone—"

He grabbed my forearm and gripped it hard. "Don't leave me."

"Okay. I won't leave." I swallowed, glancing at all the pieces of Franklin scattered across the wall and floor. Then I forced myself to block out the rest of him and just focus on his eyes. He'd brought them back under his control again. "What can I do?"

"The iPod. It's in here." His fingers brushed one of his coat pockets. "Let's listen to that song."

I nestled one of the earbuds in his ear, ignoring the black spray of blood on his earlobe and the bloody chaos that lay just a few inches farther back. The other earbud I put in my own ear. The Philip Glass song was already queued up. I started it playing, then touched Franklin's cheek and traced my fingertips down toward his chin. As usual, they left a smear behind. Not of paint this time, though.

"I'm not mad at your mom, you know," Franklin said. "I'm still glad she put the capsule in my head. When you kissed me last night, that made it all worth it. Except for Pete and Callie dying. Nothing was worth that. But all the rest. Maybe you should draw a tattoo about that kiss, Rem. *That* would be something."

In my ear, the high notes started in, the delicate thread of melody unspooling.

"This is incredible," he said. "My brain feels . . . wider than the sky." He let out another laugh, fainter this time. "I feel . . . connected to everything. There's no anger. I forgive all of us." His fingers, still tight on my arm, squeezed as another wave of euphoria passed over him. The way he looked made me think of that Tattoo Atlas picture I'd drawn of my brother and the birds flying out of his head. "You know what would make this even better?" he said. "If you kissed me one more time."

I pressed my mouth against Franklin's. He released a quiet, happy sigh. As we kissed, the shard of tooth drifted from my mouth to his. A fragment of Rem Braithwaite to mix with all the fragments of Franklin Kettle.

When his lips stopped gripping mine, I knew he was dead.

69

A week later the snow still lay several feet thick on the ground. The gazebo in our backyard had buckled under the load and blown over. It lay there now like a snowbound carcass, with rib-like planks sticking up here and there and the roof collapsed like a bashed-in skull.

I found Lydia on the rear porch staring at the wreckage and smoking. It was night, about ten o'clock. I'd just pulled my Saab into the driveway when she sent a text asking me to meet her back here. When she saw me, she stood and moved to give me a hug, but I held up a warning hand. Her eyes went to the sling supporting my left arm. "You don't look so good."

"A fall down two flights of stairs will do that to you."

"Ouch."

"Yeah, that pretty much sums it up."

We sat down on the bench. "I heard the Saab pull up," she said. "Are you sure you should be driving with your arm like that?"

"I'm not supposed to, but I had something important to do."

She didn't ask what the something was, and I didn't volunteer the information. Her eyes bounced off my Tattoo Atlas, which I'd wedged under my arm, but I didn't explain that either. A few flakes of snow drifted down and settled on the gazebo, adding to the pile slowly burying it.

"When did you get back?" I asked.

"Yesterday."

"Have you seen Tor yet? Talked to him?"

She shook her head, her brow furrowing. "What's going on with him, Rem?"

"You mean the 'For Sale' sign?" It had gone up in front of the Agnarsons' house that morning.

"Well, yes, but I've also tried calling and he won't answer."

"He just got home from the hospital a couple days ago. Give him time."

"I don't think it's just that. After my first few calls, he sent me this weird text saying he cares about me a lot but can't see me for a while. Why would he do that? Does it have to do with the abduction? Or is it something else?"

I glanced up at Tor's bedroom window. It was dark, with the blinds drawn. It had been like that for the past week.

"Listen," I said. "I should tell you something. I should've told you a long time ago."

"Okay."

Before I went on, I turned my palms up on my lap and stared at them like I could see through my gloves to the skin underneath, decorated with watercolor smudges of all different shades. Blue. Green. Red. Earlier I'd been laboring over a new design in my Tattoo Atlas.

Without looking up I said, "Tor and I, we used to mess around."

Lydia didn't act surprised. She tapped on her cigarette. A piece of ash wafted down like a gray snowflake. "When?"

"It started sophomore year. The last time was a couple weeks ago."

She studied the cigarette's glowing tip while she digested what I'd said. "So he's gay. And you didn't tell me. Not even when I showed up in tears on your doorstep."

"If he's gay or not, that isn't for me to say. I should've told you what we were doing, though. You deserved to know. I just didn't want to hurt you."

"Mr. Nice Guy."

"Exactly. That's no excuse. I'm sorry, Lydia."

"Uh-huh." She took a drag and exhaled. We both watched the cloud of smoke hang in the chilly air between us. Then, with sudden violence, she hurled her cigarette into the yard. It landed in the snow with a quiet hiss. "I just feel so effing stupid."

She got quiet again and stared at the wrecked gazebo. I watched for tears, but this time none ran down her freckly cheeks.

"It's okay," she said finally. "I'll deal. I think a part of me might've known all along." She rooted around in her purse for her box of cigarettes. "Anyway, it's probably selfish of me to get upset after what you two just went through." She looked up at me, the box clutched in her hand. "What happened, Rem? Can you talk about it? The news reports are so sketchy. Something about Franklin Kettle's capsule going haywire?"

That had become the official version of events: the capsule had malfunctioned, and the glitch had caused Franklin to kill Callie and try to kill Tor and me.

I'd struggled with how to feel about the cover-up. Knowing Mom was still lying knotted me up inside, and I hadn't even come to terms with the lying she'd *already* done. I understood it had all been for Ethan, but Ethan was dead. I was her son too, and I was alive, and her mad scientist recklessness had almost gotten me killed. How did that make any sense?

It didn't. But Mom had convinced herself her project was a means of saving American soldiers, and not just an incredibly dangerous way for her to work through her own grief. She'd bent her perception of reality to justify her actions to herself. It was a trick of the brain, something we all did, just like she'd said herself.

Hadn't I done it too?

With Tor, for example. For years I'd made excuses for him. Then when he'd broken things off with me and all my anger toward him had come to the surface, I'd gone to the other extreme and turned him into a killer.

And with Franklin. After the Big Bang, in my mind, I'd made him a monster. And later I'd made him innocent. When really he'd been neither.

Just that morning I'd finished watching the footage Franklin had sent me and setting down everything that had happened in a blank sketchbook. If I'd hoped all that writing might magically erase the story from my head, it didn't. The memory of Franklin, and of those days, would be like a capsule embedded in my skull and changing the way my neurons fired for the rest of my life.

But at least now I knew what I needed to do with my confession.

I set the sketchbook outside Mom's bedroom door, knocked, and walked away. The whole week we'd barely talked. She'd spent about as much time in her bedroom as I had in mine. I heard her open the door and pick up what I'd left there, and a couple hours later she came down the hall and returned my knock. When I opened, I had a big speech ready about how even though I knew it wouldn't be easy for either of us, and even though it was a complicated story, and even though I understood the world didn't do well with complicated stories, making this public was the right thing to do.

But before I could say any of that, she just pressed the sketchbook into my hands and said, "Go ahead, Rem."

"So what happened?" Lydia asked now, puffing on a fresh cigarette.

"Don't worry," I answered. "You'll hear about it soon enough."

A cold wind kicked up, stirring some of the freshly fallen snow. One of the gazebo beams groaned as it resettled.

"This cold's making my shoulder ache," I said. "I should probably go inside."

"Of course." She put the cigarette out, picked up a couple

other butts she'd lined up on the bench next to her, and stepped down from the porch. Before she left, she paused to hunt around in a snowdrift. I couldn't tell why at first. "We're moving away too," she told me while she searched. "My dad's had enough of Boreal Street. I tried telling him what happened here could've happened anywhere, but he's made up his mind."

I was pretty sure my mom would've liked to leave as well, but I also knew we probably weren't going anywhere. After returning my confession that morning, Mom had a long phone conversation with her lawyer to find out just how much we'd lose for doing the right thing. It didn't look like she'd face any actual prison time, but when the shit hit the fan and everything went public, she'd for sure lose her position, her lab, her reputation. Things would get hard, money would be tight, and we wouldn't get much if we tried to sell our place on cursed Boreal Street.

Lydia picked something out of the snow and held it up: the cigarette she'd lobbed. She added it to the others and started to go.

"Wait, Lydia," I said. "You don't have to do this, you know."

She stopped. The smile dropped off her face. Her freckly cheeks turned pink. "Do what?"

"I went behind your back with Tor. I lied to you. You don't have to act like everything's okay. You don't have to be nice. That's what I always did with Tor, and it wasn't a good thing. You can tell me how you feel. I *want* you to tell me how you feel. I think sometimes you have to let yourself be angry a little before you can really forgive someone."

She pulled her ponytail over her shoulder and eyed me

cautiously while she twisted it in her hands. "Okay, then. I'm P-Oed at you, I guess. Really effing P-Oed."

At least it was a start. And I needed the practice too. I'd have a lot more people angry at me once the whole story came out. Especially the part about me letting Franklin leave my house so he could go kill Callie. No one would be calling me Mr. Nice Guy anymore.

"I'll miss you, though, Rem," Lydia said. "I'll miss all of us."

She disappeared around the corner of the house. I got up and moved to go inside, but then I caught a glimpse of something and stopped. In the darkness at the back of the yard, behind the wrecked gazebo, I'd seen a flash of traffic-cone orange. My breath caught. My chest tightened. I ran to the far end of the porch to get a better look.

A fox stood peering back at me, its eyes glinting in the porch lights, as if it wanted to let me know it wouldn't be leaving Boreal Street either. For some reason it made me feel better to think those dangerous, beautiful creatures would still be there, hidden in the trees. In the distance Mrs. Kettle's wind chimes sounded. The fox padded back into the woods.

I went into the house with my Tattoo Atlas. Mom had holed herself up in her bedroom again, so I limped straight to mine. It took me about five minutes to take off my coat without causing myself excruciating pain. I pulled off my sweatshirt as well and probed the clean white bandage covering my chest. Then, in front of the mirror on the wall, I unstuck the medical tape and carefully lifted the bandage away.

Underneath, the skin was still pinkish and shiny with ointment, but you could see the image there clearly enough: my first tattoo. I had a feeling I'd get more down the road—for Callie, for Pete, for Ethan—but this had seemed like the right place to start.

At the top a pair of my imps held a banner with *FRANKLIN* printed on it. Below that stood two stylized laboratory mice, but with huge human heads, locked together in an embrace. One had a shaved skull and a twisty nose and glasses. One had a blue smudge of paint on his cheek. They faced each other, just like in that optical illusion where you look at it one way and it's a vase, and you look at it another way and it's two profiles. Except you could tell these two were moving closer together, so pretty soon they'd meet right at the spot in the center of my chest where that Philip Glass song always tugged at me. Pretty soon there wouldn't be a vase at all, just two profiles locked together in a kiss.

ACKNOWLEDGMENTS

In the acknowledgments of my first book, I described how I got a two-book deal and found out my partner and I were pregnant with twins in the very same month. That good news jackpot came with a terrifying realization: I was going to have to write a second book at the same time my partner and I were preparing for, and then taking care of, two newborn girls.

I was right to be scared. For me, 2015 involved lots and lots of running back and forth between my laptop and the changing table. Fortunately, I had plenty of help with the babies, and I know *Tattoo Atlas* wouldn't have gotten finished without it. So to Rosa Willis, Jessica Sorenson, and my partner Duncan Kerr, I owe a huge thank-you for making it possible for me to write.

As for *Tattoo Atlas* itself, it wouldn't be the book it is now without the input of beta readers Cat Vasko, Meghan Thornton, Tamim Ansary, and especially Kevin Wofsy, who commented on multiple drafts and knew just how to articulate his feedback in a clear and kind way.

And then there's my editor, Michael Strother. Michael, your positivity, your always calm and friendly demeanor, and your generosity with your time (and your exclamation points) made working with you once again a joy. You gave me the freedom to explore in my writing while still knowing when to rein me in. I loved every minute of my time with you. And big, big thanks to the wonderful Liesa Abrams and Sarah McCabe for their editorial work too.

Thank you to everyone else at Simon & Schuster who helped get this book on shelves: Mara Anastas and Mary Marotta in publishing, whose warmth always makes me happy; Lucille Rettino, Carolyn Swerdloff, Catherine Hayden, and Tara Grieco in marketing; Jennifer Romanello and Jodie Hockensmith in publicity; Michelle Leo and her ed/library marketing team; Christina Pecorale and the rest of the sales team; managing editor Katherine Devendorf; production editor Amanda Veloso; and cover designer Regina Flath, who took *Tattoo Atlas*'s cover in a direction I never would've expected but immediately knew was exactly right.

Lots and lots of gratitude go to my agent, Tracey Adams. Tracey, I adore and value you more with every passing year. I still can't believe my luck in having you as my agent. I also remain enormously grateful to Quinlan Lee for landing this book deal for me in the first place. And Josh Adams and Samantha Bagood, thanks for helping to make Adams Literary the warm, welcoming literary family it is.

Speaking of warm, welcoming literary families, I'd like to say a special thank-you to Amie Kaufman for taking me under her wing, championing my writing, and showing me how to be a writer while staying sane. And thanks to all the other writers who went out of their way to make a scared new writer feel welcome in the young-adult fiction world, including (but not limited to) Shaun David Hutchinson, Kristin Elizabeth Clark, Jim Averbeck, Jay Kristoff, Cindy Pon, Heather Petty, Suzanne Young, Delilah S. Dawson, and Margaret Peterson Haddix.

Writing is a lonely pursuit, and it's wonderful to feel like I'm at long last becoming part of a community of writers.

Most of all, though, I'm thankful for my family—and especially little Lucy and Ada, who were the best excuses for a writing break ever.